THE NAKED RUNNER

FRANCIS CLIFFORD

THE NAKED RUNNER

Coward-McCann, Inc.
New York

To
John Attenborough
and
Robin Denniston

*All men dream but not equally. Those who dream
by night in the dusty recesses of their minds
wake in the day to find that it was vanity: but
the dreamers of the day are dangerous men, for
they may act their dream with open eyes, to
make it possible. . . .*

—T. E. LAWRENCE

. . . a fear among fears,

A naked runner lost in a storm of spears.

—ARTHUR SYMONS

Chapter One

SAM LAKER watched his son serve himself with a second enormous helping of breakfast cereal then top it over with sugar and cream. Lord, he marveled, how they can put it away at fourteen. And this was merely a beginning, he knew. Bacon and eggs, half a dozen slices of buttered toast, perhaps an apple to round off with—and sure enough the hunger pangs would be back well before lunch. Only last week Mrs. Ruddick had said that when Patrick was home from Greynham it was like shopping for an entire extra household. Still, Laker reflected, he looks damn well on it, and that's the main thing. Big for his age, and chunky. Helen would have approved—except perhaps for the present state of his hair.

He folded the *Telegraph*, drained his coffee and smiled. "What's on the agenda for today?"

"The Planetarium."

"Oh yes, you told me. You and Tim Maxwell."

"That's right."

"And afterwards?"

"We thought we'd come back to the river. If the weather lasts, that is. Otherwise I'll probably go over to his place and listen to records or something."

"Didn't you do that yesterday?"

"Yes, but Tim's player conked out. He'll have had it fixed by this afternoon, though."

"I see." Laker paused uncertainly. "Well, you're all organized then?"

"Just about."

He rose, pushing away his chair. "The Planetarium ought to be interesting."

"Yes."

"Enjoy yourself, anyway."

"Thanks."

"And don't try anything too clever if you do go on the water."

"I won't. 'Bye."

They never seemed to speak much in the mornings. Patrick was invariably late down and Laker made a point of being at Gale & Watts by nine-thirty. Not that breakfast, even at the weekend, was an especially communicative time; but it often struck Laker that leaving the boy to his own devices five days a week throughout most of the school holidays was a routine act of desertion. It would have been different if he weren't an only child, or if Helen had lived, but regrets like that offered no solution. On the credit side, Patrick was nothing if not self-reliant. And, by way of amends, next week's trip to Leipzig and West Germany would help to balance things up a bit.

The mail had come. Telephone bill, a picture postcard for Mrs. Ruddick and a letter addressed to Patrick from Paris. *Patrick Laker, Esquire.* Laker opened the breakfast room door and tossed the envelope onto the table.

"Just arrived. Which particular pen-pal would that be?"

"Gilles," Patrick answered, straightening it. "Gilles Leroux."

"Formal type, eh?"

"How do you mean?"

"Esquire."

Patrick eyes widened. "Oh, glory."

"Incidentally—"

"Yes?"

"Get your hair cut, will you?"

A grin from Patrick and Laker shut the door again. A minute or two later he looked into the kitchen.

"I'll be in at the usual time, Mrs. Ruddick. Around six-thirty."

"Very well, Mr. Laker."

"Patrick will be out most of the day as far as I can gather. Meanwhile he's busy taking on fuel."

"It's a wonder where he puts it, and that's a fact. But they're all the same at his age." Smiling, efficient, dependable Mrs. Ruddick. "You ought to see my nephew."

"By the way, there's a card for you," Laker said. "I left it in the hall."

Except for a few curled feathers of cirrus the morning was cloudless. Rain wouldn't come amiss, Laker thought, glancing at the roses as he cut across the lawn to the garage. He didn't fancy an evening's watering, but all the signs were that he was in for one. He ran the Humber out, locked the garage after him, then headed along the tree-lined avenue.

It was five miles to Gale & Watts and he had twenty minutes. He slowed at the intersection, waited for a gaggle of cars to pass, then nosed into the main road that would lead him through Oatlands and on past the filling station and into Weybridge. The trees and bordering hedges wore a bloom of late summer dust. He wound the driving window all the way down, letting the air whoosh in. In Oatlands he veered out of the traffic stream, switched off, and crossed to the tobacconist's for cigarettes.

"Morning, sir." From habit the man reached for the required brand and slid a pack across the counter. "Another lovely morning."

"Certainly is."

"We deserve all we can get, that's what I say."

Laker collected the change, nodded his thanks and stepped outside. Again and again he was to trace the nightmare back to that precise moment and wonder whether Slattery would in fact have got in touch if the next few seconds had never happened. But there and then he was aware only of the woman with the pram who was in the path of an oncoming truck. With shocking clarity he saw the horrified expression of the driver in the high cab and the inevitability of disaster as the woman dithered between strides.

Instinct propelled Laker from the curb. He sprinted, canted forward, going for the woman's waist, flinging himself at her in a despairing Rugby tackle. She had begun to scream as his right shoulder crashed into her, and then she grunted, hands going up. In an overlapping blur of awareness he felt her moving with him and glimpsed the pram shooting clear and the hood of the truck shuddering to ward them in a squeal of locked brakes that was merged with the hoarseness of a human voice somewhere in the distance. Then he was falling with the woman under him, rolling the instant they hit the tarmac, twisting away from the truck's towering bulk. With his eyes half screwed he saw the red side of it loom vertically against the sky, going past him, the near wing brushing his clothes, and only then was he sure they were clear. The truck shook to a standstill with the cab door immediately above Laker's head and the next thing he remembered with certainty was the driver staring down at him, eyes and face rigid with terror through sifting dust.

"You okay?"

Laker stirred. A wheel hub was against his left calf. He tried to say "I think so," but there was a kind of dislocation between his brain and his tongue and all he could do was cough.

"Jesus!"

As the driver leapt from his cab Laker pushed himself onto his knees. The woman was stirring too, calling "Michael? . . . Michael?" in a dazed sort of way. Two or three people were between the truck and the pavement, righting the pram which had fallen sideways.

"Jesus," the driver repeated numbly to Laker, "they were goners but for you. You okay?" His face was the color of zinc.

"Yes."

Laker stood up and helped the woman to her feet. She had a graze on her forehead and her eyes were frantic.

"Michael!"

The pram was upright now, the curly-haired child bawling but apparently unscathed. The woman ran to him, her voice breaking. All the voices seemed suddenly very loud, a little unreal. Someone said: "He had a bump, that's all. Just a bump when the pram hit the curb and toppled over. He's scared, that's all. He isn't hurt."

"They were goners," the driver was insisting. "She came out from behind that parked van like a sleepwalker, she did. Didn't give me a chance."

Laker went over to the pram. The woman had freed the child from its harness and was holding him to her, sobbing. She wasn't much more than a girl. Her yellow dress was streaked with tar and a man who'd apparently retrieved her shoes was offering them to her.

Laker said, "Can I take you home?"

He reckoned she scarcely heard him. He was only one of many; part of the babel. Somebody from a shop had brought out a chair.

"A doctor, maybe? My car's here."

She shook her head. A sizable crowd had gathered. Laker looked at her. She'd be all right: no point in staying. He turned and made for the Humber, almost oblivious of the fact that the driver was asking, "Where's the fellow that pushed 'em clear? They'd have had it but for him."

He got into the car and drew away. His left knee throbbed and he was a shade light in the head, but it wasn't until he had nearly reached Weybridge that the reaction hit him in earnest. He pulled in to the side and felt the coldness blow through him and then the hot flush came. Everything went a greenish-pink for a few moments and he rested his forehead on the wheel, eyes closed, blood and brightness beating together in his mind. A minute or two passed before the feeling of nausea began to ebb. Eventually, he broke the seal on the crushed pack of cigarettes and with trembling fingers lit up.

He'd scraped his knuckles, he noticed. He blew smoke against the windshield, then took a deep lungful of air. Almost nine-thirty. Well, for once he'd be late. He wiped the chilly sweat from his face and sucked his knuckles, then prepared to drive on, a kind of disbelief possessing him as the scene began to run like a film across his natural vision. It had been close, all right, too close, and his nerves couldn't quite cope with it yet.

Gale & Watts designed and manufactured office equipment.

One of Laker's uncles, Charles Gale, had taken him into the firm soon after the war and for five years he served a kind of apprenticeship, "a grounding" Charles called it, first in the factory and then in the office, transferring periodically from one department to another. Accounts, Costing, Sales, Publicity, Organization and Methods, Welfare—Laker duly went through the mill. On his thirtieth birthday, two years after marrying Helen, he had been elevated to the position of Frank Watts' personal assistant and when Charles retired on medical advice in the late fifties Laker was elected to fill the vacancy on the Board.

It was a small company, with something under eight hundred employees, and the neat red brick and white stone offices which screened the factory bays from the road stood back from the entrance gates behind a spread of shrubs and flower-bordered lawn. Laker ran the Humber into a space in the front parking lot and got out, extracting his briefcase before locking up. He was one of those men who looked taller than his true height, which was five feet ten and a half inches, and he went to the scales around one hundred and ninety pounds. Like Patrick he was very solidly put together. His dark hair was on the wire side, a trifle crinkly, and when he smiled it was a generous smile, radiating crow's-feet from the outer corners of his eyes and showing strong, even teeth that were his own. Guessing his age, strangers usually underestimated: he was, in fact, forty-three. "How d'you do it, Sam?" Baxendale, the sales director, had remarked only a couple of weeks earlier. "What's the secret? I break my back on the rowing machine and do thirty-six holes every Saturday and Sunday, so help me, and what happens? All I get is a twin-sized paunch and a flabby chin."

Laker walked diagonally across the forecourt, the trace of a limp only slightly impairing his stride. MacDonald, the commissionaire, offered a bright "Good morning, Mr. Laker" and held the door open. MacDonald had never quit the parade ground; ramrod-straight, he marched everywhere, his left arm scarcely swinging as if he permanently carried a rifle at the trail.

"Morning, John."

It was a pleasant entrance lobby with a half a dozen watercolors framed on pastel-washed walls. "No need," Charles Gale used to say, "for an office to look like a penitentiary." Laker nodded to the girl in Reception, unaware as he mounted the stairs that her gaze followed him curiously. Ten to ten. Carol Nolan, his secretary, was busy typing as he entered his second-floor office.

"Hallo," he said. "Had you given me up?"

"I was beginning to wonder."

"Well, I'm sure Gale & Watts is still solvent." His smile briefly changed to a wince as he sat in the swivel chair. "Any calls?"

"No," she said. "There's quite a post, though, and you've an appointment at eleven with Mr. Thornton of International."

Laker nodded, glancing at the orderly presentation of his mail and the files already flagged for reference. Carol was the best secretary he'd ever had, and by far the most attractive: raven-black hair, lively brown eyes and long, slim legs. Baxendale was forever suggesting that she ought to come to him when his own Miss Grigg retired, if not sooner. "She's just what's wanted on my front, believe me." And then, invariably, the corny crack: "To my mind Development can't do another thing for her."

"What's happened," Carol was saying now, "to your jacket?"

"Where?"

"The shoulder. No, the other one—at the back." She moved around the desk. "It's torn."

Laker craned his head. White padding bulged where the seam had come apart.

"And your hand. How—?"

"That I knew about." He sucked the scraped knuckles again. "Get some tape, will you?"

"Did you fall or something?"

"Kind of."

She eyed him uncertainly. "Is that all you're going to tell me?"

"Let's say I had a slightly confused argument with a truck."

"Whereabouts?"

"Oh, not far from home."

"Is the car damaged?"

"I wasn't in it." He shifted in the chair. "Look, be a good girl and get the adhesive tape, will you?"

She knew him well enough not to press him. When she returned from First Aid she said, "May I have your jacket, please? You can't see Mr. Thornton if you're looking like that."

Laker gave it to her and she carried it away for temporary repairs. His suede shoes were smeared with tar across the toes, but they'd pass. Routine imposed itself. He got down to his mail, but it was quite a while before the day took shape in the way others did, building upon their sequence of events and problems. His mind repeatedly fled to the woman in the yellow dress. It was a long time since he had been within a hairbreadth of danger or had his nerves stroked by anything worse than some minor, passing fear. Now, in retrospect, the incident had a curiously static quality, though once he shuddered dismissively as memory and imagination swept him with the vivid reality of every split second.

Carol brought his jacket back ten minutes before Reception announced that Thornton had arrived. He was a frequent visitor, so there was no need for Laker to have to apologize for the quality of the canteen coffee. He wasn't one for hanging about, either. As soon as they had studied the drawings and discussed the test reports on a new plastic sheeting requirement, he left. It was only then that Laker discovered he had lost his wallet. Dining room accounts were presented on the last Tuesday of the month and, as soon as Thornton had gone, Carol was in with various additions to the paper work together with the August account. And he always liked to settle on the spot.

"You didn't see it when you were mending my jacket, did you?"

"No," Carol said.

"Blast. Then it must have fallen out at Oatlands."

"Is that where you had your so-called argument with the truck?"

"Yes. Ring the police, will you? Don't go into details. Just report the loss. Someone may have turned it in."

No one had, she informed him a few minutes later.

He swore more forcibly.

"Was there much in it?"

"Driving license, A.A. card—"

"Money, I meant."

"About fifteen pounds."

Carol made a pained face.

"And something from the Leipzig Fair people—flight particulars."

"*I've* got your plane tickets," she said. "And your Fair Cards and traveler's checks and hotel reservations. Are you sure you started out with the wallet?"

"Sure," he said, then gave a resigned shrug. "We'll just have to keep our fingers crossed." Then again: "Blast it!" Helen had given it to him.

He lunched with Baxendale in the private room reserved for directors. Baxendale was in his most buttonholing mood, unloading all the stories he'd heard at the golf club the previous evening including the one about the lama who unscrewed his navel only to find that his behind fell off when he stood up—a story so ancient that Laker could only imagine it must be going the rounds a second time.

"How's the delectable Miss Nolan today? On the ball as usual?"

"I'm happy to say."

"You ought to marry her, Sam. She's a guinea a box."

Laker laughed. "I thought you wanted her yourself to brighten your office."

"All in all I'm the most generous of men."

"Where'd I find another secretary to come within a mile of her?"

"That'd be the last thing to worry me if I were in your shoes. Seriously, though, you ought to marry again. Margaret agrees with me. Mrs. Ruddick's a marvel and all that, but there's more to having a woman about the house than merely having a woman about the house." The boom years showed in Baxendale's thick flesh and paunchy eyes. "It'd be good for young Patrick, too— wouldn't it now?"

"I'll think it over," Laker countered lightly.

"My eye, you will. By the way, when are you two off to Germany?"

"Tomorrow week."

"Where are you going after you've done your duty at Leipzig?"

"The Rhineland. Ever been?"

"No."

"It was Patrick's idea. The house has been full of maps and leaflets for months."

"Well, I envy you. If Margaret has her way we'll never see anything except the bloody Costa del Sol. Oh, it's all right, I suppose, but it's too damned hot for golf unless you start before breakfast and the food's off-putting. Those dreary paellas always look to me as if they've been regurgitated. Incidently, what have you done to your hand?"

An incoming trunk call summoned him away before he got an answer. Laker left shortly afterwards and went back to his office. Carol wasn't there, but she had pinned a note to the blotter.

1:10 P.M. Police rang to say crocodile wallet handed in. Thirteen pounds ten. A.A. card, driving license, Leipzig letter and two photographs—C.N.

Relieved, Laker mulled over the Minutes of the last Publicity Committee; he was due at the quarterly meeting at three. Apart from an occasional reminder either from his knuckles or his bruised knee the morning's shock had receded. If his thoughts wandered from the day's stint it was toward Patrick, wondering whether he was still in London or on his way back with Tim Maxwell. The weather had held, so they were probably bound for the river. Odd how one worried—out of a sense of inadequacy, he supposed. Yet Patrick did tend to be a shade impetuous; someone more accident-prone would have learned his lesson by now.

"What did you tell 'em?" he asked Carol on her return from lunch.

"That you'd call for it on your way home."

"Fine." He nodded.

She took letters from him for the next three-quarters of an hour. Baxendale's remarks kept echoing in his mind and once he caught himself looking at her almost as if it were for the first time. There was a bond between them—respect, trust, loyalty. Now and then he'd driven her home to Woking. She'd dined with him once or twice and he remembered her birthday religiously. But that was all.

At the door on his way to the meeting he asked suddenly, "How old are you, Carol?"

"Old?"

"That's right."

"Twenty-three," she said, coloring slightly. "Why?"

"I just wondered."

As if he didn't know. And Patrick was almost fifteen. But there it was; think an improbable thought and you got a very impractical answer.

The police sergeant on duty asked if Laker could identify himself, then produced the wallet and turned the receipt book around for him to sign.

As Laker was checking the contents, the sergeant said, "A great thing you did this morning, sir. Quick thinking."

Privately, Laker had hoped that he wouldn't be associated with what had happened; but no such luck. He shrugged and countered: "Who handed the wallet in?"

"Horne's delivery boy." The sergeant consulted the book. "Said he found it in the gutter."

"Do you know him?"

"By sight, yes."

Laker put a pound on the desk. "Would you see he gets that?"

"I certainly will, sir. Yes, a fine effort on your part from what I've heard."

"How's the young woman?"

"Right as rain, I gather."

Curiosity got the better of Laker as he was turning to leave. "Who decided it was me, anyhow?"

"I think it was the tobacconist, sir. He's the one who recognized you. You didn't give your name or anything, you see. By the time one of our men arrived the fellow from the local paper had done his work for him, you might say. And then the wallet sort of confirmed things."

He ought to have guessed, Laker told himself, that the press would latch on. There wasn't anything he could do except hope that some eager tyro wasn't going to overdramatize everything with the intention of catching the editor's eye.

On the way home he toyed with the idea of stopping off for a drink, but decided against it. At twenty past six he ran the car into the garage and went through the side door into the house.

"Patrick showed up yet?"

"He just beat you, hardly five minutes ago." Mrs. Ruddick looked at him more carefully than usual. "Are you all right, Mr. Laker?"

He wasn't expecting her to have heard; not this soon, anyway.

"A reporter rang," she said. "A Mr. Case."

"Oh." That explained it.

"This morning." She had a trace of a Gloucestershire accent which gave warmth to her voice. "He wanted to get in touch with you, but I thought you wouldn't like to be bothered at the office so I told him you'd be away all day."

"Thanks. I'm glad you did."

"He mentioned what it was about, of course."

Laker found the admiring, slightly anxious gleam in her eyes embarrassing.

"What else did you tell him?"

"Nothing. Oh no, Mr. Laker. Once I knew you weren't hurt I thought it best to let you deal with it yourself."

"Thanks, Mrs. Ruddick."

He nodded and made for the coat closet. It had been a slack day, slack enough to feel almost guilty about, but the evening was close, sticky, and a wash revived him. When he eventually entered the living room Patrick was already there.

"Hello," Laker said. "What did you make of the Planetarium?"

"It was great."

"Worth my going to sometime?"

"I'd say so, yes." With the air of a conjurer disclosing his next prop, Patrick produced the *Evening Standard* from behind his back. "Seems to me you've been seeing stars yourself."

"Meaning?"

"Look," Patrick said, and gave him the paper, pointing to an item low down on the front page.

WAR HERO SAVES MOTHER AND CHILD
SCOOPED FROM LORRY'S PATH

Oatlands Village, near Weybridge in Surrey, was the scene of high drama at 9:15 this morning when a passerby, Mr. Samuel Laker, flung himself in front of a heavily laden truck to hurl a mother and her child clear of almost certain death.

The woman, Mrs. Edna Browning, was wheeling her eighteen-month-old son Michael across the road when the incident occurred. "She gave me no chance," lorry driver Mr. Jim Smailes explained. "They would have been goners if she and the little kid hadn't been shoved out of the way. It was about the bravest thing I've seen in fifteen years' driving."

Mrs. Browning sustained slight bruising and shock. The child was completely unhurt. Mr. Laker, 43, who lives locally at Roundwood, Mill Avenue, was not available for comment. During the war he was awarded the Distinguished Service Order and the Military Cross. A widower, with one son, he is a Director of Gale & Watts, the office equipment manufacturers.

"Oh, hell," Laker said quietly.

"Tim Maxwell spotted it. He was so impressed, in fact, that he paid the fares back."

"They make mountains out of molehills, you know that." Laker glanced at the by-line. *A Special Correspondent:* Mr. Case, no doubt. But whoever it was could certainly ferret.

Patrick was grinning like a Cheshire cat. "Come on, Dad. Cheer up. It's not as if they've said anything awful about you. A million people will have seen what's there. Don't you think I'm entitled to the full story?"

Laker moved his shoulders. "They've made it full enough, flannel included." He dropped the newspaper onto a chair and started to pour himself a whisky. "It just happened— the way things do."

A million people. That Martin Slattery might have been one of them never so much as entered his head.

Chapter Two

CASE, the reporter, didn't call back, but the telephone started ringing later that evening.

Baxendale was the first to get on to him ("You old dog, you, hiding your light under a bushel"), then Cranston from across the road, then Mary Armitage, another neighbor, then a cousin from Hampstead. As a consequence, Laker neither finished watering the garden, nor gave Patrick all the time he'd promised him on the holiday itinerary.

He was of two minds next morning about dodging the tobacconist's and getting his cigarettes elsewhere, but doing so would have no more than staved off the inevitable. He endured the plaudits and the insisted-upon handshake only to find that there was no escape even when he arrived at Gale & Watts. MacDonald saluted him as if a guard of honor were drawn up awaiting inspection, and on the way through to his office he collected more nods and "good mornings" than normally came his way in a week. Carol Nolan merely said, "You realize, I suppose, that you've destroyed the image I'd cultivated about myself outside of here? When I got home last night I was the one person who didn't know. The *one* person, mind"—and she clenched her fist at him on her way back to her desk. Then the private calls began again, about one in every three, and Laker found a formula to cope with them.

Slattery came through the following day, Wednesday. The thing was as good as over by then and there was suddenly a pile of work, like a seventh wave, to set Laker's conscience to rights about having had too easy a time earlier in the week. He was in the middle of a hastily convened meeting with Wilson and Farrow, from Design Group, trying to unravel a particularly knotty problem, when Carol's buzzer sounded.

"Yes?" He was on the brusque side.

"There's a Mr. Slattery wanting you. I know you said you weren't to be interrupted but he insists it's urgent."

"What name?"

"Slattery. Martin Slattery."

Laker frowned, memory spanning the years.

"Shall I put him through?"

He glanced across at the other two. "Did he say *what* was urgent?"

"No."

"All right, I'll take it." He apologized briefly to Wilson and Farrow, then waited for the opening: "Martin Slattery here. Who's that?"

"Sam Laker."

"Sam! How are you keeping?"

"Fine."

"I'm delighted to see that your reflexes are as good as ever."

Even after so long a time the breezy, quick-fire delivery was instantly familiar.

"We must read the same paper," Laker said.

"Could be. Well, what's it been, Sam? How long?"

"I hate to think."

Farrow was pretending not to listen, whereas Wilson was making no bones about it.

"From the sound of things you're very much a tycoon these days."

"Hardly."

"Damned difficult to reach, anyhow. Almost easier to break into the Kremlin than get past your secretary." Slattery laughed, the dryish cackle Laker imagined he had forgotten.

"I'm sorry about that, but—well—I'm at a meeting."

"Then I won't keep you."

"Something urgent, wasn't it?"

"I wondered if we could lunch."

Laker raised his eyes to the ceiling. My God. "I'd like that, yes."

"Tomorrow?"

"Tomorrow's a bit sudden."

"I'm tied up the rest of the week, and most of next as well. Failing lunch, perhaps you'd dine with me?"

"Hang on, will you, while I look?" Reaching for his diary, Laker said, "Where are you? In town?"

"Yes."

"Still in the same business?" He was filling in.

"Not exactly."

Tomorrow was clear, Laker saw. But it was short notice all the same. At any other time he might not have felt so pushed to give an answer, but Wilson was surreptitiously glancing at his watch and muttering *sotto voce* to Farrow. Why was it that a first-rate designer like Wilson had to be such a difficult cuss?

"Let's make it tomorrow then."

"Splendid. Lunch?"

"Yes, lunch would suit me best." He could look in on International: two birds with one stone. "Where shall we meet?"

Slattery gave an address in Manchester Square. "The bottom bell. Don't pay any attention to the name. The bottom bell, yes? And how about twelve-thirty?" The last thing he said was: "It'll be really marvelous to see you again, Sam. A hell of a lot of water's gone down the Thames since we were within arm's length."

Laker hung up and looked across at the others. "Sorry." He smiled. "Now, where were we?"

He had met Martin Slattery in the penultimate year of the war, a few weeks after D-day.

One of Laker's more lasting memories of the Special Operations setup in Grosvenor Gardens was the time they had spent together after his return from Italy. Slattery's office was in an overflow building not far from Victoria Station and Laker shared it with him, on and off, for a couple of months. Slattery had a limp then, the result of some accident on a grenade range, and what Laker particularly remembered was the homily framed behind his desk: he was word-perfect in it even now—*According to the theory of aerodynamics, and as may be readily demonstrated by means of a wind tunnel, the bumblebee is unable to fly. This is because the size, weight and shape of his body in relation to the total wingspan make flight impossible. But the bumblebee, being ignorant of these scientific facts and possessing considerable determination, does fly—and makes a little honey too.*

It was a bitter kind of honey, though. But amid the permissible murder of war those two months were quite unlike any other in Laker's experience. Office hours, bus queues, the tube, midday sandwiches and beer in the pub around the corner. He was even able to live at home in St. John's Wood.

Slattery was one of those responsible for briefing and debriefing what were invariably described as "foreign bodies." Since Laker was due to be dropped into Germany himself as soon as conditions were right he was never present when these sessions took place: it was fundamental that field operators remained in the dark as to who else was involved, and where, unless it directly concerned them. But while his own operation was delayed he was attached to Slattery, helping out with the collation of every scrap of general intelligence that came in. And there was a mass of it coming in around that time: the lean, scavenging years were over.

Sandwiched between the fury of Italy, with its naked violence and brutal hardship, and the gamble in store for him in Germany, an office had seemed to Laker an unreal place in which to find himself. He was never quite able to adjust his mind to the esoteric argot and the academic approach of headquarters. But the work appeared tailor-made for Slattery. He would have been about thirty then: plump, red-faced and bespectacled. Whether the homily about the bumblebee was on his wall as a kind of self-justification for being chairborne, or whether it somehow pleased him for its own sake, Laker never could decide. Mentally he was very alert, with a remarkable aptitude for being able to discard inessentials and to strip a report, no matter how garbled, down to its bare bones. Though he fought his war by proxy he fought it with a quiet intent that only once, during Laker's contact with him, hinted at some hidden fury.

They'd have a drink or two most evenings before going their separate ways, but Laker didn't really get to know him. Not that he was in the mood for developing acquaintances then: he was too on edge with what was coming. But Slattery was with him when he received the call about the flying bomb near Lords, and for some reason it was Slattery he rang from St. John's Wood to say that his parents and sister were dead and it was Slattery he walked with in Green Park a night or two later when, sodden with whisky and hatred, he swore what he would do when they let him loose in Germany.

And Slattery who said, "You do that, Sam. You kill the bastards. Kill every bloody one of them you can."

Which he did. And when it was all over and he finally came home to the ruins and the emptiness, it was to Slattery that he made his last report before he was eventually demobilized and taken under Charles Gale's wing.

Laker spent a useful half-hour with Thornton at International's enormous glass-and-steel rabbit warren near Chiswick before driving on through Kensington High Street and around the outskirts of Hyde Park. The midday traffic was sluggishly heavy and new one-way streets seemed to be cropping up every week. Even reaching Manchester Square was easier said than done and when he got there he couldn't park. In the end he found a vacant meter on the fringe of Grosvenor Square ("Eisenhowerplatz" Slattery used to term it; strange how the trivia stuck) and walked across Oxford Street into the comparative quiet of the Georgian environs of the Wallace Collection.

The address Slattery had given him was on the east side of the square. The bottom bell was marked CURTIS but he pressed it dutifully, wondering while he waited why Slattery should choose to meet him here when there were half a dozen good restaurants and hotels barely a stone's throw away.

Only a few seconds elapsed before the door opened. Momentarily, a stranger stood framed in the gap, a shortish, bulky, balding man who, as recognition dawned, Laker realized was Slattery. The spectacles and brick-colored complexion outweighed any slight hesitation.

"I'm late, I'm afraid."

"Sam! Come in, come on in."

Slattery encouraged him with a gesture, remaining where he was as if to avoid the direct sunlight. Only when the door was closed did he shake hands enthusiastically, as if he were presenting Laker with an award.

"Good to see you again, Sam. You're looking marvelous, I must say."

"And you. Sorry about the time, but what with getting the car parked—"

"Oh, parking's murder around here. Murder." Slattery gestured again like a helpful department store floorwalker. "Go on through—first right."

They crossed a wide tiled hall under a chandelier: there was a staircase with a filigree railing sloping up to the next floor. Laker entered a lobby which led into a small room with numerous sporting prints and miniatures on the walls and dust sheets over the furniture.

"Keep going," Slattery chuckled from behind. "Civilization's just ahead."

There the room was spacious, bright, uncluttered. Striped paper, marble fireplace, deep brocaded chairs, rust-red drapes, a huge gilded mirror. One of the pictures might have been a Corot. Manchester Square looked misty beyond the window-length ninon.

"Would you like a wash or anything?"

"No, thanks."

There was a pause, a kind of mutual uncertainty, during which they were strangers again. Probing, Laker said, "You don't live here, I take it?"

"No. Cigarette? No, it belongs to a friend. He lets me use it from time to time. No, as far as having an address goes, mine's in Kew. What will you have? Sherry? Gin?"

"Sherry, please."

"It's a fino. Too dry?"

"Absolutely right."

Traffic rumbled vaguely in the distance, emphasizing the quiet.

"Well, here's to you, Sam. It's certainly been a long time."

He hadn't changed much, really. Less hair, a slight loose-ness about his suit as though he'd shrunk a little; and he seemed shorter somehow. But the face was unlined, almost cherubic, and his speech was as quick as ever. Behind the thick-rimmed spectacles his eyes were eagerly attentive. And the limp had gone.

They sank into the chairs and Laker said, "You stayed on, didn't you?"

"After the war?"

He nodded.

"Yes, I suppose you could say that."

"And you're still at it?"

"After a fashion."

"I guessed as much from the camouflage."

"This place? Oh, that's more habit than anything else." Beaming, Slattery crossed his legs. "Tell me about yourself, Sam. Are Gale & Watts the people you joined when things folded up?"

"That's right."

"One of them was an uncle of yours, wasn't he?"

"Charles Gale, yes."

"I remember now. God," he said, "it's been a time hasn't it?" He blew smoke. He was inclined to blink a lot. "You mar-ried, didn't you? I believe I heard that."

"Yes, but my wife died."

"I'm sorry."

"Eight years ago. Cancer. It was very sudden—mercifully so in the circumstances."

"I'm sorry," Slattery repeated.

"What about you?"

"Me? Oh yes, I'm married. Three children, what's more, all costing the earth."

They compared notes, the conversation flowing more

easily when they touched on common ground. And there were names to fall back on—Ayres, Bill Maltby, McBride, Harry Castle, Gemmell. . . .

"What ever became of Polglaze?" Laker asked.

"I rather fancy he went to the States."

"He and Harry Castle were always cheek-by-jowl in those days."

"They were, weren't they? Harry's a solicitor. *Very* prosperous. Who said crime doesn't pay?"

"Do you ever see Thompson?"

"I read him from time to time. He writes, didn't you know? Well, you haven't missed much. Not surprising considering the reports he used to put together."

They laughed, Slattery tilting the decanter toward Laker's glass.

"There's a cold spread," he said. "Do you mind?"

"Sounds wonderful."

He watched Slattery bring the trolley in. So he was still at it, still in the game—whatever the game was now. Did it never go sour on him, corrode, rot? Or was it always fresh and complicated and worthwhile; beautiful, even? He'd admitted to that once.

Laker said, "Remember Erskine?"

Slattery paused, cocked his head. "Vaguely. Polish Section, wasn't he? . . . That's one I've quite lost touch with." And there was something just sufficiently contrived about the denial to make Laker guess that Erskine was still in the game too. Not that he was particularly interested: *chacun son goût.*

An hour passed. It was a simple yet excellent meal: melon, cold lamb, a strawberry mousse with cream. Once or twice it crossed Laker's mind that he had come a long way merely to ramble over old times, but the claret and the pattern of their talk disarmed any lurking conjecture. And when Slattery eventually asked, "Is it next week you're going to Germany, Sam?" he let it drop like a stone.

"Yes." Then, looking up in surprise: "How the hell did you know?"

"I checked."

"Checked?"

Slattery nodded, quite unabashed.

"My God," Laker said. His lips curled in astonishment. "What are you? Some sort of eyes and ears?"

"We still keep tabs—though doing so isn't my particular pigeon."

"Exactly what *is* your pigeon?"

Slattery avoided answering that.

Without hostility, Laker said, "Do you mean to tell me that anyone who happens to be visiting Germany is automatically . . ."

"Of course not. But you're going to Leipzig."

"So?"

"Leipzig's in the Russian Zone." Slattery lifted his heavy shoulders. "Look," he then said cheerfully, leaning forward a little. "There's no mumbo-jumbo about this. When I read about you in the *Standard* the other evening I simply thought: That's Sam Laker. Why not get together? . . . So I called you."

"Having checked on me first?"

"I'm not apologizing. Records are usually more rewarding than the *Directory of Directors*. It was just routine, Sam. You're an old pro, so you'll know how it is."

"I don't believe I do. Are you telling me that all this time, all these years, I've been under someone's beady eye?"

"Not in the way you're implying, no."

"But someone's kept tabs—you said so yourself."

"Only certain tabs."

"Now you're talking in riddles."

"It's a rough world, Sam. Putting it at its simplest, Leipzig is behind the lines. That's the kind of tab I mean, the kind that sticks."

"I'm visiting the Trade Fair—about the largest, incidentally, and the oldest, in Europe."

"Which is precisely what's logged on the file."

"Your sources must be bloody good. All I've done is apply for Fair Cards and book a flight."

"They're good," Slattery said evenly. "Not perfect, but good."

Laker stirred his coffee. He couldn't help smiling. "Is Leipzig my only black mark?"

"Do you really want to hear?"

"Of course, I'm fascinated—and a little indignant."

"You've a boy, haven't you? Patrick."

"Yes."

"Since May last year he's been in touch with an address in Rostock, Leninstrasse 32, to be precise."

Laker snorted derisively. "A pen-pal. He's got about six of 'em."

"A pen-pal in Halberstadt took the daughter of a certain naval officer for a great ride a couple of years ago. Practically emptied her father's briefcase."

"There's nothing in mine worth having. Besides, all Patrick's contacts are thoroughly genuine. As often as not I see their letters myself. 'I am an East German boy, sixteen years old, and my hobbies are sailing, music and collecting postcards.' They're as innocent as the day's long."

"That's not the point, Sam. If you're using a net, a whole lot of innocent fish swim into it."

"But you tab them just the same."

"As a matter of routine."

"You must employ an army," Laker said tartly. "What else have you got on me?"

"Not a thing."

"After so long?"

"There's the old stuff, of course. That's still there—in a class by itself."

"I must be a disappointment to you."

"It's only background, Sam. Don't get the wrong end of the stick."

"I haven't. But I'll be a damn sight more careful in future."

Part of him accepted the necessity of vigilance, part of him objected to the form it apparently took. On balance it struck him as pretty preposterous and he said as much.

"You wouldn't think that if you'd stayed on," Slattery replied.

"I wasn't cut out for staying on."

"Why not?"

"I couldn't have kept it up."

"Kept what up?"

"Oh, I don't know." Laker paused. "But I couldn't play it as a sort of everlasting chess, not on and on, world without end."

"Is that all you imagine it to be?"

"For want of a better comparison, yes."

Slattery said casually, "What kind of spur would you need, then?"

Laker hesitated. There was only one thing, one thing, but it was dead, thank God. Anyway, Slattery would remember; he was there in Green Park that night years ago.

He glanced at his watch. He didn't want a ticket on the car for overrunning his meter time and it was quite a walk back to Brook Street. They talked more generally for a while, but the leads were tending to peter out. Once, the telephone rang. Slattery merely said "Yes?" when he picked it up and "Yes" twice more before he put it down. Presently Laker suggested that he ought to be going.

"Must you?"

"I'm afraid so."

"It's flown, hasn't it? By the way, when are you off?"

"To Leipzig?"

"Yes."

"Surely a little detail like that hasn't escaped your notice?" Laker could still smile, though a trifle sourly.

"Refresh my memory."

"Wednesday. For forty-eight hours I'm picking other people's brains as regards office equipment, after which Patrick and I are spending about ten days in and around the Rhineland."

"Very nice." Slattery stubbed his cigarette, making an overthorough job of it. "Sam."

"Yes?"

"I haven't been entirely honest with you."

"I think I understand."

"I don't mean that."

"What, then?"

"I had a particular reason for getting you to come along."

"Oh?"

"It was to ask a favor."

"What kind of favor?"

"I'm hoping you'll deliver a message for me."

"Where?"

"Leipzig." Then quickly: "There's no risk. Absolutely none."

So that was his pigeon. "Why me?" Laker said.

"Who better?"

"Have you run out of regular couriers, or what?"

Slattery blinked at him. "It's your availability, Sam. Plus the fact that you're totally uncompromised over there." The jargon hadn't changed. "In point of fact it's not such an exceptional request these days."

"A verbal message?"

"No. But that side of things will be taken care of."

"Isn't this wildly unorthodox?"

"Not with someone like you."

Laker looked away, watching a green car move toward Spanish Place through the sunlit fog of ninon.

"I'd rather not," he said.

"It would take about ten minutes of your time, Sam. Hardly more." Slattery waited, watching him. "You'll remember better than most what hanging on can be like. Well, there's someone hanging on now. And you could have them off the rack on Wednesday."

Laker kept his gaze on the windows. No, he thought.

"I'd more than hoped," Slattery said. "I was absolutely sure you'd agree." He spoke as if Laker owed him something. "It couldn't be more simple." With a ghost of a smile, he added, "No cloak, no dagger."

"I daresay."

"Think about it."

"If I must."

"Think about it and let me know."

"All right," Laker conceded.

"By this evening? It has to be by then."

"All right. Where do I phone you?"

Slattery gave him a Gerrard number. They started through the room where the dust covers were.

"It's important, Sam. I wouldn't have put it to you otherwise. I know what's on your mind—Patrick, Gale & Watts. I can understand your hesitation. It's a lot to ask, but as far as you're concerned it will be as uneventful as stepping out into the street."

Chapter Three

LAKER walked back to Brook Street, heeding the warning whispers. He hadn't collected a ticket, which was a relief. He sat in the car for a minute or two without attempting to drive, blind to the sauntering woman who slowed and offered a hopeful smile from the pavement.

It was a lot to ask, all right. And galling that he should have been asked at all. "An old pro like you"—Slattery seemed to consider this sufficient excuse. Once in the game, always in it, always an honorary member—that was his line. "When I read the file," his parting words were, "and saw where you were going it was almost too good to be true."

Irritated, Laker lit a cigarette. What galled him particularly was the implicit suggestion that if he refused he was letting Slattery down. "There's no danger, Sam, absolutely none. I wouldn't have put it to you otherwise."

One way and another lunch had been an eye-opener. It was surprising enough to have learned that one's associations with Communist territories were so indefatigably recorded. Granted, it was a suspicion-ridden world. Granted, the bureaucratic net couldn't be individually selective. But when one's willingness to be used was apparently more or less expected if circumstances provided the need and the opportunity—that jarred.

And the proposition itself was so damned vague. If Slattery had been more forthcoming it might have been easier to have reached an out-and-out decision before leaving Manchester Square. As it was, Laker couldn't for the life of him understand why he should continue to mull it over. "A simple, straightforward person-to-person delivery. . . . Ten minutes of your time." To whom? he thought. Exactly how and where?

Brooding, he switched on and went into gear; drew away. The old pals act was a kind of blackmail. And nothing was ever one hundred percent safe: nothing. Slattery could say what he liked.

Park Lane sucked him into its flow. No, he thought again. But as he headed toward Knightsbridge and the Brompton Road his initial hostility to the idea began to fade. Against his will Slattery's anonymous contact in Leipzig weighed with him. There wasn't much worse than being cut off. He didn't have to stretch his imagination to know what it was to wait, and go on waiting. Day by day the certainty of having been abandoned gnawed at the nerves. Silence of that kind was the most agonizing silence of all. He'd experienced it once, and once was plenty.

The airborne assault on Arnhem was already poised when Laker was dropped in. He went in alone more than two hundred miles east of the Rhine, touching down in wooded country to the west of Gardelegen. A reception party was there to hustle him away—Karl and Günter and the girl. If the punch through Arnhem succeeded, the way to the heart of Germany would be open, and each and every bridge that could be kept intact across the Aller would be worth its proverbial weight in gold: that was the scheme. But Arnhem failed and their radio failed and Karl and Günter didn't return from a raid on an explosive dump at Klötze.

In case they'd be taken alive, Laker and the girl left the protection of the crumbling farmhouse and holed themselves up in a thick patch of spruce overlooking the Magdeburg-Uelzen road. Night after night long convoys moved northeast and aircraft droned across the autumn sky. It was cold and it rained a lot. Laker roofed over a hollow and at night they would lie in it. Every day the girl would go down to one or other of the nearby villages and somehow find food: once she came back with a blanket.

A week after Karl and Günter were lost he got the set to work again and began calling at the specified times. There was never an answer but he went on calling long after he was certain he'd been written off. He did it more to encourage the girl than anything. She wouldn't leave him. She was thin and freckled and eighteen years old. But no. "You will starve," she said, again and again. "Without me you will be finished."

They were to have linked up with another group to the north of Gifhorn, but without instructions they didn't know how. So they continued to wait, Laker vainly risking his call sign three times a day. Twice they were forced to move. They waited in hunger and desparation. It grew colder and they clung to each other for warmth. "Sammy," she called him. They waited five days more, trying to deduce from the movement on the road what might have happened to the distant front. Eventually Laker decided their only chance was to travel west, but on the evening they prepared to start the girl became ill. He could hear her lungs bubbling as she breathed and her skin burned in the cold. By midnight her speech was rambling. He wrapped her in the blanket and carried her to an isolated house from which she had sometimes stolen eggs. He laid her on the ground where the light would fall when the door was opened, knocked hard and ran—stopping only to check when someone came; an old man.

Then he went back to the spruces again, kicked the set to pieces and retrieved his carbine and some grenades. It took him twenty-nine days to reach the Allied lines and on the way he conducted a private war, the full volume of his hatred released at last for what had befallen his parents and sister and out of grief and uncertainty for the girl. He killed where he could and when he could—an isolated sentry, two Luftwaffe corporals cycling together, all the occupants of a staff car, the crew of a stranded tank. There were others, too; he lost count. He did it out of a haunting fury and because he really didn't care whether he lived or died and because he could shoot marvelously well. And by the time he got through to the Americans he was wild-eyed as a hunted animal and grabbed instinctively for the carbine when he awoke from his exhaustion and found a nurse bending over the bed. . . .

There were things one never forgot.

After Hammersmith he took the less direct route back to Weybridge—Richmond, Hampton, Sunbury. It was always pleasant along by the river with the boats showing through the weeping willows and there was little traffic to distract his mind. Inevitably, as he passed through Oatlands, he was reminded of the woman in the yellow dress: if it weren't for her he'd have been spared the favor Slattery expected of him. Chance had the longest, most unpredictable arm of all.

He had no illusions. It was a different kind of war now— more complex, more sophisticated, yet equally ruthless, potentially as deadly. No holes in the sodden ground, little overt violence. A different kind of war, yes; but hanging on would be no less desperate. . . . Everything, nothing had changed. And Slattery, blast him, knew that he knew what hanging on was like; and that knowing would probably help to tip the scales.

He arrived at Gale & Watts shortly before four. Carol had dealt with most of the bread-and-butter chores, but there was a fair amount demanding his attention. He cleared as much as he could in fast time and telephoned the two people Carol had listed for him. Baxendale looked in briefly, ostensibly to put him on to one of Piggott's rides next day but more obviously to indulge his fascination for Carol's legs.

It was after five when Laker asked for a line and dialed the Gerrard number. A woman answered without indicating where she was speaking from.

"Mr. Slattery, please."

"Who's calling?"

He told her.

"Is Mr. Slattery expecting you to telephone?"

"Yes," he said and waited for the click and Slattery's voice. "I'm at my office," he began.

"Go ahead."

"I'm not enamored of it, but the answer's yes."

Slattery didn't exactly indicate enthusiasm. "Oh good," was all he said—rather as if Laker had found that he was free for dinner or something.

"If it's really that important and there's no one else."

"It is, Sam. And there isn't."

"And provided it's as elementary as you made out."

"It couldn't be more so."

"All right . . . What now?"

"I'll be in touch. Incidentally, about your watch—"

"My what?"

"Your watch. I'm most dreadfully sorry. It was entirely my fault. I'm arranging for it to be collected in the morning."

"In the morning?" Laker was a little slow.

"Sometime before noon if that's convenient."

"Oh yes . . . Very well." Suddenly there were a dozen questions welling out of last-second misgivings, but an open line made them impossible. "Is that all?"

"For the present, Sam. And thanks. I was banking on you, you know."

You bet, Laker thought. He fingered his watch, wondering how they would tamper with it; what it would carry. But at least he knew the means of delivery, and it wasn't difficult to guess how it was to be effected. The knowledge was curiously reassuring, underlining Slattery's insistence on the run-of-the-mill nature of what he'd agreed to do. Even so, how much of a fool was he to have committed himself?

He wasn't allowed to dwell on it without interruption. Carol plied him with a score of letters for signature and there was a joint report by Wilson and Farrow, suggesting a way out of the Design Group's difficulty, marked FOR URGENT COMMENT. Laker tried to concentrate on it there and then, but after a while he gave up. Leipzig kept intruding. Gale & Watts hadn't an export business worth talking about, so there was no possibility of doing them harm. And, as regards Patrick . . . Hell, if he started along those lines he'd better change his mind while he could. He was sufficiently lukewarm as it was without thinking in terms of the consequences of a slipup. Slattery had surely played his proxy game long enough now to have this aspect of it perfected. Behind the beaming smile and blinking bespectacled eyes he was deceptively shrewd, a realist, and Laker's lingering doubts found refuge in that. Scores of export executives toting their briefcases around Europe must have acted as unpaid postmen over the last few years—Slattery had as good as suggested as much. And this was about what it came to—being a postman.

He stayed on for half an hour after Carol left, but the Wilson-Farrow argument still demanded more of him than he seemed able to give, so he decided to take it home. Patrick was there when he arrived, the maps spread out, a sentence in one of his tour leaflets underlined: *A cable car will take you high above Rüdesheim to the Germania Monument, erected in the last century as a symbol of Bismarck's united Germany.*

"There's nothing in the papers," Patrick grinned meaningly, "but what exciting thing's happened to you since breakfast?"

MacDonald rang through from Reception sharp at eleven next morning.

"Person for your watch, sir. Shall I come up or will Miss Nolan come down?"

"Come up, John." Then: "No, on second thought ask *him* to come up."

"Right away, sir."

Laker's curiosity didn't reward him with anything out of the ordinary. A rather thin young man with a spaniel-like face and a neat brown suit presently put his head around the door. "Mr. Laker?"

"Correct. Come on in."

The suit was good; the tie instantly recognizable. It would have been interesting to know what he did with the rest of his time. For an absurd moment Laker thought of asking him whether he was in the habit of collecting watches.

"Do I get a receipt?"

"I'll write you one if you wish."

Laker shook his head. He unstrapped the watch and slid it into an envelope.

"Thank you," the young man said.

"That's all, I take it?"

"I think so, Mr. Laker. Good morning."

A minute afterwards Laker watched him from his window cross the forecourt and drive off in a plain, dark blue van.

No one more casual or disinterested entered the office throughout the daylong press of work: only the naked feel of Laker's left wrist kept sharply reminding him that the undertaking had moved a first stage from acceptance toward execution.

Slattery left him alone for twenty-four hours. It was noon on Saturday before he chose to telephone. Laker was in the book so it was no surprise to be caught at the house. But he said: "Another few minutes and you'd have missed me."

"Sorry, the weekend's always chancy, I suppose. Could we meet one evening?"

"When?"

"Tomorrow?"

"I'm playing bridge tomorrow."

"Monday?"

"It'll have to be Monday. Tonight I'm tied up and Tuesday's my last evening."

"All right, then. Let's say Monday. And to spare you the burden of all the comings and goings, how about meeting halfway?"

"Where?"

"The Mitre, Hampton Court. Nell Gwyn Bar."

"Fine," Laker said.

He arrived a quarter of an hour before the agreed time, ordered a Scotch and waited. He had managed not to think about Slattery too much over the rest of the weekend. But on the short drive from Roundwood, and now, as he looked about him at the prosperous self-sufficiency of the bar's occupants, an undercurrent of uneasiness tugged at him. Oh, he'd do it. He wouldn't cry off at this stage. But the sooner Wednesday had come and gone, the better. And in—what?— less than six days' time he'd be done with Leipzig and Pat-

rick's carefully planned side of things would have begun—
Heidelberg, Mannheim, Worms, Mainz, Rüdesheim, Kochem,
Coblenz . . . It was the boy's holiday, after all.

"Hello," Slattery said, suddenly at his elbow. "Have I
kept you?" He pulled a vacant chair from the next table and
sat down.

"What'll you have?"

"A pink." He almost changed his mind. "Yes, a pink . . . I
did explain, didn't I, that I can't stay?"

"You did."

"My wife's old father's been stomping round Kew Gardens
all afternoon and he's dining with us. He's as deaf as a post,
more's the pity, and I'm the only one in the family whose
voice has the right timbre, or whatever it is, so my presence
is virtually obligatory on these occasions."

He leaned back, brushing his sparse hair with the flat of
his hands, blinking from table to table as if innocently in
search of friends.

"Good luck, Sam," he said when his gin came. "And thanks
again."

Laker shrugged.

"Down to business?"

"I'm ready."

"How good are you on telephone numbers?"

"It depends. I remembered the Gerrard one. Try me."

"Double three, four two, eight six." Slattery repeated it.
"Salt it away." He tapped his head.

Laker's lips moved.

"Got it?"

"I will have."

They were quite close, their voices sufficiently low.

"Do you know Leipzig?"

"I was once there as a kid, but it's all a blur now."

"What's your hotel?"

"Astoria."

Slattery nodded. "There's a jeweler's in the Luisenstrasse —a five-minute taxi ride. The description's flattering, I admit, but that's beside the point. The name's Kromadecka." He spelled it out. "All right?"

"Yes."

"It's small, but you can't miss it. All you have to do is to ask them to fit a new watch strap."

"Nothing more?"

"Nothing more." Slattery's smile seemed to be prompted by a memory. "I told you, it couldn't be more straightforward."

"When do I get the watch back?"

"There and then."

"From you, I mean."

"Sorry, stupid of me. I'll have it delivered on Tuesday evening, to your home."

"I see."

Slattery signaled a waiter. "Scotch, is it?"

"Please."

Neither spoke for a few moments. People were coming and going all the time. A girl laughed nearby, content with the world she knew, safe. Leipzig seemed very remote. "Happier about things now?" Slattery beamed.

"You haven't raised any gooseflesh, I grant you that."

"Any questions?"

"Only why the hell I should be doing it."

Slattery laughed his ridiculous cackle.

"This place, Kromadecka—"

"Yes?"

"Doesn't it matter who attends to me?"

"The problem won't arise. There's only one person there."

"I don't need to furnish recognition aids or anything like that?"

"No. Merely ask for a new strap, wait while it's fitted, then push off. Get on over to the Fair and begin picking those brains you talked about. Start your holiday, in fact."

"And the number? Where does that come in?"

"It won't." Slattery spread his hands almost apologetically. "Call it insurance, Sam. Wise-virgin common sense. Has it lodged, incidentally?"

"Three three, four two, eight six."

"It's like the emergency handle on the train. It's a million to one against your having to use the thing but it's reassuring to know it's there. The least I can do is to draw your attention to its existence." He matched Laker's gaze for a second or two. "Get me?"

"I get you," Laker said. He drew on his cigarette. There was always an element of risk, no matter how infinitesimal, and he'd made his own assessment of it. But he'd somehow have liked Slattery more if there hadn't been such smooth denials at Manchester Square.

"And I'll tell you this. You'll never hook me another time, not even if you were to go down on your knees."

He smiled grimly and Slattery blinked back, fingering his glass.

"Do you want to recap?"

"Not really."

"What time do you touch down?"

"Around noon. I've forgotten exactly."

"Do it that afternoon, will you, Sam? On Wednesday. Don't wait until the next day."

"I won't sleep on it, you can be sure of that. The quicker I'm through with being one of your acting unpaid supernumeraries the better I'll like it, believe me."

"Good man," Slattery said. He drained his glass with a hint of finality. "Now I'm the one who's against the clock. What are you doing?"

"Going home."

They walked out together. After the artificial brightness the dusk seemed thicker than it was; the river air surprisingly cool. Beyond the wall and the trees across the wide road Hampton Court shaped the skyline: intrigue had no end. A man and woman passed, the woman carrying a small child, and the child was wailing out of weariness and the ancestral fear of what the gathering dusk might conceal.

Laker accompanied Slattery to his car—a gray Rover with a Royal Thames Yacht Club badge. The prefix to the registration number was UUU and Laker recalled a once-heard music hall gag—"three volunteers." Slattery unlocked the door and turned—to shake hands, Laker assumed. But he said: "There's something I haven't mentioned, Sam."

"What?"

A bus trundled by, and Slattery waited. Laker could hardly see his face.

"What?" he asked more doubtfully, suspicious of postscripts.

"At Kromadecka's. You mentioned recognition."

"Yes?"

Slattery cleared his throat. "You'll know who it is."

"How d'you mean—'know'?"

"The person who'll fix your watch strap will be Karen Gisevius."

"Sammy," she had called him.

"Karen?" Laker echoed. "Karen?"

"That's right."

"But—" His thoughts seemed to be stumbling in several directions at once. He said stupidly, "She's alive, then?"

"Oh yes."

"My God." He could grasp so much and no more. Seconds elapsed. "My God," he said. "Why didn't you tell me the other day?"

"It wouldn't have been reasonable."

"Reasonable?" Laker frowned.

"To use her as a lever. It might have come to that if you'd refused in the first place. Happily, you didn't. But it's only right that I should put you in the picture now."

Slattery's head and shoulders were silhouetted against the Mitre's wisteria-covered, softly lit façade.

"How long," Laker began, faltered, then started again. "How long have you known?"

"Known?"

"That she'd survived."

"Some time, Sam. A goodish time."

"Twenty years?" Something akin to resentment had entered Laker's voice.

"Ten's more like it." Slattery delayed for a couple to pass nearby through the parked cars. "She was recruited in the mid-fifties but even then her name didn't ring an immediate bell. She's one of our best links, Sam. That's why it's so galling to have her out on a limb like this." He seemed to imagine that more was expected of him, because he went on: "There's been a misunderstanding. Not a slipup. No one's been blown—nothing as serious as that. Otherwise I wouldn't be involving you. I can't explain, and you won't expect me to. But the result is that contact's been broken and it's imperative to make the damage good."

Laker wasn't really listening. His mind was on the house and the gasping, blanketed body abandoned in desperation to the mercy of whoever came in answer to his rap on the door, the years telescoping as he thought of that and a score of related things, one of them being the day he sat in Slattery's Grosvenor Gardens office for the last time and worded his report about Karl and Günter and Karen Gisevius and the failure of the gamble called Operation Extension.

"I could have been told," he said.

"Not once she was on our books."

"Unofficially."

"Hardly, Sam."

Slattery's silhouette moved as he shifted his legs. The dusk seemed to be shrinking all the time and the cars dipping over the bridge were jostling into position for the rotary ahead. It was a ridiculous place in which to talk about anything, let alone this.

"Why not?" Laker persisted.

"It never crossed my mind, Sam. And we'd lost touch, hadn't we? Gone our own ways."

"Until it suited you."

"Until I read the *Evening Standard* last week."

"Oh balls," Laker snapped quietly.

He was strangely confused, filled with wonder that Karen lived yet feeling cheated for not having known of it and disturbed at the sudden prospect of meeting her again. It was too much to take at once and his stunned mood compounded an unreasoning anger with Slattery that was shot through with distrust.

"If there's one thing I can't stand," he said, "it's being led by the nose."

"Sam—"

"Once a pro, always a pro. It's your claim, not mine. You can't have it both bloody ways."

"I'm sorry. I had no idea—"

"Balls," Laker snapped again. "And another thing. Do you seriously expect me to walk into this place where she is and leave a handful of minutes later—just like that? Or have you forgotten your dealing with people instead of little pins on the map?"

Judiciously, Slattery took his time. "You'd rather not do it, is that it?"

"I didn't say that."

"I don't think you've fully understood my position. The whole world might be making tracks to Leipzig, but I can't employ any Tom, Dick or Harry. *You* know that. It's a fluke if you like, about you and Karen, but these things crop up. And I certainly wasn't going to put pressure on you by mentioning her right away."

"Ten minutes, you said. Then push off, get back to the Fair. . . . As uneventful as stepping out into the street. What sort of person do you—"

"I was merely underlining the extent of the commitment." Slattery spoke as if he were justified by a set of rules. "She'll be the best judge of what's possible and what isn't."

Laker pursed his lips, still confused, still bitter. It was late in the day to have baited the hook. He glared at Slattery in the dusk. Karen Gisevius . . .

"She's one of our best, Sam."

"I don't doubt it."

It bewildered him to realize they weren't speaking of the past, or of the dead. The use of the present tense kept ramming home the shock, awakening memories which time had grafted onto him so that the longer he listened to Slattery the more moved he became. Question upon question began to queue in his mind, but Slattery's answers increasingly had the quality of protective gestures.

"Listen, Sam—and don't get me wrong. I'm not running an international social contacts bureau, nor am I holding a gun to your head. You're still at liberty to cry off. It's up to you, entirely up to you. It has been from the start. But now you know it's Karen I rather thought you'd be especially glad to help."

"You make it sound like a good turn."

"Isn't it?"

Christ, Laker thought.

"Isn't it?" Slattery insisted. "Isn't it first and foremost exactly that?"

Two worlds were overlapping as Laker drove back to Weybridge, thinking, thinking, sensing already that nothing would ever be quite the same again.

Chapter Four

THE watch was brought to the house early on Tuesday evening. Laker had left the office before the usual time and was there to take it in. The small blue van looked as if it might have been the same one, but the man who came to the door certainly wasn't and he struck Laker as an unlikely accomplice—squat, middle-aged, untidy and badly out of condition if his shortness of breath was anything to go by. If Mrs. Ruddick had accepted the slim, brown-paper package it would have been odds on his getting a tip. As it was he simply asked Laker's name, nodded and walked away, his somewhat moody glance at the roses implying that, given the opportunity, he too could make use of leisure.

Patrick had gone upstairs to try to squeeze yet another afterthought into an already bulging suitcase and Mrs. Ruddick was quietly clattering in the kitchen. There was no writing or typed label on the package. Laker took it into the living room and broke the seals, drew out the watch and examined the strap. Unmistakably, it was his own. Whatever had been done to it was completely invisible. They'd un-

stitched it, he presumed, but he couldn't detect the slightest
trace of extra bulk or resewing. Slattery had been as good as
his word on the score of technique ("Even you will doubt
that you're carrying anything, Sam.") and Laker had never
been more than mildly curious regarding the details of the
message he would be delivering at Kromadecka's. But from
the moment Karen Gisevius was mentioned the project had
taken on an entirely new dimension.

For a day and a night he had tried to convince himself
that he had no reason to feel aggrieved at the way in which
Slattery had played his cards. There was logic in his argument as to why he had avoided mentioning Karen until the
last. But, knowing the potential of her name, it was naïve to
imply that for ten years or more the thought of at least
privately reporting her survival hadn't so much as crossed
his mind. So was the specious nonsense about having lost
touch when, only a couple of days earlier, he'd been quoting
from Laker's file.

He wasn't easy to fathom, and renewed acquaintance had
reminded Laker how slight their association ever was. Outside the Mitre his apparent insensitivity to everything except
the main chance had injected anger into Laker's confusion,
obliterating from the wake of the initial shock any purity of
delight or astonished curiosity. These had emerged since,
strengthening as Laker's resentment mellowed and he tried
to reason that Slattery was inhibited by a special code of
laws and moralities. Slattery's parting words had been:
"We'll meet when it's over, Sam." In the gloom he had
fumbled a handshake like a Freemason searching for the
correct pressure point. And only then, for the briefest possible duration, Laker had thought he detected the very
slightest flaw in the bland, puzzling indifference. "No hard
feelings, I hope—now or at any time."

He gazed into the garden, thoughts focusing on Karen.
She would be about thirty-eight now, thirty-seven or thirty-

eight. He could only picture her as she once was—thin, freckled and with eyes that burned with a gravity beyond her years. Everything else was conjecture, what they had shared being merely a springboard for all the wandering question marks which filled his mind as he sought to imagine what might have happened between his leaving her at the house near Gardelegen and her now being at a jeweler's in Leipzig. He thought about her with a curious sense of unreality, as if he still couldn't completely accept that by tomorrow afternoon he would have seen her, vaguely concerned with the shape of his own life as much as with hers, drifting from one query to another, one problem to another, thinking about survival, dying, being chosen and not being chosen, recovery, living, about the war which had brought them together and the kind of peace that would do so again.

He had never been back: Germany was split from north to south even before he was out of uniform, with Gardelegen behind the wire and the freshly sown mines. He wrote, though. He wrote the Red Cross and other likely authorities, but they couldn't help. Twice he went as far as to send letters direct, addressing them as a child might—*Large Gray Stone House, 3 kms. Southwest of Gardelegen.* . . . But there was no answer and, in his heart, he had scarcely expected one. Europe was a place of ghosts and its desolation had swallowed her up along with the millions. She remained a memory, as vivid and deeply branded as the murders he'd committed on his way out; dead, for all he knew, as dead as the hate that had made them possible.

He had to keep reminding himself that she wouldn't realize he was coming. It was useless to speculate on what had brought her back into the game, yet the watch on his wrist and the telephone number stored in the recesses of his mind were proof that tomorrow was first and foremost Slattery's business. But Slattery wasn't the only one to have lost contact and it was inconceivable that the Kromadecka shop on the Luisenstrasse would lead to an exchange of watch straps and nothing more. Inconceivable, Russian Zone or no. . . .

"Dad," Patrick was calling from the stairs, "what do you think I should do? Load my camera now, or in the morning?"

It was an early flight: 8:55 from London.

Low slicks of mist threatened the approaches to the airport, but there was no delay. Exactly on time the Viscount soared into the overhanging blue. Laker and Patrick were forward of the starboard wing and Patrick had the window seat; he'd only flown twice before and it was still very much of a novelty. As soon as Laker released his belt he looked over his shoulder along the tube of the fuselage: much as he'd expected there was hardly a woman passenger to be seen. The man directly across the aisle was already browsing through a glossy catalog of toys and construction kits and the hum of conversation somehow lacked the normal defensive arrogance of English travelers on holiday; it sounded more in keeping with any expense account Pullman on its way to or from the Midlands.

They were to put down at Amsterdam and Laker's guess was that ninety percent of those aboard would transfer to the Leipzig connection. He eased back into his seat and stared past Patrick's profile at the mottled drift of Surrey and Kent. By the time the gray and pink encrustation of Canterbury was discernible on their left the morning's collation had been served, the flight particulars passed along and Patrick's concentration on the view beginning to wane. He grinned at his father and fished out a German phrase book.

"The postillion," Laker said, "has been struck by lightning."

"That one's not here."

"I honestly doubt if it ever was."

" 'Where can I obtain a good phrase book'—that is, though."

"I don't believe it."

"Cross my heart."

Laker chuckled. His own German was excellent. "What's 'The Trade Fair'?"

"*Die Messe.*"

He took the book, opening it at random. "How about 'How do we get to the museum?' "

Patrick screwed his face. "*Wie komm man—*"

"*Kommt. Wie* kommt *man . . .*"

"*Wie kommt man zu dem Museum.*"

"Full marks. They must be teaching you something at Greynham after all. Now . . . 'Is there a price reduction for students, singly or in groups?' "

"Ouch."

"No?"

"Definitely no."

"Try 'Are there any jellyfish or dangerous currents?' "

Patrick deliberated, then retrieved the book. "I'd better stop while I'm ahead. Anyway, who's swimming?"

"You never know. We'll be over the sea any minute."

"Pessimist."

Except for the eyes, Patrick didn't much resemble Helen, but in this respect they were memorably alike—blue, with thick dark lashes. "Look after him, Sam," she had whispered that afternoon before they put her under for the unavailing operation. No one had told her, but she must have sensed it was hopeless. "Look after him for me, won't you?" Laker glanced away almost guiltily, fingering his watch, torn between the slight yet ineradicable malaise that recurred every time he considered what he had undertaken on Slattery's behalf and the eagerness with which he anticipated the chance it had given him. In the room looking onto Manchester Square his rejection of the proposition had been quite automatic. No, he'd thought, the amateur in him instinctively on guard—and again as he'd brooded in the car in Brook Street. And then, somehow, by a series of mental stepping-stones which he couldn't precisely retrace, he had found himself swung over, unenthusiastic yet willing, arguing away the risk he might be running the further he committed himself until, finally, Karen dominated every aspect of the assignment.

And yet. And yet . . .

"Did you know," Patrick said, flicking through a leaflet now, "that Bach was cantor at the Thomaskirche in Leipzig?"

"If I did I'd forgotten."

"I wonder if the Liverpool guides will mention the Beatles in a couple of hundred years' time?"

Laker winced theatrically.

"It's quite a thought, isn't it?"

"Everyone will be going to the moon by then," Laker said.

A quarter of an hour passed. Toy ships floated in the wrinkled expanse of sea. Soon the coast of Holland showed, brown and wandering, flanking their line of flight. It was barely ten, but in a heavy Dublin brogue the man across the aisle asked the stewardess for a Jameson, and seemed genuinely put out when informed that Irish wasn't available: he settled for Scotch and two hundred cigarettes instead. Construction kits, Laker reflected, must be doing very nicely indeed, thank you.

Presently a girl's voice clicked on, brittle with courtesy. "In a few minutes we will be landing at Amsterdam, ladies and gentlemen. Would you please extinguish all cigarettes and fasten your seat belts. . . ."

There was the best part of an hour's hanging about at Amsterdam. The transit lounge was resonant with disembodied announcements and the occasional whine of aircraft. Outside, the day was fine: the sky still cloudless. Patrick bought a Coca-Cola from a machine and, through the windows, fired off a couple of shots with his camera at a Caravelle disgorging its load on the hard nearby.

"By the way," Laker said, "I'd be careful about using that thing while we're in Leipzig."

"Even at the Fair?"

He shrugged, aware that he was being absurdly inconsistent. "It's the Russian Zone, after all." Aware, too, that he had suddenly sounded like Slattery. "Better check what the form is first."

They flew on in a piston-engined aircraft operated by Czech Airlines; it looked like the old Dakota. After the Viscount's smoothness it was a bumpier, noisier ride, though the furnishings were a good deal more ornate: the windows had tasseled velvet curtains and the seats were covered in scarlet velour. "Wow," a bald-headed man in front exclaimed as everyone was settling in, "it's like a whore's parlor," and his companion said drily: "You ought to know, George."

No flight maps were provided, but Patrick had brought the BEA one along and it wasn't difficult to make an intelligent guess at their route. To begin with they headed into the sun, east, and they were low enough to interpret the shifting view—the metallic-looking Rhine, the industrial haze of the Ruhr far to the south; later the Ems with what could only be Munster dragging under the port wing.

Laker had been right: most of the London passengers were still with them. More names for Slattery's files—it was an odd and still unacceptable thought. Laughter, over-enunciated English to the stewardesses, voices raised above the engines' din: Spurs might have been playing in the European Cup. The person nearest to him caught his eye and asked, "Didn't I see you last year?"

"In Leipzig?"

"Yes."

"I wasn't there."

"First time, eh?"

"Yes."

"Odd. I could have sworn we'd met. What's your line?"
Laker told him.

"You're starting the young man early, I'll say that." This
with an amiable nod toward Patrick. "My name's Black, incidentally. Dargle and Tait, Ilford . . . optical goods."

Laker wasn't in the mood for shop, and to his relief the
man seemed more or less content to let it go at that. Patrick
was saying, "Do you reckon that's the Weser?"

"Could be," he answered, peering.

"It must be."

"You're the navigator."

It was impossible to block out the past. His first time to
the Fair, yes; but he'd flown this way before, in cloudy moon-
light, with a diversionary raid on Magdeburg to distract attention, and he suddenly remembered the dispatcher, a New
Zealander, leaning back from the intercom and bawling,
"Skipper says we've passed the Weser. Hanover to starboard.
Two-fifteen and not a mouse stirring. . . ." And then he remembered another time, days later, when he lay with Karen
in the covered depression among the spruce trees. Huddled
close, her breath warm on his face yet frosting in the air, she
had said, "Do you know what I'm thinking, Sammy? I'm
thinking how normal tonight is for millions of other people—
at home, out dancing, at the theatre maybe, sitting somewhere by a fire, having a bath, cooking, feeding the baby,
making love. . . . When is it going to be normal for us,
Sammy?"

He closed his eyes and let the darkness in. No need for
qualms. He was a postman. Only fools were picked up; fools
and those who risked the deep water. For all he knew, Leipzig would be swarming with front and cover organizations.

Intelligence had become a major postwar industry. Getting rid of the strap would be child's play. But meeting Karen again wasn't something that could be conducted across a counter in the space of a few brief minutes.

Surely, he thought, it was going to be possible to see her after that?

Clouds began to obscure the land. Toward noon they turned southeast, canting over, the sun swinging. They were due in at twelve-twenty. Patrick had put the map away. The white scar of an autobahn made itself visible and other gaps in the overcast offered tantalizing glimpses of minor roads and railway tracks spidered between towns and villages clustered about the gray-green countryside.

"Do you know what?" Patrick said. "I'll send a card to Hans Meiner. That'll shake him."

"Which is Hans?"

"The boy in Rostock."

"Ah." Slattery was inescapable. "What about the others?"

"Oh, I'll do them too. Gilles, Paris; Erich, Hanover; Jenny, San Francisco; Manuel Chapi, Barcelona . . ." Patrick ticked them off on his fingers.

"Only one girl?" Laker smiled. "What happened to that glamorous thing who used to write from Athens?"

"I wish I knew. She was a bit square, though."

"Don't forget Mrs. Ruddick."

"And Tim Maxwell. Still, the point is to get one off to Hans when I'm on his side of the fence. You know—wish you were here; having capitalist time."

Patrick laughed, pleased with his joke, and Laker fisted him playfully on the shoulder. Once, a year or so ago, when they were searching the storeroom at Roundwood, Patrick had come across the box containing Laker's decorations and medal ribbons, but there was no mention of Karen in the citations and Laker had never spoken about her. What would he tell him now, supposing they all could meet? "A friend," would he say? "Someone I worked with during the war, long before you were born, before I even knew your mother, someone I believed I would never see again."

The stewardess with the severely swept-back hair and the trained smile that could have masked contempt had started along the gangway, signaling everyone to fix their belts. They were lower already, the vibration more marked, wallowing a little on the up-currents.

Cloud streamed like mist past the windows and, quite suddenly, the outskirts of Leipzig slid obliquely into view like a multicolored street map. Instinctively, Laker pointed. The aircraft seemed to search for a line, then chose one and held it, slanting in, wheels down, flaps down, throttled back, flattening out as the runway rose abruptly out of a smear of crops and hedgerows.

"Dead on time," Patrick said like a seasoned traveler as soon as the jolt was over.

The airport formalities weren't too prolonged. An announcement, first in English, then in French, greeted them as they filed indoors: "Passengers are requested to present their passports and Fair Cards at the Immigration Bureau. Facilities are also available for currency exchange. All inquiries regarding the Trade Fair should be addressed to the Information Department in this building or to the Foreign Visitors' Center at the New Town Hall. . . . Thank you."

They had to queue at Immigration, but there were no difficulties. Returning to Dover after a day-trip to Calais couldn't have been easier. A page of their perforated Fair Cards was stamped and detached; a nod and they were clear. Perhaps because the Customs official hadn't expected Laker to answer in German he chalked squiggles on their luggage without asking for anything to be opened and even went as far as to wish them a pleasant stay in the German Democratic Republic. Then they were free to move into the high, echoing Arrivals hall and pass under the flags and welcoming banners which draped the exits.

Outside, another queue waited for taxis. Theirs, when it came, was a Skoda, newish, with a photograph of Ulbricht stuck on the windshield like a talisman and a driver who wore a black plastic cap with a duckbill peak.

"Astoria Hotel," Laker said.

He was sweating thinly, and Patrick remarked on it. He shrugged. "It's a bit stuffy." But he glanced at the rearview mirror all the same, deriding his caution even as he did so, aware only then of the effort the Customs had cost him. And yet they'd waltzed through. Dismissively, he concentrated on the drive, watching Leipzig straggle toward them, alien and unrecognizable. Roundwood, Gale & Watts, Mrs. Ruddick, Carol Nolan—all at once they seemed immensely remote, in time as well as distance.

The city took shape, disappointingly graceless and functional, the heavy Russian style of the outlying tenement blocks and the more central commercial area only partially redeemed by the temporary rash of decorative bunting. The treeless squares were as drab as parade grounds and there was a heavy sprinkling of uniforms on the thronged pavements. Laker had forgotten who had recommended the Astoria, but he'd booked weeks in advance and even then it had meant Patrick sharing a room with him. As they entered the foyer the Irishman from the plane was already on his way out, giving them the thumbs-down sign as he paused.

"Mr. Laker?" a plump woman receptionist inquired, studying the hotel's letter of confirmation he'd produced. "Mr. Laker and son?" She pronounced it "Larker," but he let it go. He nodded and they waited. The décor was confused—modern pastel incongruously burdened with Edwardian gilt

—and the place seemed packed. When the woman spoke to them again it was in English. She hadn't much charm but she was certainly efficient. "Yes, that is in order, Mr. Larker. You have a reservation for two days. You will both complete and sign the register, if you please."

They did so, and she said, "Your room is number fifty-four." She couldn't manage the "r" and it sounded like "womb." Then she pinged a bell and a cadaverous porter collected the key and their luggage. The elevator whined them up to the third floor.

"You're busy," Laker remarked to the porter.

"Busy, yes. Oh yes. Fair time is always busy." He looked as if life had tried to crush him, and might do so yet. "The whole world visits Leipzig for the Fairs." When it came to a tip he asked for cigarettes instead of money.

The room was on the small side, but adequate. Twin beds, a handbasin, a single wardrobe. The atmosphere seemed heavy, as if peat were burning somewhere. Patrick opened a window and they stared out. Beyond the immediate solidity of the neighboring façades there were vacant, rubble-heaped lots and bomb-truncated ruins. Nearer, a poster implored housewives to collect scrap. Everything looked gray and it had begun to spit with rain.

"Well," Laker said. "What do you think?"

"It's different."

"From what you'd imagined?"

"No. Just different—like the old newsreels. Does that make sense?"

"After a fashion."

Patrick unslung his camera and tested one of the beds. "Still, the womb's all right."

Laker smiled. Fourteen, he thought.

"Shall we lunch now? I'm starved."

"Right away." But he delayed at the window, wondering where the Luisenstrasse was.

It was a reasonable meal. The dining room was loud with the collision of voices. Laker recognized at least three of the London passengers scattered about: Black was one of them and he seemed to be fraternizing to good effect. He waved vaguely in Laker's direction.

Laker took out the folder into which Carol had put all the Fair particulars and glanced through them. There was no reason why they should go to the Foreign Visitors' Center; he'd changed twenty pounds at the airport and had no desire to "meet and converse with trade partners in your particular sphere of interest," as one of the leaflets worded it, either at the New Town Hall or at the Messedienst—"a must for information and assistance in the advancement of international Fair business."

He wasn't there for that, or for the junketing. From the first his intention had been to make a couple of visits to the Fair itself, one general, one more specifically on behalf of Gale & Watts, and to fill in with some routine sight-seeing for Patrick's benefit. A few hours' snooping around the Business Systems section was the most he'd envisaged, and even before he was hooked by Slattery he had decided to leave that side of things until the following day. The general tour of the Fair could start after lunch, so nothing had changed—nothing, that was, except having to leave Patrick to his own devices for a short while.

He said, "I'll have to duck away for a bit this afternoon. You know—business. It would only bore you."

"For how long?"

"Not so long. We'll get over to the Fair as soon as we've unpacked and then, say about four, I'll leave you to browse on your own for a while. Okay?"

He was restless now, wishing the damn thing off his wrist; but not on that account alone.

They had the choice of a dozen or more exhibition buildings and the overall effect on Laker was rather as if Earl's Court and Olympia and the old British Industries Fair had been lumped together in the city's center. Once off the streets and confronted with the panoply of the various trade displays, it was hard not to forget that, in Slattery's phrase, they were behind the lines. Plush carpeting, ingenious presentation, subtle dioramic lighting—it was the same shop-window world with the same eye-catching gadgetry, the same kind of product demonstrators, the same extrovert bon-homie of the salesmen with their little screened-off cubicles for dispensing hospitality, the same smoky stuffiness, the same sort of voices and earnest, brow-furrowed groupings. Jerry Baxendale would have been in his element.

Laker went through the motions of showing interest, but his mind was increasingly elsewhere. The television and musical instrument section was like the Radio Show in miniature and it seemed the best possible place in which to leave Patrick. Time was getting on: time to go.

"You'll be all right?"

"Sure."

"It's almost four now. I'll be back before five. But just in case I'm not, or you get bored around here, push off to the hotel."

"Okay."

He handed Patrick some money. "Don't blow it all on records."

Patrick grinned and he left him, suddenly uneasy, regretting the necessity. At the exit he turned and looked back, as if the scene would somehow offer reassurance, then made his way into the street. It was still spitting with rain. He found a taxi-rank under some plane trees at the corner of the first block and asked for the Luisenstrasse.

"Whereabouts?" the man said. "What number?"

"Twelve," he answered, guessing, not wanting to give the name or to be vague.

He sat on the edge of the seat, a tightness in his stomach. Fair directions were everywhere but he had no idea which way they were heading. "A five-minute ride"—though that was from the Astoria. Off to the right he glimpsed a railway station, then a square dominated by an ungainly piece of statuary. Thereafter the concentration of flags and banners began to peter out: there was another Leipzig and it came quickly, more nakedly drab, billboards no longer proclaiming a welcome.

EVERY INCREASE IN OUTPUT IS A NAIL IN ERHARDT'S COFFIN. . . . WE ARE LEARNING FROM SOVIET SCIENCE, THE MOST PROGRESSIVE IN THE WORLD. . . . DO YOUR SHARE AND STRIKE A BLOW FOR THE GERMAN DEMOCRATIC REPUBLIC. . . .

Bicycles were everywhere. Lights delayed them and Laker watched the passersby: they were cosmopolitan no longer and their faces showed evidence of the hard life. Some stared, as if a taxi were a novelty, and it seemed to him that the stares were suspicious; hostile, even. They gave him a disturbing sense of isolation, of having strayed out-of-bounds. This was far enough, he kept thinking, far enough. And then, as if in obedience to his silent urging, the taxi made an abrupt right turn and cruised to a halt in front of a secondhand clothing shop.

It was an unlikely destination to have chosen. He climbed out and paid the man off, then made a pretense of tying his laces, giving the taxi time to draw away. The rain had stopped. There were shops on both sides of the street, two-storied mainly, a run-down look about them: a queue of women gossiped outside a baker's opposite. He lit a cigarette and started walking. It was a hundred yards or more before he saw Kromadecka's—just as he was beginning to have an awful feeling that he must have come to the wrong place. It was diagonally across the street, narrow-fronted, the name lettered in black on a yellow ground. In the minute it took him to reach it he twice looked over his shoulder. He would have felt less exposed amongst a crowd, but the Luisenstrasse had none to offer. Apart from the queue it seemed almost unnaturally quiet—few people, no cars, hardly a cyclist.

He walked at an even pace. "Nothing to it, Sam . . ." He had talismans of his own. "Couldn't be more elementary . . ." But there was more to this than actively taking sides in a war and, despite the tension, he was strangely elated. Ten yards away he slowed, keeping to the outside of the pavement so as to widen his view of the shop. A clock centered in the window showed that it was a little after a quarter past four. There was a hand-written notice taped to the inside of the glass.

WATCH REPAIRS
ESTIMATES FREE
PRICES MODERATE

It greeted him like an invitation, something meant for him personally, and he reached for the door, eager to make an end of being manacled to Slattery and effect a beginning of his own.

Chapter Five

A BELL above the door tinkled as he went in. The place was small, cluttered, glass cases forming a counter on three sides. Through a curtained opening he could see the base of some stairs leading out of a back room.

"A moment, please."

It was a woman's voice; soft, quite cheerful. Time had blurred how Karen had sounded, but it could only be hers—Slattery had said so—and Laker heard the intensified thud of his heart above the irregular ticking of several clocks. The walls were hung with them. In the cases were cutlery sets and a few pieces of silver plate, embossed pottery, tankards and some glass: after the lavish sophistication of the Fair everything looked pitiable. He wiped his face and waited, suddenly caught between anticipation and a kind of dread, staring about him, wondering. There was a selection of watches in a wall cabinet, and an old square safe screwed to the floor in the opposite corner.

A truck ground past just as he heard her on the stairs. Before she came through the curtains she was saying, "I'm sorry, sorry." And then she was there, the curtains closing behind her. "Good afternoon. Can I help you?"

Perhaps it was vanity, but he thought she hesitated when she saw him. For a second or two it seemed as if her face clouded with incipient disbelief, her brows knitting slightly as she moved behind the counter. But, for his part, he had no need to rack his memory; reality matched the basic image. He would have picked her out in the street, in a restaurant—anywhere. The gentle freckling, the broad mouth, the blond hair; above all, the eyes—as brown and grave as he'd remembered.

"What was it you wanted?"

He mastered emotion. Again, momentarily, he believed he detected the beginnings of a frown of recognition.

As dutifully as a boy on an errand he said, "A new watch strap."

If she felt anything she didn't show it. She gave nothing, absolutely nothing, away. "Any special kind?"

"Something like the one I'm wearing will do."

He took the watch off and handed it to her. She had dropped her gaze now.

"It's an English strap, isn't it?"

"Yes," he said. "I got it in London."

She nodded and reached for a batch of cards, each displaying a choice of samples. She was very calm, very practiced.

"I can't give you leather. Imitation is the best I have; the alternative would be plastic."

She wore a darkish orange costume of tweedlike material and a white bead necklace. Her lips were only lightly reddened and her hair curled softly away from the forehead. The skin was a fine, delicate color. When she placed the cards in front of him, he saw how slender her fingers were. There was no ring, he noticed.

"Imitation will be all right."

And suddenly it seemed beyond reason that he should continue his part of the masquerade. He couldn't be bothered with the cards. He said quietly, "Don't you remember me, Karen?"

If she bore scars at all, they were in her eyes. Now, as she lifted them to his, he saw for a fleeting instant not merely wariness but a whole background of apprehension, like an illness she had learned to live with.

"Sam," he said. "Sam Laker." Then, as if it were a code word, "Sammy."

There was nothing then but the sound of the clocks. For a long time that was all. He thought her stare would never end.

"Sammy?"

Smiling, he watched her expression as she made the leap in time, her eyes widen a fraction, the line of her mouth alter. He didn't know what he expected—delight, wonder, incredulity; any or all of these. The incredulity was dawning, but there was something else as well; dismay, perhaps—he couldn't decipher it. She lifted a hand to her throat.

"No!" she said. "Oh, no!"

"Am I so different?"

She didn't answer.

"Am I?"

She shook her head, staring still, searching his face. Slowly, she began: "I didn't expect—"

"How could you have?" He leaned nearer, Patrick forgotten, Slattery forgotten. "You look fine, Karen. You haven't changed." Matured, filled out, but not changed. "As soon as you came through the curtains—"

"I . . . I can't believe it," she said. She shook her head again, closing her eyes momentarily. "Sammy Laker"—and now when she used his name the wonder was there.

"You frowned when you saw me. I thought perhaps—"

"It was the light," she said. "You were against the light."

"You didn't guess?"

"No."

"And now?"

"There's no need to guess now." Her lips were trembling. "I thought you were dead, Karen—until forty-eight hours ago, that is, when they asked me to do this."

Laker gestured toward the watch lying between them: they were safe here. Thoughts a million times faster than speech were racing through his mind. He began to talk about the Red Cross, about the letters to the house near Gardelegen, very moved suddenly, and all the time she gazed at him as if certainty hadn't quite enveloped her yet. Little by little she seemed to be shedding her dismay or whatever it was he imagined he saw; but there was no smile.

"How long have you been in Leipzig?"

"Since 'forty-seven."

"And in this shop?"

"Twelve years. It was my uncle's. When he died I kept it going."

"Do you live here?"

She raised her eyes to the ceiling. "Upstairs."

They paused then. She had hardly touched the watch.

"I wondered about you," Laker said.

"So did I," she said. "I wondered, too. Many, many times." A kind of tremor seemed to pass through her. "I still haven't grasped it, Sammy . . . You."

He nodded. "And they say miracles never happen." He offered her a cigarette but she refused, with a fluttering gesture. "Tell me about yourself."

She shrugged.

"Were you ill for long?"

"At that house?"

"Yes."

"Not so long. They were very kind."

He had the feeling that she couldn't give her mind to what

had happened all that time ago. Biting her lower lip she stared at him, denied in some way the ease to let her wonder live and grow out of the passing moments. They both faltered sometimes, lost for words. Behind Laker's back a clock whirred and struck the half-hour. He'd almost forgotten what had brought him there. Even in the silences he seemed to be learning something about her. He wasn't sure whether Karen asked him or not, but he found himself telling her about what he had done since the war; about Helen. She must have asked, otherwise he would hardly have been speaking about Helen so soon, but he was confused himself, split by many emotions.

"There are children?"

"A boy—Patrick. Not that he's a child anymore. He's with me in Leipzig, incidentally." Another clock was chiming. "Are you married?"

"No," she said.

"Were you?"

"No."

Someone went by in the street, a woman wearing a headscarf, blinking the light from the window as she passed. Karen glanced quickly that way and he realized anew how tense she was.

"You will have to go," she said.

"Not yet."

"Soon." Slattery's comment echoed in her tone—"I'm not running a social contacts bureau, Sam."

"You've got to fix my strap first."

She picked up the watch and reached into a drawer for a pair of sharp-pointed pliers.

"How many years have you been fixing straps?" he asked. "Straps from London?"

She frowned over the watch, probing with the pliers, but refrained from answering.

"Or shouldn't I ask things like that?"

Without looking at him she said, "You have never done this before, have you?"

"Does it show so much?"

She nodded.

"There's a whole lot more I want to ask."

"There won't be time."

"I'm here until first thing Friday morning. At the Astoria. Couldn't we meet there?"

"It would not be wise."

"Tonight, for dinner?"

"No, Sammy."

"Why not?"

"You know why."

"But, hell—" he began, the amateur in him hurt. He thought of Black, Black who could fraternize openly in the hotel's dining room, and the score of animated meetings he'd witnessed during that selfsame afternoon. Leipzig was packed with foreigners, its arms flung wide in the interests of trade. Openly, in the Astoria's bar, with Patrick, and then to dine, the three of them—where was the harm?

He tried to put it to her, but she only shook her head.

"I can't."

"Do you want to?"

"Of course," she said. "Of course."

"But you won't?"

"It's not a risk I can take." She looked at him. "Believe me, please."

Once she had risked so much, survived so much. They both had. Suddenly he remembered that other time, and her saying, "When is it going to be normal for us, Sammy?" Suddenly he realized that in a few minutes he would be out in the street. One wing of the strap was already detached and she had started picking at the fastening of the other. Slattery loomed once more. The Mitre, the flat in Manchester Square and the plain blue van. "She's one of our best, Sam . . . There's been a misunderstanding. You can get her off the rack."

Laker stubbed his cigarette. "I can phone you, surely?"

"No."

He stared at her, striving to accept that her coolness toward him wasn't willful.

"I can't just go," he said. "I can't just walk away. Not after twenty years. I can't just say good-bye and not see you again."

"You must."

"Can't you suggest something? Isn't there a park, or a square, or a café?"

"Don't push me, Sammy. It's no good." She unclipped the other wing of the strap, more clumsily than before, her movements showing signs of stress. "Don't you understand?"

"I do, but—"

"Already you have stayed too long."

"Ten minutes?"

"They must have told you how it would be."

He said nothing.

"I didn't know you were coming." Now, all at once, she was near to tears. "I didn't know *who* was coming, or even when it would be. I'm not expected to know, I'm not expected to ask. That isn't my part of it." Her eyes burned, brown and huge, yet her face still held its fine color. "I thought you were dead, Sammy. And not until forty-eight hours ago. Until just now. It's harder for me—can't you see? I didn't know it was going to be you standing here." Her lips trembled again. "Oh, God," she finished wretchedly.

"I'm sorry," Laker said. "I'm sorry, Karen." He seemed tongue-tied. Impulsively, reaching forward, he touched her on the cheek. For a moment she didn't draw away, but suddenly she stiffened.

"No."

Her voice was sharp. She pulled back and bent her head over the watch. Outside, there was the drag of footsteps.

"Vopos," she whispered tersely.

"Who?"

"Vopos."

The light faded as the window was partially blocked. Out of the corner of his eyes Laker saw two members of the People's Police, one taller than the other, and the taller of them was leaning forward as he peered in, hoisting his shoulder-slung carbine.

"Which strap have you chosen?"

Karen's tone had utterly changed: the cards shook slightly as she held them in front of him.

Laker pointed. "I'll take that one."

The light swelled again as the figures moved. He thought they were going away, but he was wrong. When the doorbell tinkled, his neck prickled coldly. They came in, heavy boots gritting on the worn linoleum, and stood behind him, close because of the lack of space. For an awful moment that seemed quite interminable he remained woodenly at the counter, expecting them to speak, to challenge him even. The two wings of his old strap lying on the glass looked frighteningly conspicuous.

Karen finished unfastening the new one from the display card before addressing them. "Can I help you?" It amazed Laker that she should have the ability to smile.

One of the two cleared his throat. "You have a brooch in the window."

Over his left shoulder Laker focused briefly on a fleshy, constipated face under a green fore-and-aft cap, a young face with thick lips and a snub nose. Then he turned his head away.

"Would you like to show me which one?"

"I will wait."

"It's no trouble. You can be making up your mind while I finish with this gentleman's watch."

Karen moved to the window: the Vopo who had spoken followed suit. "There," he said. "There, yes, that's it."

She returned to where Laker was standing without so much as glancing at him. In his relief he marveled at her control, but there was lead in his heart. A kind of angry dejection filled him as she began fixing the new strap into position. It was almost unendurable to wait to be dismissed, unable to speak with her again, let alone to make one more plea that their reunion shouldn't end in such a fashion. Behind him the two Vopos muttered over the brooch. "What do you think?" one of them said. "Will it do?" and the other answered, "Do? She'll fall for it. Look, if I hold it you can see it better." As if mesmerized, Laker stared across the counter, watching Karen's small-boned hands fold the last clip down with the pincers.

Then she was saying, "There, sir . . . I think you'll find that's satisfactory."

Sir. . . . He took it from her, vainly hoping to hold her gaze if only for a second, aware that she was facing the Vopos, yet hoping despite that. "Thank you."

There were a thousand questions, but nothing was possible. He paid with a note. The till was on a shelf fixed to the wall and as she turned she casually picked up the pieces of the strap and dropped them into an open drawer, for all the world like a woman for whom tidiness was everything. And when she spoke to him again, counting out his change, he might have been exactly what he was meant to be—a stranger.

"Thank you, sir. Good afternoon."

The sound of the doorbell seemed to mock him as he walked away. Yet the resentment locked within his feeling of deprivation wasn't directed against her. The Vopos had served to remind him of the dangers. Until they came the shop had seemed quite safe; Slattery's game—her game—a shade unreal, undeserving of extreme caution. But now that alarm had brushed his own nerves he more fully understood the high wire on which she existed, and it was this that he hated—its discipline and its denial.

For what? Yes, for what?

He crossed the street, his mind whirling, selfishly grateful that she had almost reached the brink of tears. The past meant something, then. He hadn't nurtured an illusion or romanticized a memory.

It was getting close to a quarter to five. An enormous effort was required to bring his thoughts to bear on where he had arranged to meet Patrick. He walked briskly, heedless of his surroundings, hoping to find a taxi. There was a telephone booth at the first intersection. She had insisted that he mustn't call but he went in and looked for Kromadecka in the tatty directory, scribbling the number, the number only, hurriedly in his diary. He wouldn't use it for a while, perhaps never; but he couldn't accept that he had seen the last of her. Tomorrow, perhaps, he might return to the shop, ostensibly to buy something. He would have to think what to do, what was best—weighing the possible risk to her against what the last fifteen minutes had aroused in him.

He walked with his shoulders hunched, embittered by the irony of the situation, unable to think very clearly. After several hundred yards he found himself passing a bookshop. *Art Is a Weapon*, the window display proclaimed. Inside, he asked where he could get a taxi and the assistant, speaking slowly as if unsure of Laker's command of the language, directed him to a rank a couple of blocks away. The driver at the head of the rank accepted him without enthusiasm and crunched through the gears on his way to the Astoria. Patrick would almost certainly have gone back to the hotel; it was as near to five as made no difference.

The streets spread themselves as they approached the area of the Fair. Under the bunting and the banners there were crowds again, people moving with varying degrees of purpose, the stiffening of uniforms among them. He was in the clear now, a postman no longer, so the uniforms conveyed no sense of personal threat; yet they were indicative of his dilemma, the outward and visible reason for care before he made a second move toward Karen.

He recognized the Ring-Messehaus, with its fringe of flags hanging limply after the rain, but he failed to see the railway station he had passed on the previous journey. Vaguely, he suspected the driver was giving him a tourist's runaround and soon he leaned forward, saying "Astoria" in such a way as to indicate that he knew his Leipzig, only to find that he didn't. Hardly had he spoken than they were drawing up outside the hotel, scraping the curb.

He suffered the driver's smirk, paid, and turned toward the steps. The heavy peatlike scent enveloped him as he entered the foyer. There was no sign of Patrick. He hesitated, wondering whether to wait for him there or to go on up to their room. And, as he hesitated, a man in a light raincoat rose from one of the tables near the entrance and approached —a shortish man with a slightly lopsided face.

"Mr. Laker?"

He didn't use the broad "a." With affected ease Laker said, "That's right."

"Mr. Samuel Laker?"

"Yes."

"I have some unfortunate news, I'm afraid, Mr. Laker."

"Oh?"

"There's been an accident." He stuttered slightly. "I'm sorry to say that your son has—"

"Accident?" Scalp tightening, Laker snatched at the words. "What happened?"

The man started on some rigmarole about stairs, a fall, but Laker couldn't wait for him to finish.

"Is he badly hurt?"

"He was unconscious when they put him in the ambulance."

"Where is he?"

"At the University Clinic."

"God!" Laker said.

He wheeled blindly for the doors, isolated by the shock, unaware that he was followed. But on the steps his arm was grabbed.

"This way, this way . . . I have a car."

He remembered being guided to an old gray Mercedes and getting into the back seat, the man in the raincoat lurching against him as the door was slammed. Another man was already at the wheel and they started to move almost immediately, nosing into the traffic.

"When did it happen?"

"Half an hour ago."

"How's he injured? Is it his head, or what?"

"I couldn't say exactly. But don't alarm yourself too much. I don't think you will find his condition too serious."

"Unconscious, you said."

"Yes, but—"

"Did you see him?"

"Not personally, no."

"Was it at the radio and television place?"

"Yes, yes; that's right."

"God!" Laker said again. He felt sick . . . stunned. "I left him alone for a while because there was some business I had to attend to and I thought it would bore him. I wondered at the time whether I was making a mistake. But his German's not bad, d'you see, and he's normally quite capable of looking after himself." Anxiety, self-reproach, spilled over. The streets blurred past. "How far's the hospital?"

"Not too far, Mr. Laker."

His hands wouldn't remain still and he brought them together, the knuckles bone-white. He heard himself say, "It's very good of you to help like this. I appreciate it." By talking he could at least keep his imagination under control. "How did you recognize me?"

"Please?"

"How did you know me? Or that I'd be at the Astoria?"

"Your son said you would be there."

Laker frowned. "He *was* able to speak, then?"

"I understand so. To begin with."

He found himself looking at his companion as if for the first time. The man had a hat on now, a brown trilby. The person at the wheel was bareheaded, wearing a black leather jacket; around the cropped blond hairline his neck was inflamed with boils. "Take a left," the one with the hat said, and Laker felt the centrifugal tug as the tires snickered. Since the shock hit him he had been in a daze, apprehensive of what awaited him, oblivious of the distance they were covering. The minutes passed. He couldn't for the life of him understand how Patrick had come to pitch down a flight of stairs, but his questions increasingly drew a blank, a shrug. Suspicion was some way from taking hold, but his wits were thawing a little and it struck him that the man was losing interest, more concerned with their route and issuing directions. Twice in succession they bore right. There was less traffic and the streets had narrowed: it was the other Leipzig again, cheerless and gaunt with factories squatting amid old untended scars.

Laker said urgently, "What's the hospital called again?"

"The University Clinic."

"Are we nearly there?"

"Soon."

But there was no indication of it. On edge, he said, "Wasn't there anything more central?" He glanced at his watch. Time suddenly took meaningful shape. Where were they? They were moving fast and the city was running more and more to seed.

"Who are you?" he said, alarmed by a wild doubt.

The man shifted position, but didn't answer. Small, bright eyes; a crease-bracketed mouth.

"Look, where's my son been taken? Where's this hospital?"

"Keep quiet, Mr. Laker."

Laker stiffened, heart missing a beat.

"There is no hospital and there has been no accident." The slight stutter emphasized the injection of menace. "Keep quiet and don't try anything foolish."

"What the hell are you talking about?"

"I'm talking about you, Mr. Laker. Do as I say and you will come to no harm."

As casually as if he were about to offer a cigarette the man withdrew his right hand from inside the raincoat. Dropping his gaze, Laker saw an automatic pistol.

"Otherwise," the man said, "I will have no alternative but to kill you."

Chapter Six

LAKER stared at the gun with incredulous dismay. Fear crawled clammily over his skin.

"Is this a joke?" he managed thickly. "Some kind of a joke?"

"No joke, Mr. Laker."

They must have covered a quarter of a mile before another word was spoken and throughout that time his thoughts spun in chaos.

Karen, Kromadecka's.

He achieved that one coherent deduction before the confusion regained its hold. With as much control as he could find he said, "What's the meaning of this? Just what do you think you're doing?"

Except with his eyes the man ignored him.

Laker licked his lips, desperately seeking to pacify himself, not to bluster. "Look," he said, "I don't know who you are, and I don't care, but you've made a mistake. A bloody silly mistake." But it was hopeless and he already knew it. Something had gone wrong, terribly wrong; the gun and the two men and the story about Patrick were an integral part of disaster.

"Where are we going?"

No reply.

"What about my son? Where's he?"

"In good hands, Mr. Laker. Safe and sound."

"Where?" he shouted. Then he tried again, more persuasively. "I'm a British subject. This is ridiculous. Intolerable" —echoing the protests of all those who had ever walked into a trap; and again, even as he formed the words, he knew the futility of them. Appeals, bribes—these were out, too. He'd fallen for the oldest trick of all and it was twenty years since he had been within reach of a weapon, twenty years since he was trained in the unarmed skills that might have led to a physical break. Pressing against his side of the car he felt unable to move, held by the gun and the other's eyes, his groping relief that Patrick was uninjured whirled away by apprehensions so tortured that they amounted almost to a physical pain.

"Who are you?" he demanded. "Police?"

"We aren't kidnappers, Mr. Laker."

"Who, then? And what am I supposed to have done?"

"You will find out." A joyless, off-center smile. "But, if it is any comfort to you, my colleague and I have official blessing."

They were leaving the fringes of the city: numbly, Laker was aware of a smear of crops behind the man's head, trees dotted about an untenanted green slope. For a moment or two his thoughts seemed to reach a state of appalled calm, but before he could attempt to reason the confusion began to renew itself, repeating his mind's instinctive cry of dismay when he first saw the gun. Patrick was at the heart of it, Patrick and Karen and Slattery. And there were others, others who were involved in that they were a part of the pattern of his life, faces and places near and far, all frenetically scrambled together, kaleidoscopic images sweeping him as if he were drowning.

Christ, he thought. Oh Christ.

He started feeling for his pockets, but the man checked him.

"I want a cigarette," he said.

"Use these."

A pack was tossed across together with some matches. Laker lit up clumsily, fingers shaking, narrowing his eyes against the smoke. Another weakening rush of panic surged through him. There had been nothing to arouse his suspicions, no evidence of being followed—no feeling the weight of another's scrutiny. Lies, denials—he must cling to these now. Karen would and so must he. They'd have picked her up as well; everything pointed to the inevitability of that. It couldn't be him without her. Her without him, yes, but not him without her.

Oh Christ, he thought again.

Pines stood along each side of the road. "Where are you taking me?" he asked a second time, but he might have been talking to himself. The sun flickered like a signal lamp through the trees and the driver grunted, reaching to retrieve dark glasses from the empty seat beside him.

They were heading northeast and it had passed the half-hour. A sign pointed to Berlin, and Laker felt an inner cold blow through him, chilling him in the marrow. Minute after minute he was stumbling around in his mind for a clue to what might have betrayed them, yet his most desperate anxiety was still for Patrick.

"What do you mean by 'in good hands'?"

"Exactly what the phrase implies, Mr. Laker."

"But where is he? What's he been told? I was meeting him at five."

A shrug.

"He's fourteen. Fourteen—a kid. And he's only once before been away from England."

He waited, but there was no answer.

"Are you deaf?" he suddenly raged through his distress. "Why the hell can't you explain what this is all about?" Then finally, in English, "You bastard. Whoever you are, you sodding bastard." And he saw the man's eyebrows contract and knew he'd understood.

An autobahn crossed their path like a dike. They took the looping underpass and gradually the trees straggled back to fence the road. They must have been seven or eight miles from the outskirts of Leipzig before the driver cut his speed. A track led off to the right. They nosed clear of the tarmac and headed into the pines, the car slewed a little as the wheels shuddered in and out of some ruts. Laker stared about him, sensing the journey was almost at an end yet baffled by the sudden change of route. The pines hemmed them in and he felt his isolation as never before. After about half a mile the track branched and they bore left, not far, debouching eventually into a small clearing in which there was a log hut. If Laker had anticipated anything beyond the certainty of an interrogation, it wasn't this.

"Listen," the man in the raincoat stuttered quietly. "No foolishness. Get out and remain still. Don't move. Don't do something you might regret."

Laker obeyed woodenly. The driver had beaten him to it. Until his companion had rounded the back of the Mercedes he stood close to Laker, close but not too close, as watchfully as a wrestler. Blue specks were sand-blasted into the coarse facial skin and the mouth was sullen. Over Laker's shoulder he must have received a signal because he nodded and turned toward the hut.

"Follow him, please." This was from behind.

Three wooden steps led up to a door. There were several

windows, none of them curtained. A board fixed to the nearest side of the hut stated in red on white FIRE CONTROL. B SECTOR. The driver fished a key from his leather jacket, unlocked the door and pushed his way inside. Laker entered as cautiously as the pistol at his back allowed. Everything seemed dark for a moment or two and then, as his vision adjusted, he found himself in a squarish room in which was nothing except a table and a few hard chairs. Another door led out of the room, but this was closed. A single bulb with a white enamel shade hung from the central rafter.

"Sit down." The man in the raincoat elbowed the door to, then removed his hat, motioning with the automatic as he did so. "Sit at the table and empty your pockets." What passed for a smile pushed his features askew. "Everything, mind."

Laker glared at him, risking stubbornness. "Who the devil are you? Just what authority have you got?"

"This." The gun. "This will do for now. And if you think I wouldn't use it you are very much in error."

The room was resonant and their voices bounced off the bare walls. Laker emptied his pockets slowly, the only show of defiance remaining to him. Wallet, pen, nail clippers, comb, handkerchief, cigarettes and lighter, some loose change, diary . . . Panic could still block his thoughts to reason and, as he put the diary on the table, he remembered with a prickle of alarm that it contained the Kromadecka number.

"Anything else?"

"No."

"It would be wise for us to make certain, don't you think? Take your overcoat and jacket off. And your trousers." There was a pause, during which Laker did nothing. "You have no option, Mr. Laker. Hurry now."

The driver went over them as minutely as if he were looking for lice. All he found were a couple of old cinema ticket stubs, but the seam which Carol Nolan had resewn on the right shoulder of the jacket interested him. He produced a clasp knife, slit it open and explored the wadding, ignoring Laker's protests. Eventually, after a shake of the head, he tossed the clothes onto the nearest chair.

Laker put them on again, his anger as impotent as his desperation. "What did you expect?" He swallowed. "Look, this is monstrous. I demand an explanation. I'm in Leipzig for the Fair, a bona fide visitor, and my son's expecting me at the Astoria Hotel. You've made a mistake, I tell you, and the sooner—"

"If there has been a mistake, Mr. Laker, you will be entitled to, and will receive, the fullest amends. Meanwhile we can only wait and see."

"Wait?"

"Wait, yes."

"How long, for God's sake? What for?"

"I mentioned, didn't I, that your arrest had official blessing?"

"Arrest? Now look here—"

"The last half hour has perhaps been a little unorthodox. However, Colonel Hartmann will be here at six and he, better than anyone, will be in a position to judge whether a mistake has been made. Colonel Hartmann, you see, is head of S.S.D.—the State Security Service."

With that the man picked up the diary, crossed his legs and began to turn the pages. "Watch him," he said, and Laker saw that the driver had a pistol, too.

Again the milling confusion of mind descended. And again Slattery was there—"No one's been blown; nothing like that . . ." Well, Karen was blown now, and he was linked with her. The two Vopos? No, no. How, then? He still couldn't think straight. There was an awful feeling of emptiness in him, as if his strength had been sapped.

It was ten to six, and the sun was splintering lower through the pines. He went to the nearest window and stared out. The immediate landscape wasn't irrelevant to his fears. Why had they brought him here instead of to some urban headquarters? He turned nervously, in need of another cigarette, but the driver warned him away from those he had left on the table and threw him one of his own instead.

"Mine aren't poisoned," Laker said bitterly, but the man only cleared his throat and rubbed the barrel of his automatic on his sleeve. You lout, Laker thought. He looked at the one leafing through the diary, and as if he had been given a cue the man said, "I see your son's birthday is the same as mine—June 14th."

Laker glared, hating him. It was imbecilic to have noted the Kromadecka number, yet it would be equally mad to deny having been in the shop. He would have admitted to that in any case. They knew, anyway. Karen was the focal point of what had happened and for him to be here at all could only mean that she must have been under suspicion long before he set foot in the Luisenstrasse. Why else had he been hijacked?—and so promptly? If only he could calm his mind. . . . He smoked about halfway down the cigarette, weakness returning like a fever. Then the one in the raincoat rose and dropped the diary on the table. He had given no indication of having noticed the number; in fact he'd appeared to be more interested in the London underground map than anything.

"You were a busy person, Mr. Laker," he remarked. "You lived a full life back there in England."

He said it as mildly as a priest reproving a common vice. At any other time Laker might have fastened in alarm to the use of the past tense, but for some inexplicable reason he was suddenly aware of the correct pronunciation of his name. The receptionist at the Astoria had called him "Larker," but this man had never made that mistake. Not once. He had been right from the very beginning ("Mr. Laker? Mr. Samuel Laker?") and the only other person in Leipzig who'd addressed him accurately was Karen.

A terrible possibility entered his head. He tried to shove it aside, attributing the accuracy to Patrick, but it insisted, boring in. With an almost convulsive movement that tore skin from dry lips he snatched the cigarette from his mouth, searching his memory for Slattery's exact words outside the Mitre—"A misunderstanding, Sam. I can't explain and you won't expect me to. But contact's been broken. . . ." In disbelief he then remembered something else. "No!" Karen had said when she recognized him. "Oh no!" And with a sense of derangement he found himself interpreting her look of dismay as one of guilt. Had she been aware of what was going to happen? Could it be that she was blown *before* Slattery ever approached him; her shock principally that of discovering whom she was forced to expose? "Oh God," she had uttered finally. "I didn't know it was going to be you standing here. . . ."

Every instinct in him clamored that he had to be wrong. It was unbelievable that he should be thinking of her as if she were a kind of enemy when only an hour ago he had been moved by her very closeness. Yet the fact remained that within fifteen minutes of his leaving Kromadecka's the Mercedes was at the hotel, *waiting for him,* along with the lies about Patrick and this devastating, slowly burgeoning seed of Laker pronounced as it should have been.

If she had been under duress he was sunk. He heeled out the cigarette on the floor, subsided onto a chair and for barren moments afterwards rested his head in his hands. He didn't hear the car coming. The others did, and the man in the raincoat went outside. But after perhaps a minute he was conscious of voices, the one that stuttered and the one he didn't know, and the clatter on the steps.

He was expecting someone in uniform, but he was wrong. Hartmann was wearing a dark brown belted overcoat and a black velour trilby, the brim of which was turned down back and front. He was tall, lean, older than Laker, and his eyes had a slightly fixed stare, like a ventriloquist's. He paused when he saw Laker, looked at him for a long moment with apparent disinterest, then motioned to the driver, who had stopped leaning against the wall and was suddenly at attention.

"I'll use the other room." The voice was throttled, as if he had had laryngitis.

"Yes, Colonel."

The driver opened the communicating door and snapped on a light. The other two went through and the door was shut, leaving Laker and the driver alone. Laker sweated, listening to the murmur which reached them through the partition, protest and apprehension compounded below layer upon layer of hopelessness. Several minutes elapsed before the door opened again and the man in the raincoat emerged.

"All right," he said, and jerked his head.

It was a similar-sized room, with a table and only two chairs, but the whole of one side was stacked with buckets, bags of sand, coiled lengths of hose and long-handled birch brooms. All but one of the windows were obscured, so the electric light was necessary. With a renewal of bewilderment Laker questioned why he had been brought to such a place. He felt scared, scared and irresolute, as if he sensed that he wasn't far from the borderline of nightmare.

"I understand you speak German."

"Yes."

"Very well. Sit down."

They faced each other across the empty table. Hartmann's swarthy complexion seemed to emphasize the blueness of his eyes. Narrow nose, straight gray hair. His hat had left a pres-

sure-weal angled across his forehead and he rubbed it gingerly.

"The two in the other room aren't the only ones who are
armed." The strained voice, the ventriloquist's stare. "Is that
clear?" He didn't wait. "Now tell me something about yourself, Mr. Laker." The "a" was correct again, feeding Laker's
newfound conclusions.

"I want to know why I'm here, first."

"We'll come to that."

"I want to know now. And I want to know what's become
of my son." He was like an actor with no faith in the weight
of his lines. "If you can't tell me I insist on being taken to
someone who can."

"To whom, for instance?"

"I don't give a damn as long as I get some answers."

"And an apology, I suppose?"

Laker shifted position.

"What would you expect this apology to cover?"

"My God," Laker snapped. "What do you think?"

"False arrest? Or is your objection to the manner in which
it was carried out?" Hartmann seemed amused. "There was
no violence, was there? If you cast your mind back you will
realize that my colleagues employed the Judo technique of
using their opponent's muscles."

Laker leaned toward him. "I was told my son was at the
University Clinic. But since I now know that was a lie, where
is he? Who's looking after him? What kind of explanation's
he been given about this . . . this nonsense?"

"The story is that you've been called away."

"He won't accept that."

"He really doesn't have any choice."

Laker clenched his hands. "Where am I supposed to have
been called to? For what reason? And for how long? I've a
right to know. And I've a right to be told on what grounds,
what possible grounds—"

"We aren't here to discuss your son. And rights, you will discover, begin and end with me." Hartmann paused to rub the diminishing weal. "You should have taken his welfare into consideration before you came to the Democratic Republic."

"I don't follow."

"No?" The tone was almost conversational, but his eyes never once left Laker's face. "You will, though. I am certain you will. . . . Now, what brought you to Leipzig?"

"I came for the Fair."

"On your own account?"

"No."

"What line of business are you in?"

"We design and manufacture office equipment."

" 'We'?"

"My firm. Gale & Watts."

"In London?"

"No."

"Where, then?"

"In Weybridge, Surrey."

"I see. . . . And have you found our Fair worth the visit?"

"What I've had time for, yes."

"How about your particular trade section?"

"I haven't been to it yet."

"When did you arrive?"

"This morning."

"By air?"

"Yes. I applied for Fair Cards at your Agency office in London two months ago—for myself and for my son."

"Never having been here before?"

"Not since I was a child."

Hartmann nodded. "How did you and your son spend this afternoon?"

"On a general look-around." Laker tried to match the stare. Now the crux was coming.

"A general look-around at what?"

He moved his shoulders. "Sports goods, photographic equipment, radio and television—"

"So you didn't visit the section you specifically came to Leipzig to see?"

"We're on holiday as much as anything and I gave the boy his head this afternoon. Tomorrow, though—"

"Where else did you go, Mr. Laker?"

"Personally?" He hadn't meant to stall, but he couldn't seem to help himself.

"Personally. What decided you to separate from your son?"

"I went to get something done to my watch."

"What, exactly?"

"It needed a new strap."

"And where did you go?"

"To a shop in the Luisenstrasse."

"The Luisenstrasse?"

"Yes."

"And the name of this shop?"

"Kromadecka."

Another skillful, demoralizing pause. The overhead light seemed to burn brighter.

"Why there?"

"How do you mean?"

"What made you choose that particular shop?"

"It was recommended."

"Oh yes?"

"I broke my old strap on the plane. One of the passengers suggested I ought to go to Kromadecka."

"Mr. Laker," Hartmann said, "there are half a dozen places which you could have gone to within walking distance of the Astoria Hotel."

"I wasn't aware of that. I haven't been in Leipzig for over thirty years."

"So the distance to the Luisenstrasse surprised you?"

"Yes—I suppose it did."

"You went by taxi?"

"Yes."

Hartmann rested his chin on his knuckles. "Your only reason for going to Kromadecka was to have your watch attended to—am I right?"

"Quite right."

"There was no other motive?"

"No."

"You would swear to that?"

"Certainly."

For a lunatic moment Laker thought it possible that there was some sort of hope. But almost at once this died.

"When did you write the Kromadecka number in your diary?"

"On the plane."

"Why not the address?"

"I wasn't given the address." Suddenly he was floundering.

"A telephone number only? By a stranger in an aircraft?"

"Yes."

"You expect me to believe that?"

"It happens to be true."

Seconds elapsed. Then, gazing across at him with what could have been pity, Hartmann said, "You are very much a novice, Mr. Laker. Those people who sent you—"

"Gale & Watts?"

"The people who sent you to Kromadecka . . . Didn't they tell you the cardinal rule?"

He stood up, walked to the door and opened it. The man in the raincoat was there, like an eavesdropper.

"Bring the Gisevius woman in," Hartmann said, and Laker's heart plummeted as he spun around.

Apart from the first frightened glance she would not look

at him. She was dressed exactly as when he saw her last except that the white bead necklace was gone. Her hair was slightly disarranged. She came in as if she had been pushed, then halted abruptly, swaying a little, terribly pale.

"Do you know this man?" Hartmann asked.

"Yes."

"Explain how you know him."

"He called at my shop." It was a whisper, almost inaudible, but there was no hesitation.

"When?"

"This afternoon."

"For what purpose?"

"To renew the strap of his watch."

Laker had got to his feet. Wheeling on Hartmann he protested desperately, "I told you. I told you this."

Hartmann's face was expressionless. "What was sewn into the old strap, Fräulein? The one he left with you?"

"Microfilm."

An insect pinged against the light. Hartmann glanced sidelong. "You see, Mr. Laker? Or do you still insist that your arrest is without cause?"

"I don't know what the hell you're talking about."

"No?"

"No," Laker shouted, dismay absolute.

"Are you making out that we have confronted you with a liar?"

Laker choked back the instinctive assent. Karen's eyes were prismatically blurred, averted from him. Hartmann allowed time for an answer, then nodded to the other man.

"Very well. Take her away."

She went without prompting, as if she wanted to run from the room, but in the doorway she turned suddenly and met Laker's gaze, sobbing, defeated. "I'm sorry . . . I'm sorry . . ." The man in the raincoat shoved her into the other room. Laker heard them cross to the outer door, heard it opened and slammed. The grass killed their footsteps after that but the sound of her crying seemed to go on and on, bitter and broken, matching his own wretchedness.

And Hartmann's throttled voice was saying, "Spare me, please, the story that you were merely doing a friend of yours in London a favor. I have heard that one before, and there is nothing more tiresome than repetition."

For perhaps another quarter of an hour Laker denied everything except having visited Kromadecka's; either that or he met Hartmann's leads with a dogged silence. In a mood of heartbreak and recrimination the ragged edges of his mind isolated themselves from the reality of Hartmann's presence and turned in hostility upon the mainspring of disaster, Slattery—Slattery who must have been aware that, at best, Karen was on thin ice and that anyone sent to contact her was running an abnormal risk. *Must* . . . So he should have been told, warned; instead of which he'd been criminally misled. And now, as at Gardelegen years before, he was as good as written off, Slattery's get-out number as useless as the wireless set which wouldn't work. And this time he was trapped, without choice of action, run to earth on behalf of an organization he didn't know or belong to and which would almost certainly disown him.

Whose game *was* this? Whose war? Not his. Not Patrick's.

Hartmann had just said, "You are either an unfortunate fool, Mr. Laker, or a benighted idealist. The Gisevius woman is clearly the latter—though in her case, since she is a German, such a phrase is a euphemism." The ventriloquist's stare was there again. "Which are you, Mr. Laker?"

Laker looked through him.

"Did it not occur to you that this might happen? How much did they tell you in London before they borrowed your watch?"

He didn't answer. They knew more than he did. Karen had

branded him from the doorway, and the remembered sound of her voice sent a pang through him as stunning as grief. She must have been as powerless as he was now. Chance had worked against them both, lain in wait for them after half a lifetime, and London would have ditched her as well. Nothing he said would help her. And he owed Slattery nothing, absolutely nothing. His first loyalty was to himself and to Patrick and it was better to stick to the lies and protestations than offer one word too many. Cooperation wasn't a way out. What was on the microfilm? What kind of postman had he been?

"I want to see my son," he cut in on Hartmann.

"That will not be possible."

"Why not?"

"There won't be time."

Time? Time? "I want to write to him, then." He licked his lips. "A note. I'm . . . I'm trying to be practical. He's got no money, to start with, and—"

"That side of things has been taken care of."

"Who by?"

"By my department."

"He's fourteen," Laker said, veins swelling in his temples. "If there's a spark of sympathy in you—"

"I'm aware of the boy's age."

"He hasn't done anything."

"I'm aware of that, too. But, as I said earlier, we didn't meet to talk about him. And remember this, Mr. Laker. You are a long way from home. What's more, your country does not recognize the German Democratic Republic. This, as you will discover, is greatly to your disadvantage since it means that what are sometimes called your interests cannot be safeguarded."

Again, for a fleeting moment, Hartmann's face seemed to register a hard-held pity. Then, abruptly, as if he had come to a decision with himself, he got to his feet and went out, taking his hat, leaving the door open. Laker heard a muttered conversation in the other room. Craning around, he saw the driver framed by the doorway, arms crossed, watching him. Half a minute later someone left the hut—Hartmann, he presumed—and presently he heard a car retch, roar, then purr away.

He moved to the solitary window, thoughts churning frantically. It was small, too small, the frame heavy. Daylight still held in the clearing and long shadows were printed across the grass. Why here? he questioned again. And what would follow? What happened to the others? Those one read about? A People's Court? . . . He couldn't understand why Hartmann had left without pressing him further, but his mind had been stretched beyond conscious usefulness and he could find no answers—to that or to anything else.

They left him alone for a few minutes. Presently the driver came to the door, the automatic like an extension of his right arm, and ordered him out. The man in the raincoat followed and the three of them walked across the clearing toward the Mercedes. The air seemed cold and Laker shivered involuntarily. A stained wash of clouds patched the gaps in the pines. Far off, a train rattled. He slowed as he neared the car but to his surprise the driver said, "Keep going." Puzzled, Laker started to round it, imagining that he was expected to get in from the far side, but the driver waved him on. When he hesitated the other one stuttered, "Into the trees, Mr. Laker."

Alarm entered him then. "Why?"

"Into the trees. Go on—move."

He obeyed, tightness gripping his stomach. Perhaps thirty paces brought them to the edge of the pines and his panic mounted with every step.

No, he thought. No. They couldn't.

The driver was three or four yards behind. "Where are you taking me?" Laker demanded, but there was no answer. The light faded as he entered the trees. The ground was springy, deadening their footfalls. The trees were well-spaced. He stopped again.

"What's the idea?"

Their faces confirmed his fears. Unnerved, he stared at them. *Jesus* . . .

"Hurry, Mr. Laker."

He seemed to have lost the ability to move. Suddenly the nightmare was on him, insanely improbable, yet happening, actually happening. He started to say something but his lips stuck to his teeth and a kind of leer resulted, dragging the corners of his mouth.

"Walk," the driver snapped. "Turn around and walk. Otherwise you can have it here."

Laker made about ten paces, a withering contraction shrinking his insides, numbing him through and through.

"Stop."

Almost immediately a rope was flipped over his shoulders, pinning his arms. He struggled as if an icy douche had restored his senses. The man in the raincoat stood with the pistol pointed at Laker's chest while the driver looped the rope around the nearest tree, then hauled so that Laker stumbled back. He began to bawl at them, demoralized, swept by a kind of frenzy, fighting against the rope, kicking, dread and disbelief compounded into an electric terror.

From behind, the driver fastened the rope across Laker's ankles, whistling tunelessly as he did so. Then he stood up, fumbled inside his jacket and brought out a thick brown paper bag. The last things Laker saw before the bag was shoved over his head were the blond hairs poking through the driver's chin and the smoke from the other's cigarette hanging on the air like ectoplasm.

The sugary smell of the bag and the acrid stink of his own sweat enveloped him. He stopped shouting, jerking his head, trying to toss the bag away. The driver was backing with the alacrity of someone who had lit a fuse; Laker could hear the crushing of pine needles. Light blurred through a small hole on one side of the bag. It wouldn't shift. Now, straining his ears, he tried to stifle the monstrous hammerblows of his pulse, desperate to identify the slightest sound.

His guts seemed to be liquidizing. Stiff against the tree, fingernails digging into the bark, teeth beginning to chatter.

No! . . . No! . . .

Silence.

Where were they?

A bird twittered somewhere in the branches. A cough, several yards away, its hoicking rasp muffled by the bag. A whisper. A metallic click . . . Time seemed to run to a halt. Laker screwed his eyes, images sweeping in raving disorder across the throbbing, blood-red darkness—Patrick, Slattery, Helen, Patrick, Hartmann, Karen . . . Patrick . . .

Body arched, the back of his legs beating a flabby tattoo against the tree, bladder beginning to empty.

Silence.

A tiny thread of awareness made him understand that time was moving on again. He cocked his head.

Nothing.

Then a sound, slow and deliberate. The soft crunch of someone walking. Half right. Coming closer. Laker held his breath. His lips moved, but nothing escaped them. His wits were resurrecting, clinging to life. The footsteps approached casually. Two or three paces from him they stopped.

Another silence that seemed to last as long as the spinning, recollected years. He flinched from whoever was there, whatever was happening. Finally the man in the raincoat spoke.

"Not today, Mr. Laker." It came with a rush as the stutter broke. "We'll forget about it this time."

And Laker vomited into the bag.

Chapter Seven

THEY helped him to the car, linking him in an underarm grip. One of them gave him some rag to wipe himself and afterwards, when he had slumped into the back seat, a metal flask was pushed into his hands.

"Cognac."

He shook his head.

"Cognac. You need it."

Through a blur of awareness he tilted the flask. The cognac caught at his throat and he started coughing. He pushed the flask away, bending over, heavily gasping for air. Then he slumped back again and closed his eyes, horror beating through him.

"Let's go," he heard.

Icy ripples were moving everywhere over his skin. The car lurched as it met the ruts and he swayed with it, limp and unprotesting. Shivering, hugging himself, he had no control over the reflexive spasms which occasionally twitched his body, nor could he unlock his jaws. He could smell the bag still and the foulness of his soiled clothes wafted up at him, reviving the tidal wave of fear and the release from it that had buckled his knees and made him sag on the rope.

Several minutes must have passed before the violence of the trauma began to ebb a little. After a while he opened his eyes and stared glazedly through the window, dimly conscious of speed, cars flicking the other way, the rubbery lick of tires. The sun had dropped below the horizon and the slopes were darkening below their gilded rim, but this didn't register. Questions were drumming a shaky tattoo against his senses, demanding an explanation. One thing and one thing only was clear—he wasn't alive because of any sudden change of heart. What had happened had been intended to happen.

A feeling of vertigo assailed him. Something else was in store, but it was beyond his powers of recovery to grapple with what it might be. He wound the window down and raised his face to the draft, ashen, oblivious of the driver's curiosity reflected in the quivering rearview mirror or the other's sideways glance.

They corkscrewed under the autobahn. Soon, Leipzig began to fashion itself, the scattered fringes rising out of the shrinking dusk.

"More cognac?"

The stutter, more than the voice itself, seemed to summon the enfeebling nausea. Laker groped forward, a gargling noise in his throat, but nothing came.

"Pull over, Hans. I don't want him messing the car."

They slowed and the man in the raincoat watched him as anxiously as a parent.

"All right?"

Laker nodded, threads of spittle hanging from his lips, wondering how much longer he was to be toyed with, cat and mouse, and to what end. Solicitude was as much a part of the nightmare as survival.

Where he was taken he didn't then know. It seemed to be the back of a building toward the city's center. A narrow entrance, a dozen or so stone steps and then a small rope-operated elevator which moaned them up to about the second floor. Several right-angle turns brought them to an expanding-metal gate which snapped behind them. The driver didn't accompany them beyond the gate, but the other one directed Laker along a short, ill-lit corridor. Nobody else was in evidence. They passed a number of plain gray doors, each with an exterior observation shutter. At the end door on the left Laker was told to halt. The man produced a key and tossed it to him, taking no chances even here, the pistol bulging his right-hand pocket.

"Inside, Mr. Laker."

There was a steel bunk, a wooden table and a galvanized slop-bucket; nothing else. Walls and ceiling were white-washed. High up, set in a chute, a small barred window framed a square of near-darkness. Two lights burned, one above the bunk, the other from a plug directly below the chute.

As soon as Laker stepped inside, the door closed and he heard the lock go on. Without as much as looking around he flung himself onto the bunk. For what seemed an immense amount of time he remained motionless, as if he had been poleaxed, staring blankly at the opposite wall, chained to a succession of appalling cameos that flitted across the surface of his consciousness. When he eventually gazed along the length of his body and saw what he had done to himself, he lacked any sense of shame. Thoughts stirred and eddied, shying from the edges of reality. But there was no refuge, no escape from whatever unfinished crisis chance and Hartmann had chosen for him, and the question marks continued feebly in the background with disordered insistence.

Soon after eight he heard movement in the corridor. He

sat up, muscles rigid by the time the door was opened. Someone he had never seen before came in, a youngish, dark-haired individual with a long penitential face who wore a white shirt and black trousers that could have belonged to a uniform. He was carrying a plastic bowl in one hand, a towel in the other.

Putting the bowl on the table he said impatiently, "I want your clothes." Then, as the towel landed on the bunk: "Your clothes. I haven't got all night."

Laker stripped to his shirt and underpants without a word, defiance bludgeoned out of him. There was warm water in the bowl and a cake of brown soap wrapped in the towel. When he was alone again he washed, then pulled a blanket over his shoulders and sat huddled on the bunk with his back against the wall, desperately trying to still his mind and to get a grip on himself.

"Not today, Mr. Laker . . ."

Whatever was coming he could find no basis for hope. Penciled on the wall to his left were someone else's initials together with a year-old date, and there were others when he looked for them, half a dozen or so, one spidered into the brickwork as if with a thumbnail, the date more recent. From the depths of shock Laker wondered who these people were and whether secrecy and half-truths had erupted into madness for them, too.

Toward eight-thirty the same man kneed the door open and brought in a tray on which were soup, a hash of some kind, coarse dark bread and a mug of coffee. On his way out he delayed to drop matches and a pack of cigarettes on the bunk, but Laker was beyond the reach of surprise. The sight of the food almost turned his stomach; he couldn't touch it. He drank the sharp black coffee, though, and lit up, inhaling so fiercely that it made him dizzy.

Patrick, Karen, Slattery—his mind revolved endlessly. It was absolutely quiet except for the small sounds of his own making and these seemed to increase his isolation. A star or two glittered in the dark square of the window. The hash formed a wrinkled skin as it grew cold. For what might have been hours he relived what the day had done to him, traveling again through expectancy charged with tension, tension with action, action with dismay, dismay with that awful escalation of fear; and now the savage, impenetrable remorse.

God, what a fool he'd been. What a blind, uncalculating fool. . . .

But it wasn't hours: when he next heard movement in the corridor he saw that it was only ten past nine. The man entered again, this time fully uniformed in black, carrying Laker's suit draped across his arm. His eyes, his expression, conveyed nothing.

"Put it on," he said, and waited.

The suit had been sponged and pressed; the tear in the right shoulder resewn.

"Where am I going?"

"Colonel Hartmann wants you."

Laker had guessed as much, but he was too exhausted to care. When he started to walk, his legs felt as though he'd been bedridden for weeks.

To reach Hartmann's office they descended an iron spiral staircase to the next level and made their way through a maze of windowless, yellow-brick corridors that smelled of disinfectant. Again they passed no one, saw no one. Presently they reached a door with a green light glowing on the lintel. The man ordered Laker to stop, then motioned him in, not following, closing the door as soon as Laker had passed through. And Hartmann was there, behind a desk in the center of a largish room, waiting for him with the choked, unforgettable voice.

"Sit down, Mr. Laker."

There was a chair on the near side of the desk and Laker

went to it, dry in the mouth. Hartmann studied him in silence, reverting at once to this particular weapon in his armory, using it now almost as if he hoped it would produce a reaction; hatred, perhaps.

"How do you feel?"

Laker swallowed.

"How was it in the pines with a bag over your head?"

No reply.

"An experience, eh? To be remembered?"

His shoulders were so square that he might have had the chair-back under his jacket.

"To be remembered?"

"Yes."

"Not pleasant, eh? Not willingly gone through again?" He tapped the desk. "Answer me."

"No."

Framed behind his narrow head was a color print of a healthy-looking Ulbricht. The desk was empty of papers. Glass ashtray, blotter, two telephones—that was all. Some filing cabinets lined one of the walls; slatted blinds shut out the night. But Laker's gaze didn't wander far.

"Why do you suppose you continue to be alive, Mr. Laker?"

"I don't know."

"Have you wondered?"

"Of course."

"Have you also wondered how it came about that you were ever taken into the pines?"

"Yes."

Hartmann cleared his throat to no effect. "With more success?"

"I can only think that you must imagine me to be somebody else."

"Somebody else?" It seemed to surprise him.

"Yes."

"Who, for instance?"

"Somebody more important."

"You aren't being very logical. The Gisevius woman identified you."

Laker gestured weakly. He would have tried to shield her once, but that was hours ago. Lies, denials, pretense—these were pointless now. She was sunk, too. There was no one to betray. "In which case," he said, "you've thrown her away on account of a nobody."

"Thrown her away?"

"As far as using her is concerned."

"Is that what you are? A nobody?"

"Yes."

"You're too modest. I wouldn't say that. I wouldn't say that at all." Hartmann leaned back, crossing one leg over the other. "In time I shall explain." He swung his free leg and let the silence settle for a few moments. With a kind of admiration he then said, "You are remarkably resilient, Mr. Laker. Not many could sit there and be so self-possessed so soon after what has happened. It was an outrage, was it not?"

Laker clenched his jaws.

"An outrage," Hartmann repeated as if he found pleasure in the word. "And I shouldn't like you to think anything so drastic is normal practice. The S.S.D. and its agencies have certain responsibilities, certain functions, within the Democratic Republic. I won't bother you with what they are. But, in the usual way, when a courier is intercepted he—or she—is most rigorously interrogated. How rigorously I am sure you can imagine. In your case, however, interrogation has been kept to a bare minimum. This is not because the Gisevius woman has volunteered all we might have wanted to know about you. Far from it. The fact is that, for once, we aren't particularly interested. All that interests us is your being here." He flicked a speck of dust from the blotter. "Does any of this make sense?"

"No."

"We have plans for you, Mr. Laker. You are about to work for us . . . Oh, yes. There is a job to be done. A very special job. It will mean your being taken from here and set free."

Laker frowned his disbelief.

"I assure you. Tomorrow you will be on your way. And you will do the job as surely as a puppet dances when the strings are pulled."

"I don't understand."

"Soon you will. First, though, I want you to get used to the idea."

"And if I can't?"

"You are not in a position to object. You're as good as dead, Mr. Laker. Don't tell me your memory's that short."

Now it was Laker who paused. "You said I would be released."

"That is so. By tomorrow evening you will be in Copenhagen."

"*Copenhagen?*"

Hartmann nodded.

"Why? What for?"

"To kill someone."

"*What?*"

"To kill someone," Hartmann repeated evenly. "Does it shock you so?"

He was met with an appalled stare. Laker heard himself say, "You must be mad."

"We're talking about you."

"I couldn't do it."

"You could, Mr. Laker. And you shall." Hartmann leaned on the desk. "I can read you like a book. I can almost see your mind working—do you know that? Copenhagen, you are thinking. How will he make the puppet dance at such long range? I will have a frontier behind me. He can't control me then. Why should I kill anyone for him? The idea's preposterous."

Laker dropped his gaze.

"Am I not right? You underestimate me if you believe I'm so naïve." Suddenly there was a trace of venom. "I thought you would be quicker to appreciate the situation. Must I explain what will operate the strings?"

A fearful possibility had begun to dawn, but Laker couldn't bring himself to utter it.

"Why do you think you were made to stand against that tree? . . . No? All right, I shall enlighten you. Imagination is a poor substitute for experience, Mr. Laker. You were put there so that you would know exactly what your son will experience if you fail in Copenhagen. The only difference being that, in his case, there will be no last-second reprieve. . . . Have I made myself clear? From the moment you are liberated until you complete this assignment it is going to be— how shall I say?—zero hour for him."

Hartmann watched the blaze of horror in Laker's bloodshot eyes.

"This is the crudest form of blackmail, I admit. However, I can assure you that the old-fashioned pressures are far and away the best. A few hours ago you were terrified in the marrow of your bones—and who can blame you? This is not to say that you wouldn't offer to be taken into the pines again to spare your son. It would be a natural enough gesture. Unfortunately for you, *I* choose who goes there and who doesn't."

Laker's voice shook. "You can't mean that." The nightmare had reasserted itself with the same demented improbability. "You can't . . . you wouldn't dare. He's innocent."

Hartmann blew through his lips. "I'm not concerned with that. But you are, which is as it should be."

"He's a schoolboy. A schoolboy, do you hear? On holiday. He was keeping me company, that's all. After tomorrow we were going back to the West, to the Rhineland." The protests spilled over, words, words. "You can't mean this, any of it. You *can't*."

But he did. Oh Christ, he did.

"I want to see someone else." Panic brought Laker to his feet. "Where am I? Where is this place?" Desperately he struggled to control himself. "Who are you to decide what becomes of us? Look . . . listen to me. I want to speak to someone else. All I've done—"

"There *is* no one else—not for you. Contrary to what you may believe, the Soviets give us a very free rein in certain matters. Now sit down. This is between you and me, Mr. Laker."

In vain Laker searched for the glimpse of pity he had once detected. But Hartmann's fixed blue stare was implacable. He looked very sure of himself, as if he'd inhabited this room for a long time, proposed such things before. Even as his thoughts reeled and blundered Laker knew the futility of pleading.

"Where's my son now?"

"Unaware that he is under discussion, I promise you."

"That's not an answer."

Hartmann half smiled, as if a thought had that moment struck him. "All this has come at you very quickly. How much of it do you doubt, I wonder?" He reached for one of the telephones and dialed a number, unhooking the earpiece extension as he did so and pushing it in Laker's direction.

Laker lifted it in time to hear: "Astoria Hotel, good evening."

"Reception, please." Then, when they were connected: "I'm inquiring about two of your guests. They are British, and the name is Laker . . . Laker, yes. L-A-K-E-R . . . Can you tell me if they are still with you? The room number is fifty-four, I believe."

Hartmann's fingers drummed the desk. A hum throbbed along the line. Muffled voices sounded in the background—sane, unaware.

"Are you there, caller?"

"Yes."

"The people you are inquiring after checked out earlier this evening."

"Thank you." Hartmann hung up. "You see, Mr. Laker? I have your luggage, incidentally. Only yours, of course. Your son has kept his own."

Laker swore at him.

"You can say all you wish, but it will change nothing. And you have only yourself to blame. Deep waters are for those who can swim. You should have reckoned on the possibility of getting beyond your depth. Now, for want of a better phrase, you are an instrument about to be put to practical use. And, human nature being what it is, you will take every care to see that you operate with maximum efficiency."

Silence and heartbreak closed in on Laker. "You're asking the impossible."

"I think not."

"You've got the wrong man. I'm not a murderer."

Hartmann pressed back in his chair. "You are old enough to have been in the war. Were you in the war, Mr. Laker? A soldier, perhaps?"

"What's that got to do with it?"

"Killing was a duty then. A daily duty."

"I wasn't in the S.S."

Hartmann colored slightly. "All it needs is provocation. Provocation or necessity. Listen very carefully. If you change your mind and don't go through with this your son will never rejoin you, safe and sound. And if you try, yet fail, the result will be the same. Either way I promise you that on whatever you care to name as sacred."

Laker closed his eyes, what remained of his spirit crumbling.

Hartmann was saying: "The psychology is soundly based. I am quite certain you will give me your fullest cooperation. Everything has been most thoroughly considered. On the face of it you will be your own master. You will go to Copenhagen, you will take certain actions, and you will ensure that the job is successfully completed. Then, and then only, will you and your son be reunited."

"How can I be sure of that?"

"You have my word."

Clutching at straws now, Laker said thickly, "If my son were harmed in any way there'd be an outcry. What you've done already is a violation of every international—"

"Listen, Mr. Laker. Keep listening. I've no qualms about the story you'll tell London when you eventually return there. But do you suppose the people who sent you will care to broadcast it to the world at large? Two years ago something went badly wrong for a certain Mr. James Wyatt. Were you, as a member of the British public, ever made aware of Mr. Wyatt's objectives or what became of him? Was there an outcry then? Have you ever heard of him, in fact? . . . No. And why not? Because, unless the circumstances are exceptional, outcries are an embarrassment to those who make them. They should have told you of this in London. In effect, Mr. Laker, you and your son have ceased to be public property. Here, in this room, you may well be of the opinion that there is no such thing as justice. But you will find it doesn't exist where you come from either. Sympathy there may be; generosity, no doubt, if your silence has to be bought. But if your son suffers as a result of your failure in Copenhagen the world will never be allowed to know. London will see to that. They have too many skeletons in too many cupboards. They'll go along with our account of an accident; accept our post-mortem certificate. You yourself will know it's all a lie and so will they. But an outcry? . . . No, Mr. Laker, particularly in view of the seriousness of what we can level against them and the degree of your involvement."

Laker looked away, overwhelmed by the imagery of vicarious terror, trapped and committed by it. A shudder racked his shoulders.

"Now do you understand?"

He didn't answer.

"You have no choice, do you see?"

Laker ungummed his lips. In a low voice he said, "What am I to do?"

"I told you. You will go to Copenhagen and kill a man."

"Who? How shall I know him?" Christ, he thought hysterically, what's happening to me?

"We have photographs. Have you ever been to Copenhagen?"

"No."

"Denmark?"

"No."

"We will brief you before you go, both as regards the city and the person concerned. We will speak about the details tomorrow. You will be given every possible aid. But the timing must be yours and yours alone. And you must not fail—remember that, should freedom affect your judgment." Hartmann yawned almost theatrically. "Now, though, I suggest you sleep on it. There has been enough for one day, wouldn't you agree? Unless, that is, you have any questions?"

He was cold, ruthless, perfectly equipped for the business of murder. And yet, when he indulged what could only amount to a sadistic pleasure, there was something contrived about his manner as if at all costs he wanted the satisfaction of Laker's hatred before he was done.

"Do you believe it yet?" He tilted his head. "Or do you

imagine it all a joke? An elaborate, unforgivable, farfetched joke?"

Laker dug his nails into his palms.

"Like this evening's charade in the pine trees, perhaps?"

"No."

"What, then? . . . This room, S.S.D. headquarters, you who were so very nearly dead—and the talk is of Copenhagen and your son and London and an assassination." Hartmann's leg swung back and forth, back and forth. "It's not a dream, do you suppose? A bad dream that morning or some other awakening is going to wipe away?"

"No," Laker heard himself answer. "It's not a dream."

Chapter
Eight

IN the labyrinth of empty corridors that led back to the cell Laker's despair was like darkness, like night, and when the lock crunched home, shutting him away, he lay on the bunk in the grip of an awful stillness.

The enormity of the blackmail was too appalling for reasoned thought. He kept telling himself that, given time, he would find a way out—tomorrow, the next day. But now he was weak with the assault of weariness and shock, hollow, a sensation that was mental as well as physical, and while it lasted he numbly accepted that his will was tied.

The wall close to his face and the scrawled initials and the barred window reinforced reality. He fell asleep and woke and fell asleep again, over and over. Always when he woke the lights were burning. Sometimes a dream broke into his sleep like an intruder, once bringing him out of it in a fit of shaking, propped on the bunk, hearing the tail end of his own voice. There was a time when he found himself running along an echoing passage vainly searching for a door; another when he was talking to Karen and Slattery in the forecourt of Gale & Watts, looking across Karen who was at the wheel of the blue van with Slattery sitting beside her, and Slattery beamed: "Tell me, Sam—what's Hartmann like? What tricks do you fancy he might have up that S.S.D. sleeve of his? Incidentally, I warned you about him, didn't I?"

No! . . . No!

Toward five he surfaced once more and remained awake. He chain-smoked despite a fierce thirst, the intimidation and the purpose of it as devastating as before, his mind back on the treadmill. There had to be a loophole, *had* to be, but he was no closer to finding it. He couldn't even begin to make a coherent assessment of what might be possible until Hartmann told him more. Disbelief was stone dead. Yesterday's terror had hammered acceptance into him. He was being sent to murder someone.

Who? . . . How? . . .

In desperation he drove his thoughts elsewhere. Jerry Baxendale, Carol Nolan, Mrs. Ruddick, Roundwood, the Humber in the garage, Mill Avenue, Oatlands, the woman in the yellow dress with the pram. . . . They had receded, yet always, always, they drew him back to Slattery and what had followed since and the monstrosity of what was still to come. He watched the new day beginning to fill the small, high window, wondering where Patrick was, thinking of him with terrible grief and guilt, thinking of Helen and the last time, other times, Karen, vainly trying not to be confronted with the question of how he could ever bring himself to kill in cold blood and what was promised if he failed.

His suitcase was in the cell, unopened. He was in his pants and shirt. For the fifth time within an hour he lit a cigarette. Presently he put his shoes and suit on, then walked up and down or sat on the edge of the bunk, fretting for someone to come and take him back to Hartmann so that he could know all there was to know.

He was fed first—black bread, some mottled slices of cold sausage, the same sharp, gritty coffee. This was around seven-thirty. The man who brought the food didn't speak, either then or when he returned to take the tray away. Laker found his razor in the suitcase, plugged it into the socket below the window chute, shaved, then sluiced his face in the bowl of water the man had brought when he removed the tray.

Another hour dragged by after that. Death and violence were commonplace when he had found it possible to kill. The whole world was at it then and one could somehow hide from what it meant and what it cost. But he had grown, learned to pity, acquired sentiment, softened. Jesus, how could he go about it now? Even for Patrick's sake?

There were no more cigarettes. He put his head in his hands and stared at the floor, trembling.

Hartmann was seated behind his desk in the same attitude as when Laker had last seen him, for all the world as if he hadn't moved. It was just nine o'clock. A gray brick wall showed through the open blinds.

"Did you sleep well?" Hartmann asked with soft hoarseness.

"I slept."

"And so, I understand, did your son. That will be a relief to you, I'm sure." The taunting smile. "When did you last handle a gun, Mr. Laker?"

"What kind of a gun?"

"Any gun."

"In nineteen forty-five."

"Not since then?"

"No."

"You don't possess one? Privately?"

"No."

"Then the first thing on this morning's agenda will be for you to get some practice. I told you, didn't I, that you would be assisted as much as possible?" He glanced at his watch. "However, there is a little time yet. . . . I have no doubt you've given the proposition plenty of thought. Who wouldn't in your shoes? So I ought to touch on something which must have crossed your mind." He paused briefly. "Rid yourself of any idea of approaching your Embassy in Copenhagen or telephoning your associates in London. Inevitably, they would take steps to see that the person in question is removed from harm's way. And that, in the circumstances, is precisely what you cannot afford to have happen. Do you follow? This is between you and me, Mr. Laker. Until everything is over you have no alternative but to keep it so."

"When will that be?" That Laker could even ask was the measure of the hold on him.

"By Saturday. The moment we have confirmation that you have successfully completed the assignment your son will be on a London-bound plane." Hartmann studied his fingernails before glancing up. "It's an ugly business isn't it, Mr. Laker? Medieval, one might say—without the medieval sanctity, that is."

Saturday . . . two days. Two days from now.

Hartmann went on: "We'll come to the person's identity presently—after you've practiced at the gallery. But in case your imagination is running away with you let me tell you now that I doubt if you will ever have heard of him. He isn't the Mayor of West Berlin, or the American Secretary of State, or the Secretary-General of the United Nations. The history books won't be interested." He glanced at his watch again, like a man who calculated every move. "What kind of marksman were you, by the way?"

With sudden dread Laker burst out: "Why me? Why've you picked on me?" All at once it had struck him that there might not be a loophole after all. Incredibly, everything was pointing to his doing exactly what Hartmann had planned.

"You want a killer, an out-and-out killer . . . a professional."
His voice cracked. It was the nearest he came to abasing
himself.

Hartmann stood up, smoothing his jacket. "You suit me
very nicely, Mr. Laker. When the time comes I am certain
we will find that you excel yourself."

They rode down in the elevator, as close as friends, as silent
as strangers, then descended the flight of stone steps. An
official on duty at the exit into the street saluted as Hartmann
approached. A dark green limousine was drawn into the curb.
The official hurried out and opened the near-side door. Hartmann motioned to Laker to get in, then joined him, round-
ing the car and squeezing behind the wheel.

The street was narrow, one-way. They swung into a
crescent-shaped thoroughfare with tall buildings on one side
and a railed enclosure on the other. Only yesterday, watching the flocks of pedestrians, Laker had presumed of their
joylessness natures corrupted and made stone-hard by prom-
ises and exhortations; and pitied them. But now, as the car
threaded through heavy bicycle traffic into the world of post-
ers and statues and other bolsters of hope, a crushing envy
filled him for the sheer drab normality of their lives. From
nowhere, ringing in his mind as if it were an echo-chamber,
he remembered the girl in the Mitre laughing happily while
he and Slattery sat together and he said: "You haven't raised
any gooseflesh yet . . ."

Hartmann turned left and right, then left again. Laker
glimpsed a string of lettered bunting forming the word
Textil and some colored direction indicators, but the Fair
and everything to do with it seemed utterly unreal. Except
that they appeared to be leaving the city's center he hadn't
the least notion where they were. Peace Is Our Profession
a hoarding announced. Within five minutes they were
crowded by warehouses and the gaunt shards of some dere-

lict buildings. Soon afterwards Hartmann nosed into a cobbled street and brought the car to rest outside what looked as if it might have been a bowling alley.

"We have numerous rifle clubs and galleries in the Democratic Republic, Mr. Laker. Shooting is a very popular activity—in the schools, among factory organizations." Hartmann spoke like a guide. "Mainly it is the responsibility of the Association for Sports and Technology, but this particular gallery is administered by the Leipzig Division of the State Security Service. I think you will find it more than adequately equipped."

They got out. The entrance was round a corner. Half a dozen steps led up to a reinforced glass door. Hartmann let them in with a key. A cloakroom led off the tiled lobby and there was also a door marked GUN ROOM. The enclosed air had the stale tang of expended cordite.

Hartmann said, "Normally a caretaker would be here, but on Thursdays the gallery is closed. There are two ranges, one for recruits, one for those who are more advanced. It would be sensible—don't you agree—to treat you as a beginner?"

Laker didn't reply. It was all nightmare.

"No stupidity, Mr. Laker. I'm armed, remember—though that isn't the real deterrent. You're a marionette already, as you surely know."

He opened the gun room, selected two rifles from the racks and took some ammunition cartons from a drawer. Emerging, he pointed: "That way." Laker walked along a short passage which brought him to another door. "Go on through," Hartmann said, flicking some switches, and Laker found himself in the intense brightness of what looked to be about a twenty-five-yard range.

There were fiber mats for six firing-points on a low, planked dais. The walls were a light gray except for the far one, which was black, and this was spattered raw above the sandbagged, boxed-in target area. The air's bite was very

strong, catching the throat. The door padded behind Hartmann, who went immediately to the control panel and started
extractor-fans humming. He placed one of the rifles and a
carton of ammunition on the dais, returned to the panel,
fiddled with it for a few moments, then raised a small, ringed
target on the butt numbered 3.

"Get down on the mat and load. I've given you a Walther
.22. It's a single-shot and the magazine holds a clip of eight.
The catch on the side releases the magazine." Hartmann
moved around behind Laker. "One last thing. We aren't expecting the impossible of you in Copenhagen. Average ability will suffice and this is your chance to bring yourself up to
that standard. . . . Now, take your time."

Laker made a deliberate botch of thumbing a clip home,
muddled snapping in the magazine, then settled into a position on the mat. Even after so long a time the rifle had an
easy, natural feel, but he made a show of awkwardness. With
what he believed was cunning he aimed interminably before
snatching at the trigger. Nothing happened and he tried to
look puzzled.

"Push the safety catch forward."

He did so, aimed slightly off and fired. Sand spurted.

"Again."

Another miss, well wide.

"Again," Hartmann said tartly.

Laker missed six times in succession before Hartmann told
him to stop.

"You aren't that incompetent."

"I am. And I always was."

"Try once more. Finish the clip."

The target remained untouched.

"What kind of idiot are you, Mr. Laker? Don't you value
your son's life?"

"Not everyone can shoot," Laker gritted.

"All but the blind can do better than that. Get this into

your head, once and for all. You've a job to do. In terms of skill required it won't be so difficult. And I've given you the best incentive I could think of."

"Why me?" Laker shouted once more. "Why not do your own filthy work?"

"A wise dog never fouls his own doorstep, Mr. Laker."

"What's that supposed to tell me?"

"You'll find out. Now—reload and try again."

Laker obeyed, anger filling him; helplessness. He took a sighting shot and squeezed the trigger, shutting his mind to thoughts of bone and muscle, flesh and blood. The electrical device above the target area recorded an inner at two o'clock.

"That's more like it," he heard Hartmann concede.

He fired again, cutting the black edge of the bull on approximately the same radial line.

"Good . . . Good."

With sudden contempt Laker emptied the magazine at speed, the crack of each shot punctuated by the trickle of ejected shell cases on the floor beside him. Five clear bulls and one just clipping the line were recorded. He heard the hiss of Hartmann's indrawn breath.

"Good. *Very* good." For once there was neither threat nor mockery in the voice. Hartmann crossed to the control panel and switched the extractors off. "You make a poor actor, Mr. Laker. How long is it since you used a rifle?"

"I told you."

"Twenty years?"

"I told you."

"It's hard to believe."

"I don't give a penny damn what you believe."

"Isn't it a relief to you that your son's future may not be so precariously balanced after all? It certainly is to me. Come —I want to see how you make out on the other range."

In size, coloring and layout the second range was a duplication of the first. They reached it through a pair of communicating steel doors. This time Laker was given the other rifle.

"It's a Russian weapon," Hartmann said. "It has recently been superseded as a standard infantry issue, but it will serve your purpose very well and approximates in caliber and velocity to the one you will use. Make yourself familiar with it for a few moments. Then, at five-second intervals, I shall raise a selection of random targets."

Laker got down on the mat, legs splayed. He was shackled by a situation that was foul and crude and utterly compelling. Whatever chance there was of breaking free of it lay in the future, and the future was unmapped territory which his mind shrank from examining too closely lest he become convinced that it would offer nothing but the same hopeless subservience. He could not, dared not, think about it.

"Are you ready?"

He nodded, propped on his elbows, waiting, the catch off. Hartmann pressed a button on the control panel and a small white pear-shaped metal cutout sprang up to the right of the butt's center. Laker fired and missed; nothing showed on the electric indicator-board. Hartmann grunted. The cutout was already on its way down when Laker fired again, and this time he clipped it, taking Hartmann by surprise. Almost immediately another target appeared ten degrees or so to the left, identical but higher, wobbling on its arm. Laker scored a hit. The rifle was beautifully balanced, the recoil hardly noticeable. He missed the third cutout, got the next, drew a blank on the indicator with the fifth, then put in two shots at the sixth, scoring both times, five seconds already seeming an overgenerous exposure.

"Try again," Hartmann said. "Reload and be ready for a three-second interval only. And a different target order."

Laker scored seven hits. He was a born shot, relaxed, controlled, rock-steady, and he used the rifle now as if what remained of his pride depended on it. After he had emptied the magazine he loaded another and, on instructions, took the cutouts from a standing position, Hartmann mixing both their order and the duration of exposure. When the last puff of dust erupted from the protective wall of sandbags a full eight hits had been registered.

Hartmann nodded approvingly. "Remarkable, Mr. Laker. Quite remarkable. I would say you are exceptional. Chance isn't always so obliging. It was a fortunate day for me when you decided to go to the Luisenstrasse." He smiled. "We have a saying; perhaps you know it? If you start with certainties you can end in doubts. But if you start with doubts, and are patient with them, you can end in certainties. . . . I don't think we need continue with this, do you? The most useful place for both of us is back in my office."

They were there by ten-thirty. It had begun to seem to Laker that there had hardly been a time when he hadn't faced Hartmann and met or avoided the pale blue stare, hardly a time when his mind hadn't hovered between dread and loathing and despair.

"Now," Hartmann said, lighting a cigarette. "About this person of ours in Copenhagen."

A thin stream of smoke flattened and spread as the desk deflected it. He withdrew a pink folder from the drawer in front of his stomach. Opening the folder he tossed a photograph toward Laker: it was about half-plate size.

"There," he said. "As I told you, the history books won't be interested. You won't achieve fame, Mr. Laker. It won't be like Dallas, Texas."

Laker picked the photograph up. A broad, heavily jowled face confronted him. Bushy hair, thick eyebrows, nipped-in ears, bulbous nose with flared nostrils, large mouth with a slightly pendulous lower lip.

"Who is he?"

"Rudolf Frenzel."

The eyes looked more Slavic than German. And surprise was in them, alarm, as if they had begun to flinch from the flash or even from the upward movement of the photographer's hands.

"If you were a student of the Democratic Republic's affairs, Mr. Laker, you would recall that Frenzel was once a member of the Politburo of the Socialist Unity Party. Four years ago he defected to the West. Until quite recently he hid himself away. But at last he has ventured out of his hole. He has become a sort of errand-boy—in which connection doesn't matter. What does is that tomorrow he visits Copenhagen."

"How do you know?"

"We know," Hartmann said, and the manner of his saying it somehow reminded Laker of Slattery. "We know where he will have traveled from, the time of his arrival, the time of his departure. And we also know where he will be most exposed during his stay."

He seemed to think that Laker would ask him where this was, but Laker was staring at the photograph. "Did you hear me?" The tone was harsh again. "When you arrive in Copenhagen yourself you will realize that we have given you what help we could. Nothing can be perfect, of course, but fear can remove mountains, I assure you." He raised a finger as if he were at an auction. "The photograph, please."

It skidded across the desk and fell to the floor, but Hartmann didn't bother to retrieve it. Laker's expression seemed to gratify him.

"You will be supplied with another picture before you leave, more convenient for your pocket. It would be rash to rely too much on your memory. After all, when you are about to kill a man it is important to be certain you have picked the right one—isn't that so?" Hartmann opened the folder again and glanced at some typewritten notes. "Our friend has a reservation at the Metropol Hotel and my information is that he has been allocated room sixty-eight. When you are contacted in Copenhagen you will realize the significance of this."

"Contacted?"

"Your passport photograph has been copied and prints sent in advance. You'll be recognized, don't worry." He picked up the typewritten sheet and passed it over. "It would be better if you looked at this while I explain." He might have been discussing a sales campaign, a holiday schedule—anything; anything except the preliminaries to a murder.

Laker read:

Axel Bar, Tivoli. Thursday 20:30
Copenhagen-National, Sunderspladsen. Friday 10:00–15:00.
17:00–18:00.
Metropol Hotel, Halmstergade. Friday 18:00–Saturday 14:00

"This afternoon," Hartmann said, "you fly to Copenhagen via Schönefeld, Berlin. You will be there—in Copenhagen, that is—around seven. Contact will be made at the Axel Bar at eight-thirty tonight. Not only will you find that accommodation has been provided for you, but once you have taken your bearings you will discover also that it is directly across the street from where Frenzel will be staying. A narrow street—no wider than the range where you have reluctantly demonstrated your skill."

He paused. He was talking about a real place, a real man. And Laker could not hold his gaze.

"Frenzel arrives tomorrow, on an SAS flight from Paris, due at six in the evening. He leaves again next afternoon— on Saturday. That means you will have a maximum of twenty hours, during a proportion of which he will be as close as I can bring him to you. Across a street, Mr. Laker, a narrow street. Third-floor window to third-floor window. His will be the one directly in front of yours. With a telescopic sight it will seem almost as if you are prodding him."

He paused again, stubbing his cigarette in the glass tray. "You see there is reference to Copenhagen-National."

"Yes."

"Copenhagen-National is a bank. We have rented a safe deposit for you in the name of George Marshall. In it a rifle is waiting to be collected. The rifle is in a special case and no one will raise an eyebrow. The fact is that you will be in no personal danger until the moment you decide to put an end to Rudolf Frenzel's existence. Then, of course, your real difficulties will begin. But you can be down a fire escape and on a bus or in a taxi within three minutes of pressing the trigger. It has been timed, Mr. Laker. We gave it what we call a dry run."

He kept using "we," but as far as Laker was concerned there was no one but Hartmann. And every time Laker's mind moved he was there to block it.

"You can't afford to fail; I hope I have made that crystal clear. By three o'clock on Saturday afternoon, at the very latest, we will know whether you have succeeded or not, and I won't labor the consequences. We want Frenzel dead, Mr. Laker. Dead at all costs—even if it means jeopardizing your own chances of escape. If time begins to whittle down or there are other difficulties it may be that you will have to abandon the role of sniper and seek him out—cross the street, go to his room. These will be things for you to decide. But remember this—the Danish police are very efficient. The more you expose yourself the greater will be the risk of their laying hands on you. And—should that happen—I cannot warn you strongly enough not to open your mouth until you have been advised by your colleagues in London what to say. They will think of something, Mr. Laker. What is more, they will expect to be given the opportunity. Never forget that. They used you in the first place, after all. They will have something at stake too, remember."

A muscle was jumping in one side of Laker's face. "When will I see my son?"

Hartmann consulted the folder. "Assuming all goes well, his plane will reach London at eleven o'clock on Saturday night. Incidentally, there is a letter for him here which you have to complete."

He pushed it across. It was typed, bore yesterday's date and was headed Leipzig Airport:

I'm terribly sorry. After I left you this afternoon I got caught up in some urgent business which has made it essential for me to travel to Copenhagen immediately. I tried to find you, but couldn't. The only other thing I could do was to ask Mr. Rauter to keep an eye on you while I'm away and he has kindly agreed to do so. He suggests you ought to stay at his house rather than at the Astoria and this of course you will be doing before this hurried letter reaches you.

Expect to see you by Saturday at the latest. If I can't manage to rejoin you by then I have asked Mr. Rauter to put you on a flight to London that evening. Then we'll be able to start for the Rhineland and pick up the planned schedule. Once again I'm very, very sorry, but it couldn't be helped. Mr. Rauter will have explained.

Enjoy yourself meanwhile. I've had to dictate this, by the way.

"Who is Rauter?"

"A family man. He has a pleasant apartment, a homely wife, two children of his own. As long as your mission is successful I can promise you that your son will have nothing but happy memories of his time in Leipzig." Hartmann gestured. "Sign the letter, Mr. Laker. We've done our best not to alarm him, and you of all people should approve of that. Sign it, then listen."

Laker fumbled for his pen. *Dear Patrick*, he wrote: then,

Your affectionate father and his initials. He would never forgive himself, he knew.

"Listen," Hartmann said. "Your own flight is at 14:40. Your passport is in order. You will be provided with ample funds. Before you leave Leipzig you will have memorized the details of that piece of paper—the Axel Bar and so on. Above all you will memorize the deadline."

He waited, watching, always watching.

Laker ran his hands over his face. A full minute must have elapsed. Faintly, from the street below, a horn blared like a cry of pain. He felt stunted, smashed. Mercy was what men wanted most; quarter. And Hartmann was able to offer it—at a price.

"If I do this—"

"Yes?"

"What can you promise for Karen Gisevius?"

"Who?"

"Karen Gisevius."

Hartmann leaned forward, one eyebrow raised. "Why should she interest you?"

"I know her."

"Naturally."

Laker shook his head. "During the war. I worked with her. I haven't seen her since. Until the other day I thought she must be dead. She . . . She was . . ." And suddenly he couldn't go on. All he could do was to stare and see Hartmann slowly dissolve, solidify.

Through a blur, as if from a long way off, he heard: "You have enough to worry about."

"What will happen to her?"

"Does it matter?"

"Yes. *Yes.*"

"Then I am sorry for you."

Once before Hartmann had come to an abrupt decision

with himself, and so it was again. He pressed the buzzer on the desk and rose.

"That's all, Mr. Laker. Go and memorize those Copenhagen details. In—what?—something over three hours your plane will be leaving. On it there are likely to be businessmen. But not one of them, I assure you, will be en route for home with a contract more binding than yours."

Chapter
Nine

LEIPZIG Airport sank below. Soon it was smothered by clouds—the ragged fringes of the city, too; everything.

Laker pressed back in his seat. The last thing Hartmann had said was: "There's no way out, Mr. Laker. Racking your brains won't help. The longer you live with the situation the more you will realize that you have to go through with it to the end. One word to anyone—*anyone*—and you risk having your quarry spirited away. We have our reasons for wanting Frenzel killed just as you have reasons for making sure that he is. Until then this is between you and me. Always remember that. You and I have become partners." And in the shadows of Laker's mind his narrow face presented itself, half-smiling, eager for drama, looking for it with eyes for the most part empty of everything except a cold, lonely light.

The twin-engined aircraft was about three-quarters full but mercifully the seat beside Laker was vacant. He couldn't have coped with a stranger intent on trivialities about the

Fair. There was a yawning gulf between him and anything rational and nothing could bridge it. He had clung to the hope that once he got away he would somehow be able to detach himself from the dementia of the past twenty-four hours, continuing to cling to it long after he knew in his heart that freedom would alter nothing, clinging to it even now when doing so was no more than an act of despair. Hartmann held the strings. Distance was irrelevant. He had two days in which to go about Patrick's salvation, two days in which the memory of yesterday's terror in the pines was to goad him into becoming an instrument of vengeance.

He shook his head as if still trying to deny that anything so monstrous could have split the fabric of his life. Things like this happened to others; never to you and yours.

Behind his back someone was saying in a flat, Midlands' brogue: "I found 'em charming. Couldn't have been friendlier. It's dreary there, God knows, but they're all right. If you ask me there's a damned sight too much drivel talked about the Curtain and all that. I'm not denying it's a fact, any more than I'm saying there isn't a flaming great wall across Berlin. But what I *am* saying is that the whole political thing doesn't make the sense it once did. . . ." The knowing voice insisted through the engine's roar. "The tension's easing all the time. We aren't at each other's throats any longer. If we imagine we are it's largely the fault of the press and the television people. They need news, that lot, so they balloon every trivial little incident in the hope it'll burst and make a bang. That's my view, and I've been here twice now. Seeing's believing, after all. . . ."

Laker opened his eyes and fixed them blankly on the empty sky. Patrick, fresh from some junior book of instant knowledge, had once said: "People think the sky's blue, but it isn't, not really—did you know that, Dad? When you get beyond a certain point it's black, pitch-black."

It seemed fantastic that he should be scared to make a

move when he was within arm's-length of people who could pass a message for him. Inaction seemed a crime, yet it was part of the measure of reality. He was even nervous of being spoken to; when the stewardess offered him coffee he was brusque and dismissive, as if he were under surveillance from somewhere in the rear.

He thought of Frenzel, Frenzel with his hours already counted. Frenzel was the linchpin. Warn him, spare him, fail to get him—and Patrick paid; those were the equations. "An outcry, Mr. Laker? Oh no. You and your son have ceased to be public property. You should have asked more questions than you did before you so casually set out for Leipzig. . . . And another thing. We'll want proof about Frenzel. Nothing short of a 22-carat job will do, and we have means of telling whether you will have undertaken it honestly or not. . . . I'll know, Mr. Laker. I'll know for sure."

He was in quicksand, trapped. And if he struggled or called for help they would close over Patrick's head, not his. The more he strained his mind the more scared he found himself, the more crammed with useless hatred. And, deep down, he was aware that if the nightmare persisted, if he lived it through in puppet-like obedience, self-disgust would be the final horror.

The man behind was still plowing on: "East Germany's all right. And it's got a tremendous market potential if only the British Government would take its finger out over the recognition business. The people I met were touchy about that, and no wonder. Still, I got nothing but courtesy wherever I went, and I'm damned certain no one comes to any harm nowadays unless they deliberately go looking for it. . . ."

It was a short flight to Schönefeld; forty minutes. They were down punctually at three-twenty, down through the clouds, and everything was gray again. The accents were different, but the uniforms were the same.

There were almost three hours to wait for the Copenhagen connection and to Laker they seemed interminable. He sat in the peeling transit lounge along with a score of people, men mostly, some of them bleary from lunch and liquor, who sprawled on the couches and dozed. Every half-hour or so a cafeteria trolley was wheeled around. On and off he paced the floor, submerged within himself. If he didn't contact London he felt he would go mad before the next forty-eight hours were over. But he seemed to have lost any capacity for trust, in Slattery most of all. Slattery had bungled where Karen was concerned, miscalculated—and he might again. By comparison with Hartmann he now seemed a child, an amateur, a dabbler; but there was nobody else to bring pressure to bear. He might have strings of his own . . . *might.*

And Hartmann was there at once to push the pendulum the other way—"One word to London and, inevitably, Frenzel will go back into his hole. You can't afford to have that happen."

Laker's throat burned from incessant smoking. He couldn't remain still for long. Sometimes when he glanced at his watch he thought it must have stopped. The new strap, the wad of kroner in his pocket, the safe deposit key, the deckled edges of the photograph he dared not look at—there was no refuge. Tides of panic ebbed and flowed as his thoughts swung between Slattery and Hartmann. Slattery would have no choice but to act, and act quickly. Patrick was his responsibility. Or was the situation so insane that he would be forced to yield to Hartmann's stranglehold himself?

One moment such a thing seemed inconceivable, the next a terrifying probability. Hartmann had been so sure, so cast-iron sure, as if he knew exactly how far London would be prepared to go. "There are unwritten rules in this business, Mr. Laker. And one of them is to be wary of having your own dirty washing blown into the scandalized face of the world. London, believe me, has more than a fair share on its hands and they will guard it more jealously than you would think possible. They'll muzzle you when the time comes—quite shamelessly if their treatment of Mr. Wyatt's unfortunate widow is anything to go by. Meanwhile, Frenzel is valuable to them and they won't willingly allow him to be obliterated. London, I suggest, would only confuse you. So keep away from your Embassy, Mr. Laker. And don't ring anyone—I'd take it as a sign of weakness, do you see?"

But he would. He must.

And yet . . .

The Copenhagen flight was called at ten to six. Along with thirty or so others Laker trailed across the oil-slicked hard to a turboprop Ilyushin. With the resignation of the powerless he belted himself in and gazed out at the red-black-and-gold flags fluttering lazily along the rim of the airport buildings. The nightmare had been many things already; now, once more, it took the form of finding himself surrounded by people whose lives were wholly normal.

He wanted to shout at them, to protest, to shake their smugness, their boredom, to confide. Above all, to confide. There were files in London, he wanted them to understand, in which the names of every one of them armed with a British passport were automatically recorded once they ventured to this side of the Curtain. And there were men like Slattery who would use them if time and opportunity provided a need and they were fools enough to acquiesce. And there were men like Hartmann who could manipulate them to such a degree and with such cold certainty that they could find themselves inhabiting the same world as everyone else yet secretly terrorized, unable to cry out, committed to something that, only hours before, they would have considered utterly impossible.

With a whining crescendo the Ilyushin lifted off, graceful in its sudden buoyancy, the violence of the noise and the feeling of thrust diminishing. Second by second the horizons widened. Berlin tilted like a display model beyond the port wing and every head turned. Then the clouds intervened and spread below like crusted pack-ice.

The thickset crew-cut man beside Laker was galloping through a Swedish translation of Fleming's *Casino Royale*. Laker shut his eyes. Hartmann's stare and throttled voice, the sound of Karen's sobbing as she was taken from the hut, Patrick's parting grin as he left him, the ghastly stutter muffled by the paper bag, Slattery's naïve Boy Scout enthusiasm, Frenzel, Rudolf Frenzel—all were there again to torment and tear at his mind and his heart together with the remembered feel of the rifles and the smell of cordite in the shooting gallery and the prospect of a strange city and a rendezvous at the Axel Bar at eight-thirty. And then . . .

The palms of his hands were unnaturally moist. Twice he lit a cigarette only to stub it out after a few nervous draws. The man in the next seat smiled and turned yet another escapist page. Time passed. Coffee was served again, but Laker ordered a cognac and drained his glass in a single gulp. After a longish while he heard someone say "Rostock, I reckon." Peering down he saw an amoeba-like sepia smudge at the center of a radiation of lines and scratches and the apparently motionless sea pressed against the map of the coastline. "Having capitalist time, wish you were here"— Patrick's joke echoed brutally. Then Slattery claimed priority: "Since May last year he's been in touch with an address in Rostock; Leninstrasse 32, to be precise"—Slattery who knew so much, so bloody much, Slattery of the homily about the bumblebee, of the time before and after the Gardelegen

debacle, Slattery of the Mitre and the room in Manchester
Square and the talk of helping out—"No risk, Sam. Absolutely
none. . . ."

Never-do-it-yourself-Slattery. What match he was for Hartmann? As an ally he'd diminished, yet who else was there?

The Ilyushin made short work of the Baltic. Copenhagen
was under them several minutes before the scheduled seven
o'clock. The tanned young Customs officer who eventually
dealt with Laker said "Holiday or business?" as a brisk preliminary to letting him go and Laker answered "Business,"
at the mercy even of a chance word.

He slumped in the coach that would take him to the terminal. A B.E.A. Trident screamed in while they waited for the
coach to fill and the sight of it made London seem closer
suddenly; attainable. Why delay? There were telephones in
the Arrivals building. . . . The pendulum started swinging
again. But he was suspicious of freedom, suspicious of everyone in the immediate vicinity. Wait. Lose everyone first.
Wait until they all reached town; scattered. And then . . .
Should he? Christ, should he? More and more the power of
decision was draining out of him.

Anxiously, as the coach began to roll he glanced at his
watch: seven-twenty. "How far's the terminal?" he asked a
stout woman beside him. Fifteen minutes . . . There'd be
time enough to call London—yet what if Slattery made another balls of everything? And he could. One rash move, one
hasty indiscretion, and Hartmann would complete the equation. But would Slattery believe that? Could he make him
understand—quickly, and on a public line—how desperate
the balance truly was? Panic renewed itself the nearer he
came to chancing it. If he didn't, now or later, there was
only one alternative.

Copenhagen's outskirts scarcely made a mark on his mind.
A bridge and the evening glint of water, some laden coal

barges—not much else registered. A man nearby remarked as if he'd been an old friend, "There's the Europa"—but Laker didn't even look. He stared straight ahead, rehearsing what he would say, compressing it, trying to keep Hartmann's threats at bay. "Listen, Slattery. They were waiting for me. Kromadecka's was blown before I got there. They picked all three of us up—all three, did you hear? Karen, Patrick and me. I'm in Copenhagen now and this is why, this is what's happened . . ."

The light was still good. He noticed trees; a verdigris-covered spire. Some of the passengers were already getting to their feet. Two minutes after the half-hour. . . . The coach turned right and veered toward the curb. "Is this it?" somebody asked as movement ended. Laker took his turn at the door. Neon blinked and cascaded palely around a large square. He collected his suitcase then walked away, any-where, anywhere, it didn't matter. Several times he glanced back, but singled no one out. He left the square and crossed a street, passed through an arcade, then turned left, min-gling, one of many, moving faster than most though not conspicuously so.

After a few minutes he paused in a shop doorway; there was a post office opposite with telephone booths flanking the entrance. Several people passed, one with a brown dog on a lead, and the dog sniffed at his ankles. But there was no other interest taken in him, nobody loitering to keep their distance. He delayed for some cars to go by, then went over to the post office, certain he wasn't followed. Inside, at the counter, he asked the cost of a call to London. The clerk, who spoke English, changed two 100-kroner notes for him. There were booths along the facing wall but the clerk said, "We close at eight. I suggest you use those in the street. You may have some delay on a call like that."

Laker nodded and went outside. One of the booths was occupied. He stepped into the vacant one, put his suitcase down and studied the English version of the procedure instructions. The booth was glassed on three sides. He looked all around; no one watched or waited, yet the back of his neck prickled. A moment's hesitation, then he dialed.

"I want to make a person-to-person call to London . . . London, England, yes . . ."

A click and a different voice, slightly singsong, very precise. He gave the Gerrard number, repeating it twice, touched by a sudden alarm that Slattery might not be there at such an hour.

"Is there a delay?"

"I don't think so. There wasn't half an hour ago. What is your number, please?"

Laker read it out.

"Have you the right money?" The girl quoted the tariff.

"Yes."

"What is the name of the person to whom you wish to speak?"

Laker ran a hand through his hair. "Look," he said urgently, "I don't want it person-to-person, after all. I want a straight call on the Gerrard number."

"Not person-to-person?"

"No."

His alarm grew. Say no one was there? Suddenly everything had narrowed down to this. All he could remember was that Slattery lived in Kew.

"Hold the line, please."

He straightened, moving his feet. Turning slightly he glanced out. A short, hatless man was leaning against the post office wall, reading a newspaper. For a second or two Laker had no qualms. Come on, he urged, as the wire crackled. Come *on*. . . . Then he realized that the man was looking at him over the top of the page.

A tentacle of suspicion fastened around Laker's heart. He tried to drag his eyes away, but couldn't. For what seemed an impossible length of time he stared back. Then the man lowered the newspaper, making no bones about his purpose, and with a chilling stab of dismay Laker recognized him. He had been on the plane from Leipzig, in the transit lounge at Schönefeld, on the Ilyushin. In the toilets at Schönefeld they'd been alone, just the two of them, shoulders almost touching. . . . Suddenly Laker was certain. His brain seemed to stall as the man prolonged the blatant warning, pushing away from the wall and moving nearer.

"Have your money ready, please. I will have London for you in a few mo—"

Laker's nerve broke then. He slammed the receiver down, grabbed his suitcase and backed out of the booth. And he ran—as if something were yapping at his heels. Only when he found himself in the square where the coach had deposited him did he slow to a walk. He rested against a lamp-post, sucking in air. Despite the fading light he attracted attention: somebody stopped and spoke to him, hand on arm. Laker shook his head and walked on, frightened still, very frightened. Leipzig was three hundred miles away, behind the Curtain. But he wasn't free, he couldn't choose. Hartmann had as good as twitched the strings to prove it.

The dark was coming. Blocks of light fell from expanses of plate-glass window and the pulsing neon took a more gaudy hold. It was five past eight and his legs ached. Someone was still on his tail; he could sense it. He hadn't tried to lose himself again. Sick in the stomach he had stayed with the crowds; conformed. "Don't allow Copenhagen to affect your judgment, Mr. Laker . . ." Hartmann kept pace with him like a second shadow, Hartmann whose mind was sharp with years of suspicions and who wielded the power of life and death. "I'll know if it does, you see. I'll know for sure."

Near a bicycle park Laker hailed a cruising taxi. "Axel?" the driver queried. "Tivoli?"

It was only a short ride. He was put down at one of the entrances to the Gardens. The driver tried to explain something, pointing, but the Danish defeated Laker. He went to the arched gateway where he spoke to an attendant. "Axel Bar?" he asked uncertainly and was rewarded with a nod. He paid to pass through the turnstile. There was a restaurant immediately to his right, the Wivex, and he heard the throb of music. Pustules of colored lights bordered a choice of paths between avenues of brilliantly lighted trees. A direction-arrow showed him which to take. Couples strolled hand in hand under the faery glow, animated, dreaming, the world shut out for a while. Presently he passed an open-air stage where a clown was performing on a trampoline before a seated audience. Some scattered applause startled him, reminding him that he was different from everybody in this place, from everybody in Copenhagen, and again he felt the swift breeze of fear in his belly.

Lugging his suitcase he walked perhaps another hundred yards before he saw AXEL in electric blue on the fascia of a small, low building. As he approached he wondered if the same man would again disclose himself. Some of the tables were alfresco, spaced about a hedged enclosure, and others were roofed over behind a glass screen. He chose not to go inside. A waitress with a pink beret came for his order. He didn't want anything but he asked for a beer. Then he lit a cigarette, apprehensive, heedless of the sauntering passersby, suspecting that his contact was already present.

A military band played in the tinted distance. He sat alone with the suitcase beside him, fingering the checkerboard cloth. Again and again he checked his watch. Eight-thirty . . . Eight thirty-two . . . Eight thirty-five . . . No one yet. But there would be. Someone was waiting to show him where this room was, biding his time before closing in. There was beginning to be a dreadful inevitability about everything now.

"Can you manage a light?"

It was a girl's voice, the accent transatlantic. Laker jerked around, taken off-guard. Unknown to him she had seated herself at his table.

"A light?" she said.

Dark eyes, dark hair, white teeth, a mouth redder than blood—his glance was cursory. He nodded and fumbled in his pocket. She looked like a tart. As the flame spurted he held it to her cigarette and she steadied his hand, fingers touching his. Fawn coat, collar up.

"Thanks."

The smoke swirled. He was turning his back on her.

"The picture didn't do you justice."

He frowned.

"You were very punctual. I'll say that."

Now he stared, pulse quickening. "Aren't you making a mistake?"

"Hardly." She smiled. "Shall we go? I don't want a drink."

He didn't move.

"It isn't far. And it's getting chilly here." She smiled again. "Yes?" she prompted.

He emptied his glass. They rose together. As they moved away under the lights she said, "Tivoli closes next week for the winter, did you know?" But she was talking to someone who wasn't altogether listening.

Chapter Ten

WHEN they reached the exit by the Wivex he asked if they needed a taxi, but she said they didn't. It was the only time he spoke to her on the way. They walked for about five minutes, her heels clacking briskly as she strutted by his side. Familiar names occasionally showed amid the indecipherable welter—PETER O'TOOLE . . . CARLSBERG . . . ELIZABETH ARDEN . . . SHELL—but to Laker they seemed to belong to some other stage of his existence.

They turned a couple of corners; crossed a tram-clanking street. The crowds thinned out; soon they were almost alone. They were passing a line of shops when the girl stopped by a door next to a delicatessen.

"Here we are."

Opposite were more shops with five or six rows of windows above. Laker glanced at them quickly before following her in. There was a small hallway with stairs leading up. She went first, slim calves level with his face. On the first landing she said, "Are you fit? There are two more yet," and again there was that smile. Already Laker was confused. He had expected an anonymously rented room, bare perhaps, and then to be left alone—watched and followed only when he went out. But he was wrong. On the second landing he suspected it, on the third he was sure. He wasn't to be trusted for a minute.

Even so he asked, "Do you live here?"

"Of course."

She let him in, surprise in her tone. He found himself in a comfortably furnished bed-sitter. Doors opened off to either side of a curtained window. Quilted double divan, a radio, some framed photographs, a square table with some bottles on it, a couple of deep, soft chairs—those were among his first impressions.

She tossed her coat onto the divan and bent to plug in an electric fire. A wild doubt took Laker to the window. He pulled back the drapes.

"What's that place?"

"Across there?"

"Yes."

"The hotel, do you mean?"

"What's it called?"

"The Metropol."

He turned, the enslaved part of his mind bewildered, unable to grasp that these terrible hours were to be shared. There had been no mention of it in Leipzig.

He said, "Are you here all the time?"

"Of course," she said again. "Where else?" And then she said, "My name's Anna. What's yours?"

He didn't answer.

"Knowing it will make things easier."

"David."

David would do. In one respect he'd been right about her. Men came here in search of an hour's safety, an hour's trust, release, a breath of comfort. But Laker had forgotten what desire was. He studied the room again, his thoughts racing a full round of the clock ahead, entering a new dimension of uncertainty.

"Are you tired? You look tired. There's a Scotch if you want it." She chuckled softly, kicking off her shoes. "It's all paid for. Everything is—so make yourself at home. Everything's paid for the two days—so that's out of the way."

"Who paid?" He was cautious.

Again she seemed surprised. "I could describe him."

"When?"

"This morning."

He poured a whisky. There was no sign of a telephone. "Where do those doors go?"

"Bathroom there. Kitchen there." Sitting on the divan she watched him check. Her lips curled. "Why not look under here as well?"

He shrugged. He felt caged.

"Are you English?"

He hesitated, unsure to what extent he was bound, not knowing whether to lie, how much would be reported back, what mattered and what did not. Hartmann had left such details in the air.

"Well, are you?"

"Yes, I'm English." Then, probing once more, "What about you?"

"Oh, I'm a local girl."

"Not German?" She could have been. The transatlantic veneer camouflaged another, more basic, accent.

"No."

She laughed, tossing her hair, and the laughter mystified him. She seemed so at ease, so indifferent to why he had come. Yet the Metropol was across the street and tomorrow he was expected to bring a rifle here; kill from here. She knew that, she must know that. . . . He pulled the drapes aside once more, peering at the window directly opposite. It was in darkness, but several others were lit and in one of them, a floor down, he could see a maid turning back the bedcovers. She was close, all right; against his will the fact registered.

"When are you going to relax?"

He swung around, facing the unfamiliar room. The girl was putting a match to a cigarette. As if for the first time he noticed that she was wearing a green skirt and a white, frilled blouse. Twenty-five or -six; it was hard to tell. She proffered the pack.

"Do you want one?"

He shook his head.

Her eyes lacked something; the mouth, too. Whore's eyes, hard yet friendly, bold yet cautious, never quite certain. "What's your work?"

"Office work."

"In England?"

He avoided answering. He drank, haunted by others, further confused, wishing he were alone. He hadn't reckoned on this. Nothing was constant except the guarantee of climax. Desperation could drive him in search of another telephone; he could even take a plane to London—somewhere, sometime, he'd already considered that. Yet what would Slattery *do*? What *could* he do? That was the ultimate uncertainty. Hartmann had been in no doubt, and he believed Hartmann; the clearing in the pines and the bag over his head encouraged him in whom to believe. "A joke, Mr. Laker? A dream?" Neither; Jesus, no. Something filthy instead, filthy and cowardly and merciless. Something he didn't know the half of, yet which had him by the throat whichever way he turned.

"Have you eaten?"

"I'm not hungry."

"It's no trouble to fix something. Smørrebrød, say? Yes? . . . I'm going to the kitchen anyway."

"All right."

He was curt. She was linked with Hartmann, paid by

Hartmann, and that was enough to stoke what he felt. He
went to the window for the third time, thinking distractedly.
No one, as far as he could tell, stood in a doorway or in the
bars of shadow between the shops on the other side of the
street, but he was past being deceived or deceiving himself.
They had warned him off Slattery once and the moment he
left this room they'd be told; she would see to that.

He poured another whisky, numbing a little the crisis
within him and the stark chill of many fears. He moved
nearer the fire. A tear-off calendar on the wall carried a
thought for the day, attributed to Ibsen. *"I" is the capital city
of the underworld in which all things happen to us.* Close by
there was a colored print of the Matterhorn framed in black
passe-partout, and over the divan a beach scene with the girl
in a bikini waving at the photographer. *Klampenborg, August*
was scrawled in ink across one corner.

She was singing quietly in the kitchen. They would have
made plans for her; there was no other answer. For him
there was a fire escape—off the landing, probably: three minutes to a bus or a taxi. . . . He remembered everything,
every word. They'd done a dry run, timed it. So she was
aware of what was to happen—and she would hardly wait to
be a witness. She would go while the going was good, before
a light showed where it mattered across the way, before six
tomorrow evening when Frenzel was due. Surely . . .

His thoughts jerked on and on. Yet she lived here; it was
a home. Clean, cared-for. His eyes traveled over the pictures
again, the furniture, the strewn magazines, the bright dress-
ing table with its glass top, the amassed trivia, the long mirror facing the divan. . . . Would she abandon it all? He
was mystified still—and frightened simultaneously that he
should be thinking this way, weighing only this, as if he knew
in his heart of hearts that for him there might be no option.

"Switch on the radio, will you?"

The whisky in him obeyed, sullenly. He went to the table

and poured another glass, then sat down, staring at the coiled red bar of the fire. Presently he took out his wallet and extracted the picture of Frenzel, studying the startled eyes, the flared nostrils shadowed by the flash. "One of those for whom the world will never be safe, Mr. Laker. And it shows, don't you see?"

"There," the girl said, emerging with a tray. "Was I long?"

He shoved the photograph away like someone found out. She set the tray down on the table which she then drew closer to the chairs and the fire.

"I made coffee," she said. "Okay?"

Her face was conventionally attractive, well boned, a fringe of dark hair low on her forehead, her skin ivory-smooth. The eyes were green, he saw now, not black as he'd supposed them to be under the Tivoli lighting. He tossed back some more whisky, feeling its dull glow. She reduced the radio's volume to a background throb, then settled into the other chair, legs curled up.

"Better?" Smiling, she took a plate from the tray.

"Better?" he countered.

"When you came in you were wound up like a spring." She held herself stiffly. "Like that—you were, you know."

She baffled him. What she had brought him there to do would incriminate her if he went through with it. Unless he could wriggle free, devise something—either in conjunction with Slattery or alone—she was involved up to her slim white neck. Yet she was there to prevent him from doing just that, a jailer, ready to report on his comings and goings.

He said, "How long have you lived here?"

"A couple of years."

"Do you rent it?"

"Uh-huh." She was eating.

"So everything in the place is yours?"

"Except the bath and the wallpaper. Do you want a bath, by the way? The water's hot."

He shook his head.

"Aren't you going to eat?"

There was ham garnished with lettuce and shrimps on light rye bread. He munched without really tasting anything. He was beginning to feel so weary that everything was muted—the play on his nerves, the gnawing sense of dread, the mental confusion. She didn't look like a fanatic or someone on the eve of drama. She looked slim and young and unconcerned and well content. This was where the abandoned rifle would be found, but she didn't seem to care. He couldn't fathom her; couldn't think properly.

She sipped her coffee. "Tell me about yourself."

He was silent.

"You're quite a way from home."

Oh God, he thought, caught on a backwash of panic.

"Don't tell me nothing interesting has ever happened to you. Interesting things only seem to happen to interesting people, and you're interesting. Very."

The sensation of madness seemed to touch him again. He rose from the chair and went to the whisky bottle. She more than most would know what it was to receive confidences: men must have fed her with them, unloading their complaints, their failures, sure of sympathy, buying that too. Yet he dared not speak of Frenzel. Hartmann's warnings to stay mute couldn't apply where she was concerned; she'd already been bought—with one specific thing in view. So why not have it in the open? There was so little time. But he could not. He had doubts about her, and they were growing. Once, when a backfire in the street made him start, she chuckled: "Easy. You've too much imagination. This is a quiet neighborhood." Right or wrong he was ready to consider that she didn't know about Frenzel after all. Somewhere in the tired depths of his mind he was finding reasons to believe that she might have been lied to, misled. For all he knew she had been deceived about him and would be sacrificed when the time came. It was possible. Nothing about her was clear-cut any longer except the certainty that she expected him to share the divan, make love, sleep, wake and perhaps make love again when morning came. It was part of his right, paid for, but he was far from sure to what extent she had sold herself. Yet precisely because she had made the Axel rendezvous and had brought him to where Hartmann had promised, it was dangerous to assume too much. Either way he couldn't trust her, couldn't ask whether there was a telephone in the building, couldn't chance the offer of a bribe or think of pleading.

The whisky spun his brain. If he broached the truth and discovered that she was, in fact, ignorant of it, disaster could ensue. She would turn him out, call the police, warn the Metropol—any or all of these. When he thought of her as someone tricked and used like himself he read into her a capacity for horror and instant action. Frenzel would survive, but there would be another victim; Hartmann had left him with the certainty of that and it governed him.

Some of the time he matched her small-talk, sometimes not. She seemed to fence when he questioned her obliquely as to what she knew, yet she warmed to him with explorations of her own as if anxious—and grateful—to be spared for once some hasty, wolfish stranger. She laughed frequently, juggling almost coyly with words and meanings, but her eyes, her gestures, made it plain that she would ease his nerves, deaden whatever tortured his mind, whenever he wanted.

Eventually she turned off the radio. Laker put down his glass, seeing nothing, never so alone. And weary beyond words, exhausted by everything the endless day had done to him. He gazed at the ceiling as if he were suffocating. Tomorrow he would think again, balance everything, think and decide which gamble to take, with her, with Slattery.

"Have a bath and freshen up." She was calling him "David" now. She came to where he sat and knelt in front of him. "Yes?"

He shook his head. It was past ten-thirty: when he glanced at his watch the new strap claimed his thoughts, dragging them back through the nightmare's web.

"Bed, then?"

He shrugged. She took his hand, leaning closer, smiling, enjoying the unaccustomed luxury of play.

"There's nothing like it."

He got up again, abruptly. She watched him confidently. He drank another whisky, as if he were in a hurry, then went to the bathroom. His reflection greeted him in the wall mirror and he stared at it as if amazed by the sanity of his appearance. He washed his hands and face, then returned to the room. All the lights were out except the one beside the divan. Without surprise he saw that the girl was wearing only pants and brassiere and he remembered thinking how full her black-cupped breasts were. But he felt nothing, not even when she released the brassiere, turning expectantly as she did so. Nothing. He took off his jacket and slung it on a hook on the kitchen door, then pulled the two soft chairs together.

"What are you doing?"

He didn't answer.

"David!" She made it a complaint.

"I'm sorry," he said.

She came toward him, silhouetted. "Don't joke."

"I'm not."

"Nonsense." A little laugh. "Nonsense."

"I mean it." He punched the cushions. "I'm sorry, but there it is."

For a moment he was prepared for an outburst, but it didn't come. For what seemed a long time as he softened the cushions he was aware of her standing close, aware of a tiny part of him numbly crying for comfort and escape, aware of her lips parted in astonishment.

"Truly?"

Then she knew it was truly.

"Are you married?"

"No."

"Why, then?"

He shook his head and started unknotting his tie, still expecting anger, scorn—he wasn't sure what it would be. But, instead, her mouth twisted.

"Well, that's the first time ever. I'd like you to know that— the first time ever."

She went to the divan, pulled back the covers and tossed a blanket at him before flouncing between the sheets, indignation in the violence of her movements. But she said nothing more. Laker heeled off his shoes, got out of his trousers, then fitted himself onto the chairs and covered himself over.

The girl switched off the light almost at once. The sodium-white blur of the street lamps softly filled the room through the curtains. And Laker lay heavily on his side, huddled as if in protection against the coming day of obligation.

Karen whispered: "Sammy? . . . Sammy? . . ." She was clinging to him in the hollow and the cold was like death. Even in the shadow-play of the dream he knew that the memory would brand him throughout his lifetime; that heartbreak would come of this. "When will it be normal for us, Sammy?" He held her tight, close, their breath like ghosts, her face pinched and freckled, her eyes burning with the onset of fever. "We'll have to go," he said. "We'll have to work west. It's no good waiting. They've given us up. We're no use to them anymore." She was coughing already. "You know best, Sammy." He gazed down at her, moved, frightened for her. She'd never make it. There were planes droning in the sky. "Now?" she asked. "Right away?" But he shook his head. "When it's dark."

The picture fragmented. For a while he seemed to be nowhere, floating, not cold. He felt his body heave. He heard the crack of his carbine and saw a helmeted figure double up, saw another opening the lid of the stranded tank, aimed quickly, fired and ran. Then he was floating again, aware of the stench of decay, of destruction. And Slattery was saying, "And then, Sam? What happened then?"—Slattery blinking across the desk in the Grosvenor Gardens office, tapping his teeth with a silver pencil. "How many did you get, Sam?"

Then everything was changing once more, dissolving, focusing anew. "A favor, Sam, that's all. Nothing to it. I wouldn't be asking you otherwise . . ." In a voice that didn't sound like his own he heard himself answer: "I couldn't do it. I couldn't. Besides, Patrick will be with me." Slattery beamed: "Do what, Sam?" There were stars now, darkness, a child wailing. "Kill anyone. That's what you're asking, isn't it?" Slattery had vanished, though Laker could still hear him—"You did once, so why not again?" He began to shout back: "I had a reason, the only reason. I hated them then. *You have to hate*." And all at once it wasn't Slattery anymore, but Hartmann, Hartmann with his head tilted, saying, "Either that or you need an incentive, Mr. Laker. And I've seen to it that you've been given the best there is."

The dream went out of him with a rush. He was mumbling, grinding his teeth. It was night and he knew where he was, remembering the room, the girl, the reasons why—everyone, everything.

"What is it?"

He grunted, twisting on the chairs.

"What's the matter?"

The lamp clicked on and he squeezed his lids together. He could smell her scent, the room's stuffiness. Gradually his eyes took the brunt of the light. Sitting up, she was holding the sheet across herself, alarm making her seem prudish.

"Were you dreaming?"

"Time." He licked his lips. He was in a sweat. "What's the time?"

"You scared me."

"Huh?"

"You were saying things. Shouting."

"What?"

"Names."

"What names?"

"Frankel."

He stared.

"Frankel, Frenzel—something like that."

"Frenzel?" he said thickly.

"Yes."

He paused, then let it go. "Who's Frenzel?"

"God knows. It was your dream." She frowned. "Are you in some kind of trouble?"

"Is that what you were told?"

She shook her head. "I'm guessing."

"What *were* you told?"

"That you wanted a girl."

"Just that?"

"Just that. I must have got the story wrong, though." The hurt was still there. She gazed at him for several seconds without speaking. "Is it bad? Something bad?"

He lay back. So she didn't know. That at least was clear. He believed her. His briefing had been incomplete. Hartmann hadn't warned him she would be a stumbling-block.

"I thought you were in town for some kind of conference."

"That's right," he lied.

But she wasn't satisfied. "What is it, then?" she said after a pause.

"Nothing."

"You sounded terrified. And now you look like death. And when you first came in tonight you were—"

"It was a dream," he said.

He wiped the sweat from his face, suddenly afraid that she might not be prepared to harbor him. Her anxiety didn't sound as if it were altogether unselfish. And he'd wounded her pride as it was. Yet it was vital to stay. He must. This place was his last resort. Indeed, he might have to get her out of here—and keep her out.

"Nothing worse than that?"

"No," he forced himself. "Nothing."

He could feel her eyes on him. Inwardly he groaned. "The old-fashioned pressures are still the best, Mr. Laker." He turned away from her. God, oh God. He didn't hate Frenzel.

Chapter
Eleven

THEY must have slept again. A whimper of tires in the street finally made Laker stir. He awoke quickly, tense at once, reality boring in. He got up immediately and went to the window; looked across. In the dullness of morning the window facing him seemed almost opaque: he couldn't see to any depth beyond the open slats of the blinds. A pigeon perched itself contentedly on the sill. Peering right he noticed that the entrance to the hotel was at the corner of the block. It was early for crowds, and those who walked moved briskly, intent on destinations, unaware of Frenzel, of Patrick, of Hartmann, buying their newspapers from a shop away to the left, glancing at the headlines as they hurried out, informed of violence and disasters and tyrannies around the globe but ignorant of what fear was doing to someone above their heads, what tomorrow's editions might carry.

He let the curtain swing back and pulled on his trousers, then lit a cigarette. The girl was still sleeping. He gazed at her for a moment, then took his razor and a towel from the suitcase. The sharp click of the locks roused her. She rolled lazily onto her back, the sheet slipping from her breasts as she stretched.

"How long have you been up?"

"A couple of minutes."

"Is it late?"

"Five to eight."

She yawned and reached a long arm to the radio. He entered the bathroom, shaved and washed. He ached from the chairs. He sat on the edge of the bath when he'd finished, Hartmann's remote control guiding the rabid course of his thoughts, endlessly warning him, daring him. After some time the girl thumped on the door and he opened it. She was in a pink housecoat. "I reckoned you must have made camp," she said tartly, brushing past. He was drawn to the window again, held there as if by a magnet. The light had improved and now he could vaguely discern the interior of Frenzel's room-to-be—a cupboard, part of a mauve-covered bed. . . . But there was a point beyond which his mind refused to go.

He turned away sharply, a tightness in his chest. Yesterday's date had been torn from the calendar. *Do not men die fast enough,* he read, *without being destroyed by each other?* Friday . . Almost with disbelief he realized that he and Patrick were to have been en route to Heidelberg. "Lucky mortals," Baxendale had said. "Heidelberg, eh?" It seemed a lifetime ago.

He looked out onto the landing. It was squarish, the walls papered in silver-gray, the carpet dark blue and showing signs of wear. There were two doors, one presumably the entrance to another apartment. The second was in the angle of the stairs. He went to it quickly. There was no lock. It opened outward onto an iron platform and he saw the steps leading down, wire-meshed on both sides and roofed with corrugated sheeting. Below were garages and the service yards to the ground-floor shops; beyond, a tangle of buildings, the partial view of a back street where traffic crawled as if in obedience to a promise. Three minutes? Instinctively the query lodged.

He returned to the girl's sitting room and a calypso jerking from the radio. She emerged from the bathroom shortly afterwards and dressed in front of him with complete indifference, once asking "Hungry?" but saying nothing more. They ate in the small kitchen—boiled eggs, toast and coffee. Her mood had changed. He was wary of her, sensing that her doubts about him were unallayed. The green eyes, a little puffy now, bleary, wanted no problems, no trouble. But at least he could be open about one thing.

"Where's the nearest telephone?"

"In the shop—the delicatessen."

"Not downstairs?"

"No." Her tone was surly. "Will you be at your conference today?"

He nodded, remembering.

"What time?"

"Ten."

"Where?"

He named the place where the bank was, Sunderspladsen, and she repeated it, correcting his pronunciation with a touch of scorn. Last night she would have teased him, but she'd made a bad bargain and her feelings showed.

"And then?"

"Then what?"

"What will you do?"

"I don't follow."

"You won't want to come back here."

"Of course." Alarm chilled him. "Of course I will," he repeated.

"Why?"

"Why not?" he stalled.

"What's wrong with the Metropol?" She tossed her head. "You look across there often enough."

"This place is fine."

"For what?"

"It suits me."

With difficulty he held her gaze.

"On a couple of chairs?" she said. "You get a bed in a hotel."

He tried to laugh.

"There's no need to go on with it. Mistakes happen. How were they to know you didn't want a girl? You'd be better off elsewhere."

"I like it here."

"But I don't. It's . . . it's stupid. If you're sick or something, okay. Let's forget it ever happened." More than pique was niggling her. "Or is there another reason? One I haven't been told about?"

He snapped, "You took the money, didn't you?"

"That was yesterday."

"And tomorrow I'll have gone."

"Then I'm counting the hours."

She ground her cigarette in the saucer and went into the other room. Laker ran his hands over his face, dreading the depths of self-discovery to which he might yet be dragged. He had to keep a foothold here. And then, if need be, take the place over. God alone knew how. The imperatives controlling him made her presence unforgivable. Because she menaced an act that stabbed his mind with horror she prompted a terrible malice in him. He was too far gone in desperation to appreciate the irony. All he knew was what Hartmann had done to him, what Hartmann wanted, what was at stake.

The girl was straightening the crumpled divan when he left the kitchen. As if from habit he glanced toward Frenzel's room, the marksman in him automatically noting snags, thinking in terms of fleeting opportunity.

Nine twenty-five . . . Eight and a half hours before Frenzel's plane touched down; ten, say, before he was installed. So there was time yet. Time and Slattery. For too long he'd discounted Slattery. More and more he needed him, despite the risks, the misgivings. Alone he would crack.

"Have you got a spare key?"

"I'll be here," the girl said.

"Say you aren't?"

"I will be."

He didn't press it. He took his coat from its hook and went out to the landing. In case she listened he walked all the way down. There were glass panels on either side of the front door and he studied the street through one of them. Nobody obviously waited for him, but he was taking no chances. He opened and shut the door loudly enough for the girl to hear, then went quietly up the first flight of stairs to the fire exit.

Again there was no evidence of being under observation. The fire escape put him down by an outside lavatory at the rear of the delicatessen. The yard was stacked with wooden crates and a delivery van was parked close to the wall. No one was about. Laker walked between the crates and entered a storeroom where a woman was loading shelves with jars of pickles. She didn't notice him. He elbowed through a door into the shop, surprising an overalled youth on a ladder at the near end of the counter, but drawing no comment. It was a long rectangular shop. Half a dozen customers were either being served or waiting their turn. A solitary telephone booth stood in an alcove. Laker checked his mass of small change, then stepped inside. A light clicked on as the door thudded. He paused before dialing, staring blankly at the activity behind the counter, the cheeses, the cooked meats, the pâtés, the hung salamis and knackwursts, isolating himself, visualizing Slattery, putting his trust in him.

"London?" a voice echoed. "A moment, please."

And then it began again, the repetition, the waiting, the

rising tension. "No delay for London. Shall I book the Gerrard number?"

Three minutes after the half-hour. Someone would answer. Someone would be there. Laker closed his eyes, willing it, praying for it. The wire hummed, clicked, gabbled unintelligibly. An assistant sliced ham on a machine, a customer loaded her shopping-basket. . . . If Slattery wasn't available they would tell him where he could be found. He'd make them. And Slattery would have a solution; institute countermeasures. . . . Hope fed upon hope.

Every second lengthened, every minute. The booth was stifling. Outside, a man pointed at some mortadella, nodding, lips moving soundlessly. All the time people were either entering or leaving the shop.

"Hold for London, please."

He had the money ready on a ledge, a pencil to hand. Aloud he urged: "Hurry, for Christ's sake . . ." Another pause, another clash of tongues. On instructions he thumbed a succession of coins into the slots, waited, hands restless, eyes fixed, whispers like the sea filling his head. All at once there was silence, a moment's complete silence, before he heard the Gerrard number quoted. He hesitated, somehow unable to release himself from an intolerable strain.

"You're through, caller," the operator prompted.

He swallowed. "Mr. Slattery, please."

"Who's calling?"

It sounded like the same person, the woman who'd answered when he rang from Gale & Watts. He told her, adding, "It's urgent." But she stuck to her careful drill.

"Does Mr. Slattery know you?"

"Yes."

"Is he expecting you to telephone?"

"Yes," he snapped.

He waited again, trying to prepare his mind. Then, following a final click, Slattery was there at last, incredibly clear, seemingly in the booth with him, as close as ever he'd been. And cautious.

"Sam?"

"Listen—"

"Where are you?"

"Copenhagen."

"*Where?*"

"I'm in trouble. Bad trouble. . . ."

It came in a spate. He was never able to remember where he began or exactly what he said once the initial rush spilled over. He knew it was vital to be precise, chronological, absolutely accurate, but Slattery's interpolations confused him from the start. "Hang on, Sam. . . . Hold your horses. . . ." He ignored them for a while, blundering on, but they became more frequent, louder, sharper, eventually cutting him off between words.

"You're on an open line, man. *An open line.*"

"I've no choice."

"Then use your head. Scramble. Wrap it up."

"How can I?"

"Try."

"To hell with that. Listen—"

"I'm warning you, Sam."

Laker bit back another retort.

"Do it my way," Slattery said. "*My* way."

"Very well."

"Question and answer."

"All right."

The sound of Slattery's breathing raced along the line. "You dropped in at K's?"

"Yes."

"And found you were expected?"

"Yes."

"After which they had a talk with you?"

"Yes."

"Who did the talking?"

"Hartmann, S.S.D."

"About Patrick?"

"In part."

"Patrick's stayed on, I take it?"

"Yes."

Slattery delayed for a second or so. He hadn't missed much. "I didn't get the other person's name."

"Rudolf Frenzel . . . He flies out of here tomorrow afternoon, at two."

"Is he there now?"

"No. Tonight at six. From Paris."

"And it's a case of either, or. Either, or—is that the proposition?"

"Yes."

Silence.

Very quietly Slattery said, "Christ." Then: "The bastards."

"What are you going to do?"

"Give me time."

"I tried to get to you last night, but they objected."

"From Copenhagen?"

"Yes."

"Someone's with you?"

"Not at the moment. But I may not be able to contact you again."

The wire spat. Laker licked his lips, staring as if mesmerized at a shop assistant weighing cheese.

"Slattery?" he asked sharply, frightened by the lack of response.

"I'm here. Got my thinking-cap on. . . . Is Patrick aware of the situation?"

"He's been told he's with friends of mine."

"When did it come to a head?"

"Wednesday afternoon."

"At K's?"

"After I left. Karen's been arrested. I saw her—"

"Easy, Sam."

"She was blown. They knew I was coming—"

"*Easy!* Simmer down."

Laker glared, seething. "Get Patrick back and I'll simmer down."

"All right, all right. But—"

"I'm not asking a favor. It's a matter of life and death. No one's playing a game at this end."

"Look," Slattery said. "I'll alert Paris—that's the first thing. Our friend won't fly, do you understand? He won't arrive."

"That's no help."

"It'll take the pressure off you while we—"

"It won't, it won't." Frantically, Laker beat a fist against the coin box. "He's got to be here. *Got* to be. Don't stop him coming, for Christ's sake. They threatened me about that. He must arrive. Must, do you hear?"

"To be an Aunt Sally?"

"It's him or Patrick."

He began to talk about Hartmann, the words pouring from him again. He couldn't stop himself, straining desperately to convey the terror to which he had been subjected, the certainty that Hartmann wasn't bluffing, quoting him, restating the equation. Slattery seemed to have given up trying to interrupt.

"I haven't any choice, don't you see? Unless you intervene I've got to do what he wants."

"You couldn't."

"Put yourself in my position."

The operator cut in to say that his time had expired. Urgently he asked for an extension, for Slattery to accept the charges, and Slattery agreed.

When it sounded as if they were once more alone Slattery said icily, "Listen, Sam. I've got the message. If you go off the rails like that again I'll hang up—is that clear?"

"You wouldn't dare," Laker snapped. "You got us into this. Now get us out."

"That's easier said than done."

"Why?" He was trembling. If anything happens to Patrick I'll raise the roof. You'll have to answer for it—I'll see to that. You, personally. So think of something. And it had better be effective."

"Such as?"

"How the hell do you expect me to know? But you aren't powerless, are you?" He paused hopefully, but there was no answer. "Are you?" he echoed.

"I'll do what I can. It's tricky, though."

"Can't you offer anything more than that?"

"Not off the cuff, no."

Laker gazed wildly at the continuing mime in the shop. A woman in a fur coat waited near the booth. Slattery was saying something about "playing it by ear." Despite his blandness he sounded harassed and the jargon had a terrible sterility. In dismay, Laker shouted, "What are you going to *do?*"

"Good God!" Slattery retorted. "What do you expect? I can't promise miracles. And even if I could I wouldn't be fool enough to broadcast them."

The woman was tapping on the glass. Laker turned his back on her.

"Don't sidetrack Frenzel," he urged Slattery. "I want him here—tonight."

"Sam—"

"He's the only safeguard I've got."

"Sam, listen—"

"You listen," Laker shouted, beyond himself. "Leave Frenzel alone."

A frizzling noise filled the line. Through it Slattery was saying, "I'll be in touch."

"How?"

"Ritchie Jackson, at the Embassy."

"I can't go there. Haven't you got the picture yet?"

"Can't you telephone?"

"I'm not sure I can risk it."

The woman tapped on the glass again, harder now.

Almost hysterically Laker flung out, "Hartmann said that Patrick and I had ceased to be public property. He said that because of circumstances I don't know about you'd be unwilling to lift a finger. Well, if you won't or can't, I will. I'll have to go through with it—and don't try to stop me. Leave word at the Metropol. The Metropol. If there isn't something by six tonight I'll know where I stand. And, so help me, I'll lay the whole bloody issue at your door when the time comes, whatever happens. . . ."

He went on, goaded toward a kind of dreadful bravado. But after a while he was aware of a dribbling sound in his ear; he was talking to himself. Like someone betrayed he hung up and backed out of the booth. "*Tak!*" the woman said with heavy sarcasm. He stood amid the bustle and sudden chatter of the shop in a daze of anger and confusion. Whatever hopes he'd had had dwindled. But the upstairs room, the problem of the girl, the rifle awaiting collection at the bank—these were certainties, as real as the shoulders that jostled him.

Behind the counter an assistant cocked his head. "Nothing," Laker muttered. "Nothing." Turning away he wished to God he'd had the sense to withold Frenzel's name.

He went out through the back, crossed the yard and mounted the fire escape. Then he walked down to the front door and let himself quietly into the street. After a few paces he paused to light a cigarette, glancing both ways as he did so. Once again no one caught his eye, but this time the feeling of menace was there. Where the block ended he waited for the lights to change before going over to the

Metropol. It was shaped like a blunt V with traffic flowing along both sides. He made his way past the cars squatting in the forecourt and entered the deep-carpeted foyer.

The tall blonde on duty in Reception smiled politely, waiting to discover what language she was expected to match.

"I'm inquiring after a Mr. Frenzel."

"What name?"

"Frenzel. Rudolf Frenzel."

She consulted a list, running a scarlet nail down the side of the type. "Frenzel," she said, reminding herself.

"That's right."

"There's a Mr. Frenzel expected. He has a reservation for this evening."

Laker could see the number against her fingernail: 68. And Hartmann loomed as if to remind him that one more thing had been proved; one more guarantee honored.

"Mr. Frenzel would hardly be here yet, sir. Overnight visitors do not vacate their rooms until midday, but I can have him paged if you wish."

"No, thank you."

"Will you leave a message?"

"No." Laker shook his head. "Thank you," he repeated, then walked away.

She would remember him, but he had hardly begun to concern himself with hazards of that sort. He was still trying to assess Slattery's tone, his attitude, still dismayed that his reaction hadn't been more appalled, more encouraging. Incredibly, his main concern had seemed to be for Frenzel. Nobody else could twist Hartmann's arm, and unless that were done there could only be one end. And Hartmann had been certain what that end must be; confident. "I wouldn't care to be in London's shoes, Mr. Laker. No one likes humiliation, London least of all. But then, if I *were* in London's shoes, I wouldn't be aware of the situation, would I? You wouldn't have been stupid enough to tell me about Rudolf Frenzel, would you?"

For a while Laker walked aimlessly, blinkered by old and new fears, willing Slattery to act, to better Hartmann in some way he couldn't himself conceive of, yet dreading a blundering move aimed at sparing him which would result in tragedy. For a day and a night he had never quite abandoned faith in Slattery's ability, but he was nearer to it now than ever before. He despaired of him, viewed him with bitterness and alarm. But his hatred was for Hartmann, Hartmann who knew the lethal fury to which a person could be driven and who chose the victims and set a zero hour. Hartmann deserved what he meted out to others. Yet hatred without opportunity was as hellish as time without the certainty of hope.

Thirty to forty yards to the rear a man in a gray overcoat kept his distance. He looked like the one who'd been in the foyer of the Metropol, but Laker wasn't sure about him and he didn't experiment. But he thought: All right, all right. So you know why I went there. . . .

It was after ten and the banks were open. He would collect the rifle; he must. He was a puppet still. Nothing had changed.

A taxi brought him to the Sunderspladsen, a neat cobbled square centered on a fountain with a church filling most of one side and what Laker took to be municipal offices on the other. They had crossed a bridge to get there. The Copenhagen-National branch occupied a corner position. He paid off the driver and went in, affecting unconcern, as George Marshall requesting access to his deposit box. Once again the stepping-stone was ready and waiting: there were no snags. A clerk accompanied him down the strong room, used his master key on Laker's locker, then discreetly withdrew. Hartmann's key opened the steel door. Inside was a narrow black case, about three and a half feet long and ten or twelve inches high. It wasn't new; the rexine covering was worn along the edges and slightly scratched. Laker slid it out and took it to one of the cubicles at the end of the room. To his surprise the case was secured only by catches. He sprung them simultaneously, then lifted the lid.

The weapon nestled in a bed of yellow velvet—the stock, the barrel and the telescopic attachment, each separate. Laker didn't touch them. They looked immaculate; the polished wood, the thin film of oil on the blue-black metal, the protective caps over the sight's ends, all gleamed dully under the overhead strip of light. In a recess at the top right-hand corner was a brown fiber box and he opened that, discovering what he expected—rimless ammunition packed in cotton wool. A dozen rounds or so; he didn't count. There was an envelope taped inside the lid: *Key* was written on it in German. He removed this and shut the case, locked it, putting the key into his hip pocket as he left the cubicle.

The clerk said, "Are you taking the case with you, Mr. Marshall?"

"Yes."

"I see." He was inclined to fuss. "And are you continuing to rent your compartment?"

"Yes."

"Very good." He pushed the door to. It snapped shut and he turned the master key, giving Laker a conspiratorial smile. There was nothing to sign, but the clerk entered the date in his ledger against the locker number.

"Thank you, sir."

They walked up to the ground floor together. A nod, another smile, and they parted. Laker was sweating slightly, his face set. The case was heavier than its slimness suggested. He stepped out into the quiet square, armed now, equipped, yet as unremarkable as a musician on his way to rehearsal or a salesman hawking his particular brand of samples.

It was barely half-past ten. Only the waiting and the hoping remained, but he couldn't go back to the room so soon. He must use up a few hours first. The girl was the major flaw in Hartmann's planning. And as he walked from the bank he once more began to realize how much hinged upon his ability to handle her—the lies, the blandishments, the persuasive wheedling that might be necessary; even the violence. But he had to have that room.

Chapter Twelve

 E couldn't make up his mind whether any-
one tailed him or not, but he took no deliberate avoiding
action. It was strangely inefficient tailing, crude, apparently
spasmodic; either that or immensely skilled. Where he
walked he didn't remember, but after a while he found himself on a tree-lined embankment overlooking a stretch of
water in which the morning's white, ribbed clouds were mir-
rored. He paused there, the case at his feet, studying his
wavering reflection.

Slattery would fail him; the feeling grew. For the hun-
dreth time he went back to their meetings in Manchester
Square and at the Mitre, dismayed yet again by the amateur
enthusiasm and cheerful understatement which had roped
him in. If only he'd refused him at the outset, never learned
of Karen's existence, been spared that aching wound along
with the blackmail and its merciless carrot. Karen was already in the net by the time he was recruited, as helpless as
he and Patrick were now. And Slattery should have known
it: the grim, secret wastes beneath the surface of daily living
were his province, his bread and butter.

It was futile to theorize, yet the question marks persisted, throbbing through layers of hostility and desperation, blaming the years of deceit which had blunted Slattery's once sharp-eyed keenness for detail and his almost reflexive ability to read between the lines. At the very least Karen's position must have been suspect. Yet all he had thought necessary was to throw in a Leipzig telephone number—and that almost apologetically, as if it really weren't done even to imply that anything could go wrong.

Laker gazed into the water, despair returning like a cancerous ache. The rhythmic clatter of a train reached him, making him raise his head and stare blankly at the buildings opposite. How glib Slattery had been. "Wise-virgin common sense, Sam . . ." That was then; and just now he was cagey, slightly flustered, not shocked enough, as if he still didn't fully understand what he'd started, what Hartmann would finish. *Not shocked enough.*

Laker moved on, scared again as his thoughts clipped nearer and nearer to Frenzel, picturing the hotel window with its slatted blinds. Say they were kept closed? Would he be forced to go to Frenzel's room—confront him? The sense of panic was never far off, and now it swept him anew, compounded with a foretaste of horror and disgust. Aloud, almost dementedly, he heard himself ask, "Why me? . . . Why me?"—and a couple passing on the embankment glanced at him with surprised amusement.

Intermittent sunshine cast his shadow on the paving stones; that of the case looked out of proportion, elongated. He crossed the road, imprisoned within himself, unaware of the car forced to swerve and the driver who shouted. Soon there were shops on either side. He went into a café and ordered a cognac, needing its fire, its strength. For a while as he sat there his mind fastened wildly on the possibility of somehow entering into collusion with Frenzel, enlisting Jackson at the British Embassy, the press and the police, between them faking a story and a photograph that would fool whoever waited to inform Hartmann of what had happened. But the idea withered like others before it.

The self-sufficient chatter at the neighboring tables filled him with an extraordinary viciousness which presently drove him into the streets once more. He paused outside a newspaper office, its windows filled with enlargements of a military parade, the King and Queen arriving at the ballet. "One word to anyone, Mr. Laker. *Anyone* . . ." The throttled dictum turned him away, stayed with him, warning him that Slattery was hamstrung, too—"An outcry, Mr. Laker? Public outrage? . . . Oh no"—reminding him all over again that Frenzel and Patrick were privately in the balance and must remain so. Yet hope could be stubborn. He dared not chance another personal visit to the Metropol, but under the pressure of stress he impulsively waved a cruising taxi into the curb.

"Do you speak English?"

"Some. Where you want?" Cropped hair, blue eyes, a jaw like a boxer's.

"The Metropol."

"Okay."

"Go there for me. Ask at the desk if there is a message for Laker. Then come back here."

"A message?"

"For Laker." He spelled it quickly.

"You don't come?"

"No."

A frown. "You stay here, is that it?"

"Yes."

"Okay—but for twenty kroner."

"All right."

"Twenty kroner first."

Laker paid, repeating the name, the hotel.

"Okay," the driver said. "Five minutes."

He drew away, grinning, and Laker waited nervously. He wasn't clever, but it was the best he could do. For what seemed a very long time he gazed into a window where a model of a black bull, pinned with paper banderillas, blinked electric eyes at him amid a display of sherries. He watched the traffic's flow in the glass, convinced he wasn't watched in turn. But he fidgeted, on edge, then paced up and down. Just as he was beginning to conclude he'd allowed himself to be robbed, the taxi slid in from behind a grinding tram.

"No message."

"Are you sure?"

"Sure. Nothing for Laker."

A muscle flicked by Laker's mouth. It was early yet, only ten to twelve. Even so . . .

"Thanks," he said.

"Okay." The driver grinned again. "Perhaps she send word another time, eh?" He, too, was a man of the world.

Laker decided to give Slattery another couple of hours. Meanwhile there were practical things to be done, preparations to be made. He couldn't cling indefinitely to straws.

He found his bearings, then explored the area to the rear of the delicatessen, timing himself over the distance between the service yards and the nearest taxi-rank, walking briskly toward the street he'd seen from the top of the fire escape earlier in the day. It took him almost six minutes, but that included mistakenly entering a cul-de-sac. The second trip took under five, the third, cutting corners, only a fraction over four. And this was walking: against that there were three levels of fire escape to be negotiated. It was an all-night rank, he noted.

Eventually he took a taxi and was driven to the BEA office. There were several flights to choose from and he booked on one leaving for London at four-thirty on Saturday afternoon, two and a half hours after Frenzel's own proposed exit from Copenhagen. That part of him which had already lost confidence in the chances of a reprieve was dismayed by the gap between the unpredictable moment Frenzel was going to be squarely in his sights and four-thirty on Saturday. It might amount to hours, half a day, perhaps a night as well. There were so many imponderables. Where would he go after that headlong rush down the fire escape? The Embassy? His mind wouldn't stretch that far. Self-preservation was the least of his concerns.

He chose a place to eat within a stone's throw of the Tivoli. It was small, crowded, and he shared a table with a middle-aged man with a voracious appetite who read a newspaper and whose feet kept coming into contact with the gun case. Twice Laker moved it, apologizing. He wasn't hungry. He was killing time. He could only toy with the food, but he drank three large whiskies and several cups of black coffee. At a quarter to two he pressed some kroner into the waiter's hand and asked him to ring the Metropol. The reply was the same: nothing, no message. Anxiety hounded him into the streets again, the weight of the case insisting that the nightmare was going to run its prescribed course after all, all the demented way.

He followed the route he and the girl had taken the previous evening. As he neared the delicatessen his eyes went up to her third-floor window and the one directly opposite. The sun glinted like gold on Frenzel's.

"Fear can remove mountains, Mr. Laker . . ."

He pressed the doorbell and thought of Patrick, hardening his heart.

"Oh," she said when she saw him. That was all—"Oh," without inflexion.

She let him in and he followed her up the steep stairs. The room seemed to have shrunk since he was last there. A cigarette burned in a tray beside the divan and the covering was pulled back, the pillows dented. He put the case down at the foot of the divan and tossed his coat over it. She was wearing dark slacks and a striped sweater and there was a pale blue velvet band across her hair. Last night she'd been bright, talkative, eager to draw him out and have him relax, to have him laugh. But he'd put paid to that and the grudge still showed.

He muttered something about a wash. "Please yourself," she said and curled on the divan, reaching for a magazine.

The bathroom window was narrow and rather high. Laker moved the plastic curtain aside and gazed across the street. It surprised him how much of Frenzel's room he could see now that the sun was behind him, streaming in. He could even pick out the light switch by the white door through which Frenzel would come and go. He wouldn't inevitably be deciphering shadows, then. And, sometime or other, Frenzel would surely attend to the blinds—close them, open them; it didn't matter which. A couple of seconds would be long enough, a couple of heartbeats. Four windows to the left a plump, bald man was at that instant polishing his spectacles and Laker drew an imagined line on him. It would be easy, given the occasion, given the chance of maintaining a vigil.

He felt no relief: every fiber of him ached to be spared. In an hour or two, somehow, he would check with the Metropol again. Meanwhile he must consolidate his position and make the vigil possible. Everything hung on what was said, how it was said. He sluiced his face from the cold tap, then looked at himself, in the grip of his own helplessness. His vision seemed to cloud. He was a businessman, a widower with a house in Weybridge. Weybridge, Surrey, England . . . Who was Frenzel? Frenzel who would never know Patrick and whom Patrick would never know. What had Frenzel done except to change sides? . . . But he mustn't start thinking about Frenzel—not as a man, not like that. Only of the awful necessity and how to cope with the girl.

He finger-combed his hair and joined her in the room, mastering his nerves. She glanced up from her magazine, then went on reading.

"Have you been out?"

"No."

"You're missing a fine day."

She shrugged. He sat in the chair nearest to her and fastened his shoelaces. Money might interest her, but first he had to establish contact, rapport. She had gone cold on him; the glance just now was full of surly surmise.

"Where did you learn your English?"

"Huh?"

"Your English. It's good."

"At school. Here and there."

"It's good," he said lamely.

"I was with SAS for a while. That helped."

"Flying?"

"For a while."

She sounded bored, as if she had been asked these things a thousand times. Laker watched for a smile, some softening of her features, but there was none. He asked about her flying, the places she'd been, in what aircraft, where she liked best, not caring what her answers were, not interested, his mind simmering in the employ of a situation three hundred miles away. If she warmed to him it was barely noticeable. He got up and went to the table where the bottles were, the lava flow of doubt and anxiety endlessly pressing through him.

"Do you want one?"

She shook her head. He poured himself a whisky, deliberately avoiding looking toward the window, seeing in her green eyes a lurking background of suspicion. Given time she would probably relent; tenderness was her professional stock-in-trade. If he had been hungry for her he would have had confidence in his ability to thaw her out. But he was angling to enforce the small print of an agreement she knew nothing of, and the prospect of failure daunted him, inhibiting his approach. He carried the glass back to the chair and sat with his fingers locked around it, trying to hide his thoughts, afraid of showing that he was afraid.

"How was the conference?" she asked.

"All right."

"Isn't there an afternoon session?"

"No."

"Don't tell me you came to Copenhagen just for a morning's meeting."

"We started yesterday," he lied.

"On what?"

"Business efficiency."

It was twenty to three. He began talking again, about her, working for a return of the smile which would be a beginning. Hartmann's funds weren't exhausted and he had traveler's checks of his own: together they totaled around two hundred pounds. She could have the lot if need be. For money like that she might be willing to leave, stay the night somewhere, allow him the run of the place until the following afternoon. It was possible. It would be tempting. Two hundred pounds and no questions asked—yes?

He finished the whisky, reached over and switched on the radio. She arched an eyebrow, measuring him with a look while he struggled to mask his nerves, his tension.

"I'm sorry about last evening. I . . . I'd had a hard day—you know how it is."

She didn't answer. He lit a cigarette, the hard core of his mind intent, the rest uneasy, uncertain. If he couldn't buy her absence he would somehow have to keep her prisoner—that or quit the room entirely and haunt the Metropol until

Frenzel arrived and could be tackled squalidly at close quarters. For two days now he had existed in loneliness, anguish burning into him like the sun focused by a glass, eating away hope and pity and self-respect. It was worse than fever, worse than hysteria. Yet he was absolutely rational, absolutely clear as to what the issues were, feeling Hartmann's corrective tug whenever his very sanity questioned how it could possibly be that he was committed to a killing while the world went by outside and neither he nor Slattery could let it know. "There are rules to this game, Mr. Laker . . ." Memory never let up.

"Anna," he said.

He moved to the divan and sat beside her. She turned her head on the pillow, wary still. He took the magazine, sliding it from her grip, and tossed it aside.

"What's become of that smile?"

"It's not my smiling day."

"Why not?"

She shrugged again, lifting her shoulders like a piano player, narrowing them.

"Come on," he said.

She grimaced, lips pressed together.

"Is that the best you can do?"

"I'm not a tap," she said.

"I'm sorry about last night."

"I heard you the first time."

He still believed it was only a matter of patience. He touched her callously, as if he were just another man for whom machine-like responses would suffice. "Anna," he said, despising himself, reduced to this so that she might feel sorry for him, glad to be necessary, and then be ready to listen, more willing to consider what he had to propose.

"What's got into you?" she said flatly.

She was stiff, unyielding. He ran his fingers over her white neck and into the softness of her hair. He felt no thrill, no excitement. He was using her, or seeking to. They would find the rifle here, but he didn't care. The contract permitted no stab of regret or sorrow or repugnance. Only the end mattered, and she was in the way of Frenzel's mortal danger.

She didn't move. Her eyes seemed harder, as if he were one of those who haggled when everything was finished.

"Where's this conference of yours?"

"The Sunderspladsen."

"Where in the Sunderspladsen?"

"Where?"

"Where, yes."

"Near the bank."

She glanced away from him. The radio was pulsing out a staccato beat. Laker should have been warned, on his guard: but no. Ruthlessly he traced the line of her lips.

"You're lying," she said after a few moments.

"Lying?"

"There is no conference."

"Nonsense."

"Not in the Sunderspladsen."

"Of course there is." He forced a laugh.

"I checked," she said.

He saw the spiky glint of anger as she pushed his hands down. He sat back, alarm knotting in his chest.

"Look," he began, "this is ridiculous."

"No, it isn't."

"What's a conference got to do with us?"

"There isn't any conference."

"All right. Have it your own way. But how does that matter?"

"It matters."

"Tell me how."

She twisted off the divan and reached for a pack of cig-

arettes, fumbled one loose and lit it. He watched her,
thoughts in turmoil. Later, time and again, he was to recall
how she looked at him then.

"I want you to go."

"Why?"

"I do, that's all."

"Listen—"

"You can have the money back."

"It's not mine."

"The one who laid your perks on, then." Her nostrils flared.
Instinct was warning her, it could only be that, warning her
not to allow herself to be involved in something she sensed
yet did not understand. "I don't want you here anymore."

He got up. "You're being stupid."

"Perhaps."

"You are."

"That's my affair."

"Anna," he said desperately. He took hold of her, making
one last try, fondling her roughly in the way she knew best,
his mouth finding hers. "You must be out of your mind."

She wrenched herself free. "I mean it." She reached for a
bundle of notes on the mantelpiece. "Here," she said furiously.

"I'm staying." His voice had thickened. "You can't turn
me out."

"I can and I will."

She flung the money at him and started for the door. He
caught her by the arms as the notes scattered about his head.

"Be reasonable, for God's sake."

"Let—me—go!"

Even then he could hardly believe that disaster was land-
sliding down in a cheap brawl. If she hadn't struggled he
might have been able to control himself, quiet her—at least
quiet her. But she was vicious, kicking at his shins, her voice

rising all the time and the ugly, selfish sound of it sliced into his brain like a knife. He slapped her, horrified by what she was doing, knowing that it had to be stopped. She spat at him, kicking again.

"Don't be a fool!" he shouted. "Don't be—"

She was strong, absolutely wild. They crashed into the table and all the bottles went over. He freed a hand and slapped her a second time, hard, full on the cheekbone. She screamed. He tried to drag her toward the divan but she broke away, her gaping red mouth doing its best to destroy Patrick—in panic he could think of nothing else and in panic he went after her, thrashing around the cluttered room. With a convulsive movement she grasped one of the bottles. He closed, warding off the expected blow, but before he could check her she hurled the bottle through the window. For a moment they both stared, panting, silent, until the sound of the brittle smash below reached them and a yell came from the street. And then she ran to the broken window and screamed piercingly again, with her hands clenched beside her head.

Laker seemed unable to move anymore. Aghast, he watched her retreat from the window and sink onto the arm of the nearest chair, shaking, sobbing now. He felt as if the whole of his stomach was going to come up.

"Go away," she moaned. "Go away."

Vaguely he was aware of a noise in the street; feet thudding on the stairs. Stunned, he couldn't think. He heard himself say, "Do you know what you've done? Oh Christ, do you know what you've done?"

Someone banged on the door. The girl scurried to open it. A uniformed policeman came in, then another, big men who seemed to fill the room. There was a brief interchange between them and the girl before they motioned Laker out. He could understand so much, but no more. He thought he was merely being ejected and he picked up the gun case and his coat and the suitcase. With a hand to her swelling cheek the girl flinched as he drew level. He paused, staring into her uncomprehending face, trying to speak; but words wouldn't come.

The taller of the policemen pushed him onto the landing. It was only then and on the way down the stairs between them that he realized they were taking him with them.

Chapter
Thirteen

IN a daze Laker leaned against the side of the wagon jolting him away. There had been people on the landings, people around the street door, people outside the delicatessen—all gawking, all a blur as he was bundled across the pavement. He hadn't protested; he seemed to have been deprived of his strength, his will, his wits. And now, sitting between the two policemen in the enclosed back of the wagon, he was still beyond reasoning, the girl's screams still vibrated in his ears. "Where am I going?" he kept asking, but either they didn't understand him or they weren't disposed to answer.

When the wagon stopped, the rear doors were opened and he lurched out, clutching his coat and the two cases. One of the policemen attempted to grasp him by the arm, but he shook the hand away, beginning to react at last, dismay shot through with anger. Stone steps led up to heavy double doors. Inside was a brightly lit lobby with corridors branching left and right. He was taken past a railed barrier and brought to a standstill in front of a counter where his escorts conferred with the gray-haired policeman on duty.

Without fluency this one asked him, "What is your name?" A sheet of paper was briskly torn from a pad. "Name?"

Laker stared at him, shattered, thoughts beginning to race. He was sweating.

"Name?"

"Laker."

"Other name?"

"Samuel."

"English? American?"

"English . . . Look," Laker blurted, "you aren't thinking of keeping me here, are you?"

"Passport?"

"What?"

"You have passport?"

Laker drew it from his inside pocket and the photograph of Frenzel nearly came out, too. Glimpsing that startled expression again all but overwhelmed him with another surging rush of alarm. The light above his head seemed clinical and fierce and he was suddenly unnerved lest someone decided to examine what was in the black case.

"Will there be a fine?"

The policeman pursed his lips and turned the pages of the passport, studying the visa stamps with earnest, puckered eyes.

"I'm in a position to pay if there's a fine. Or if there's any damage to be made good."

Laker faltered, every moment of the brawl fresh and stark; frantically asking himself how it could conceivably have happened. There hadn't been reason enough: she'd almost manufactured it. He wiped his face, obsessed by what she had cost him in terms of angles and opportunity; what she might cost him yet. A clock behind the counter showed a minute or two past three.

"There was a misunderstanding." He pressed against the counter. "A misunderstanding. The window was broken by accident . . ." He swallowed. "If you'd only listen I'd like to explain . . ."

Ominously, the passport was set to one side.

"You wait," the duty man said, then corrected himself. "You *will* wait."

"What for? . . . For how long?"

"Long?"

"When can I go?"

"Not to go. Wait."

"Yes, but for how *long?*"

There was no answer. "Look here," Laker exploded, then stopped, warned by a hint of exasperation in the other's solid glance. More quietly he managed: "Am I being charged? And if so, what with?"

"Charged?"

With as much calm as Laker could dredge he said, "if there's any question of my being held I insist on being put in touch with the British Embassy—a Mr. Jackson. A Mr. Jackson at the British Embassy, is that clear?"

It didn't seem to be. He leaned across the counter and snatched up a pencil; swiveled the pad around. *Mr. Jackson,* he wrote, *British Embassy.*

"Yes?"

The man nodded. "Understand," he said. "But now you wait."

Laker fought down another distracted protest. With his coat draped across the gun case he went where the escort directed, turning into a corridor, entering a room the door of which was opened for him. The window was barred, but it was more like an interview room than anything, with a trestle table and some tubular steel chairs, cream-painted walls, red linoleum. Outside, cars were parked in a courtyard. He put the cases on the floor and sat at the table, trembling so much that he could hardly light a cigarette, reliving the swift crescendo of words and scuffling which had ruined Hartmann's basic plan, still flushed and sweating ice and fire.

He had botched everything, or had it botched for him. But it was no time for postmortems. Blaming the girl, blaming himself, wouldn't put the clock back. He'd never set foot in that room again, so there was only one course left—sickening even to contemplate, yet imperative, Hartmann's threat more urgent now than ever, more demanding, already pointing him toward a moment when squeamishness and revulsion would be numbed. He shuddered. Once he got out of here he would have to go on, on, with his senses gutted and his mind like that of an animal, deprived even of the sop to his conscience which the width of a street, the impersonal pressure on a trigger, might have given.

They hadn't locked the door; he tried it after a while and looked into the corridor. But he wasn't tempted. It would be madness to cut and run; the exits were sure to be guarded. What was more they had his passport. And he needed to contact Jackson—not merely so as to smooth his release but because Jackson was his link with Slattery, perhaps the only one now.

Less than three hours remained to Slattery: six o'clock was his deadline for producing a formula. And if he couldn't, if there wasn't one, Frenzel was as good as dead. This was what terror did to you; what Hartmann had achieved by threat and argument and what he'd known could be sustained on the strength of a promise.

Nerves several times propelled Laker to the door during the next half-hour. Once a girl passed carrying some files, and she smiled at him, interested. Shortly afterwards what he took to be an officer went by with a couple of civilians; these all ignored him. At twenty to four a policeman came into the room with a cup of tea. Laker was too eager to talk with him to be surprised. "Have you been in touch with the

British Embassy? . . . Is Mr. Jackson on his way?" But he got nowhere. Even when he followed the man into the corridor in an attempt to persuade him to fetch someone with a better understanding of English or German he failed to extract more from him than a series of gestures, shrugs and one repeated word—"Soon."

But for the rifle he would have stormed back to the counter in the entrance-lobby. There was nothing to stop him, yet he was afraid of incurring official enmity by creating a scene. If they took it into their heads to retaliate by checking his luggage, his pockets, inevitably he would find himself the focus of attention. Instead of being left to cool his heels there would be questions, questions he couldn't satisfactorily answer, and he might be held indefinitely, pending further inquiries. A sordid little shouting match with a tart was one thing; explaining away a sniper's rifle would be very much another.

He left the door open to minimize the feeling of being cut off. Four o'clock gradually came and went. He couldn't settle. At ten minutes after the hour the same man returned to collect the cup. "Soon," he said when Laker tackled him.

"Soon what?"

"Yes."

A nod and he left. Jesus . . . Another thirty minutes elapsed, inflaming Laker's despair, stretching his control almost to breaking-point. It was nearly five before anyone else acknowledged his existence. Then an officer put in an appearance, a blond giant with protruding ears and an unexpectedly amiable manner. Laker hardly gave him a chance to shut the door.

"How long am I to be detained like this?"

"That is what I have come to explain." At last the English was excellent. "It depends."

"Depends?"

"On whether the young woman decides to take action against you."

"Prefer charges, you mean?"

"Exactly. Unfortunately, she has gone out. So far we have not been able to check with her."

"But that's ridiculous. I've already been here two hours."

"I realize that."

"Am I under arrest?"

"No."

"What could she charge me with?"

"Assault."

"Say she did—what then?"

"You will be released on bail pending the hearing. And we will continue to keep your passport."

Laker somehow kept a grip on himself. "I asked at the desk for a Mr. Jackson at the British Embassy to be contacted."

"That has been done."

"Is he coming?"

"I could not say, but he has been informed."

The officer turned to leave. Laker could feel the veins bulging in his temples. "You can't hold me indefinitely."

"Not indefinitely, of course."

"Overnight?"

"I should not think that would be likely."

"Can't you be more precise?"

"I have told you—it depends. The woman should have been brought here at the same time as you. That is the normal practice. She would then have had the opportunity of asserting her rights and you would have been spared this rather unfortunate delay." In the doorway he paused as if anxious to show that he wasn't without sympathy. "However, it may be for the best. She might not want her pound of flesh—is that what you say, her pound of flesh?—once she has calmed down. Her sort rarely does."

A meal was brought to him around seven. Earlier a young policeman came with a tattered copy of *Reader's Digest*. Laker touched neither. Imperceptibly the sky darkened. The lights were put on. Most of the cars in the courtyard drew away. Whenever footsteps sounded in the corridor he stiffened, but the only times they had anything to do with were when the covered tray and the *Reader's Digest* were left on the table. Twice, imprudently, he quit the room and went to the entrance-lobby asking for news of the girl, of Jackson, once insisting that the Embassy be telephoned in his presence; and the imperturbability of those on duty, their stubborn adherence to a petty technicality, seemed more and more grotesque, a conspiracy.

Frenzel was installed in the Metropol by now. And Slattery had failed, failed even to respond, Slattery who outside the Mitre had said, "No hard feelings, I hope, Sam—now or at any time." Jackson was a dead loss, too. It was unbelievable; unforgivable. Laker rocked back and forth on a chair with his eyes hard closed, wishing to God in a kind of delirium there had never been any woman in a yellow dress with a child in a pram and a lorry bearing down on them all that distorted lifetime ago.

With an enormous effort he gathered himself together, knowing the futility of questioning anything, steeling himself to be patient, trying not to dwell on what he was being patient for. Yet he took Frenzel's picture from his pocket and stared at it, feeling hollow, drained, asking why either of them had been born.

Jackson arrived at twenty-five past eight. Laker guessed who it was from the slightly drawled "This way?" that heralded his approach along the corridor. And then he was there, about Laker's age, slight, sandy-haired, a dinner jacket showing beneath his unbuttoned overcoat. "Thank you," he said to the accompanying policeman. "Thank you very much."

He stepped into the room, offering a well-trained smile and a seemingly boneless handshake.

"Ritchie Jackson. . . . I'm sorry to have been so slow. I gather you've been kept dangling for quite some while."

"Since three o'clock."

"As long as that?"

"At least."

"I really am sorry. But I didn't get your message, you see. I wasn't in my office during the afternoon and it was only just now, half an hour or so ago, that the Embassy switchboard knew where they could catch me—glass in hand, as it were."

Laker didn't know whether to believe him; not that it mattered. Tersely, he said, "They're holding me on an idiotic technicality. I'm not under arrest and yet they say I can't leave—not, that is, until they know whether or not a complaint—"

"It's all fixed," Jackson cut in smoothly. "I've had a word with 'em."

"I can go?"

"Yes. They're feeling just a little guilty—and no wonder. They really didn't need much persuasion. They reckon the—er—other person concerned has had every chance, so they've agreed to forget there was ever any trouble. It was pretty much a storm in a teacup from what I hear, anyway. So—"

He spread his hands, smiling like a magician awaiting the applause. Laker's relief was minimal. He was searching for an indication that Jackson appreciated he wasn't rescuing just another tourist who'd run out of money or gone off the rails. But there was no sign of it, no hint that Jackson realized what was at stake. He closed the door.

"Slattery told me to ask for you."

"Oh yes—I was coming to that."

"Well?"

"He wanted you to know he's doing everything he can." Jackson paused. "Everything he can, unquote."

Laker's mouth dragged at the corners. "Is that all?"

"As far as I know. The switchboard passed the message on, you see, while I was drinking the Italian Ambassador's health."

"When was it received, for God's sake?"

"About five, I understand."

"And there was nothing else?"

"No . . . Does it make the sense it should?"

Laker was incapable of answering. Desolation plowed through him, leaving a scouring trail of bitterness. For an awful nauseous moment a part of him recoiled from what now seemed inevitable. All day he had clung to one last shred of hope, and it was part of the nightmare that Slattery's uselessness should be conveyed at second hand, casually, with gin on the breath and small teeth bared in an anxious little smile.

"Does it?" Jackson repeated like a fool. "You fellows always—" And then he stopped, on the fringes of the game and keeping there.

Dumfounded, Laker picked up the two cases and his coat. Jackson opened the door and they walked the corridor's length to the counter, where the gray-haired policeman interrupted booking a drunk to give Laker his passport.

"Can I drop you somewhere?" Jackson asked. "My car's around the side—unless it's been pinched, that is."

The night air was cool. Jackson drove with a flourish. He was wearing a hat now, its angle slightly jaunty. When Laker recognized the square where the airport coach had put him down the day before he said curtly, "This'll do," and Jackson edged into the side.

"Sure?"

"Quite sure."

"You don't want a hotel?"

Laker shook his head. Neon jazzed through the windshield.

"Well, if there's nothing else," Jackson said, holding out a hand and smiling the smile he did best, "I'll be off to claim my wife before all that Italian charm bowls her over. Glad I was able to help. A police station's no place to spend one's time and I'm sorry I couldn't get to you earlier. Still, better late than never I suppose."

Laker got out. From the curb, he said, "How soon can you get word to Slattery?"

"Practically right away."

"Tell him I had no choice, no choice at all."

"Just that?"

"Just that."

" 'No choice at all'—will do."

"There's more."

"Yes?"

"Tell him also that it Patrick suffers as a result of this I want him to know in advance that my name isn't Wyatt . . . James Wyatt."

Jackson frowned. "You can't enlarge a bit, I suppose? Or will that be clear to him?"

"It'll be clear," Laker said.

His voice shook, yet he was unnaturally calm. He watched the car ease into the traffic, then began to walk. It had ceased to concern him whether he was tailed or not. Hartmann had all but won. Shrink from murdering Frenzel and Patrick vanished, fail to murder Frenzel and Patrick vanished. . . . Nothing had changed; nothing *could* change. In his depths he realized he had asked the impossible of Slattery. The blackmail embraced them both. But he'd never excuse the callousness of almost total silence, the apparent indifference, the continued implication that once a pro always a pro and that, as such, he must fend for himself.

From the girl's room Laker would have been forced to take the first chance that presented itself, not knowing if another would follow. If she hadn't screamed him out of there Frenzel might have been dead already, the hunt in full cry. But he could delay now, choose his time—and pay the price in terms of horror. He walked slowly, on the lookout for a telephone, mentally leapfrogging forward to the moment when Patrick would touch down at London Airport tomorrow night, trying to reconcile everything with that.

It was nine when he found a public booth. Three hours had elapsed of Frenzel's twenty. He got the Metropol's number from the book, then dialed.

"Reception, please." When he was connected he said, "Have you a Mr. Frenzel with you? Rudolf Frenzel? . . . Yes, that's correct."

He waited, beginning to screw himself up for what would follow this preliminary reconnaissance. He could hear a rustle of papers; somebody coughing in the background.

"Did you say the name is Frenzel?"

"Yes."

Another crisp rustle.

"No, caller, there's no Mr. Frenzel booked here."

"There is," Laker retorted. "I checked earlier in the day."

Alarm was slow to spiral. The plane must be late. Frenzel had delayed booking in. . . . Yet he was saying urgently, "Mr. Frenzel has been allocated room sixty-eight. Rudolf Frenzel —from Paris."

"When did you check, caller?" The voice was helpful.

"This morning."

More rustling; a mutter. Then: "Ah yes, I see it now. Frenzel, sixty-eight . . ."

"Thank you."

And then it came.

"But since then, caller, the reservation has been canceled.

Mr. Frenzel relinquished his booking at four o'clock this afternoon."

It must have been five minutes before he could get a taxi. He had no recollection of hanging up or quitting the booth. In a frenzy of disbelief he signaled every passing cab, bawling at them through the traffic's rumble until at last one acknowledged him and took him to the Metropol. And there, by a quiet-spoken woman with blued hair who met the full force of his distress with impeccable politeness, dismay was made absolute.

He turned from her with a dead, beaten stare. By the Inquiries desk he stopped and asked if there was a message for him, doing so with the numbness of a person whose mind had congealed beyond sensible usefulness. And there was one. He snatched it from the man who took it from the pigeonhole, capable as he did so of assuming that Slattery finally had a germ of hope to offer, guidance, instructions, even an explanation that the miracle had been achieved and Frenzel kept out of harm's way as a precaution.

He fumbled open the folded slip. *You should not have contacted London.* And the sender's name leaped at him—*Hartmann.*

Chapter
Fourteen

HE moved blindly out into the night, oblivious of the flow of people, the gaggles of traffic, the guano-green fairytale roofs above the floodlit buildings. He felt his legs would give and he entered a bar and sat there staring, motionless, leaving untouched the whisky he never realized he ordered. Then he walked again, God knows where. Finally, on a public bench under a streetlamp, he extracted the slip of paper which was crushed between his fingers and the handle of the gun case and gazed at the scrawled writing of whoever had taken the message down. *Message for:* Mr. Samuel Laker. *Received by:* Telephone. *Time:* 16:50. The printed headings were in three languages. *Message:* You should not have contacted London. *Sender's name:* Hartmann.

He read it over and over, protest groping in the stupified darkness of his brain. And every time it turned in agony on Slattery for what had been done, Hartmann was there to intervene, claiming priority, inviting the hatred he had seemed to relish from that initial meeting in the hut.

"Between you and me, Mr. Laker. Always remember that . . ."

Laker crumpled the paper into a ball, split by an emotional cleavage beyond control, guilt and rage beating behind his eyes. He should never have given Slattery Frenzel's name. Slattery could wait, though. Slattery was a reckless incompetent and would answer for it. But Hartmann was a destroyer, the begetter of horrific sins for whom mercy was a word, pity a word. "Then I am sorry for you," he had said when Laker pleaded for Karen—and sorrow was a word, too.

"You and me, Mr. Laker . . ." So be it. There was another kind of equation now and it had Laker silently in tears. He felt an urge like lust, ugly and savage, demanding satisfaction, deeper than the will to live or preserve life.

He was going back to Leipzig.

He nursed the hatred, letting it fester, drawing on it to drug his grief. He put on his coat, picked up the cases and walked until he reached another bar; and this time he drank, blinkered by the fierceness of his intent, numbing what he could of a hundred other memories. He drank until the place closed at midnight, heavily, effectively, but he was steady on his feet when he left.

It would be morning before he could make a move, nine o'clock at the earliest before he could set about getting himself another Fair Card, nine before the airline ticket offices opened. Despite the drink, and the pain that drink could never tranquilize, he saw the essentials clearly. He wandered into a park at one time, alone by a small lake except for some furtive lovers. The streets were emptying now; more and more he had them to himself. Nobody kept that careful distance, and the lack of menace hammered in the fact that Hartmann had finished with him—emphasizing what this meant, what it could only mean. He believed Hartmann. All along he'd believed him. He'd have made himself kill for Hartmann, so there was no chance of not believing him now. "On whatever you care to name as sacred, Mr. Laker..."

Only revenge was left, and he felt the lust for it grow in the sodden depths of his spirit as he walked the night.

Sometime in the small hours he found himself passing the airline terminus. He entered and sank onto a vacant couch, aching in the thighs and calves, surrounded by a scattering of passengers waiting for dawn flights. The effect of the whisky was wearing off and with a kind of horror he knew how close he was to breakdown. His jaw muscles quaked as if a fever threatened. He shut his eyes, clinging to hatred as once he had to cling to hope, bolstering himself with it. The place filled up. People moved back and forth, bored, expectant, their hand luggage labeled, carrying guidebooks and magazines, about to venture somewhere new, returning home.

Home ... Jesus, what could home be now?

He watched a coachload depart. An indefatigable porter came to take his cases for weighing-in, but Laker stopped him.

"What is your destination, sir?"

He shook his head. Perhaps he looked ill, lost, incapable; perhaps he'd been there overlong.

"Do you know your flight number?"

"I'm all right," he retorted hoarsely. "All right."

He searched the leaflet racks. SAS listed a Czechoslovak Ilyushin at 12:15, arriving Schönefeld 13:20. The fact registered dully. SAS would confirm the time of the Leipzig connection when he bought his ticket. He'd be there before evening. The temporary visa that went with the Fair Card would see him through. There was one unavoidable hurdle, but he would face that when it came.

He urged the time away so that he could make a start. There was a discarded London newspaper on the couch; the

Express, yesterday's. He dragged it toward him distractedly.
HELICOPTER SNATCH OFF BEACHY HEAD . . . "I WON'T
BUDGE": FRANCO . . . RECORD POOLS WIN. . . . His eyes
glossed over the headlines, the centered wedding picture,
the Lancaster cartoon, and it all seemed totally unreal.
ALBRIGHT HERE, MOSCOW SAYS . . . *Matthew Albright,* he
read, *the Sino-Soviet expert missing for several months from
the U.S. State Department was today officially admitted by
Moscow to be in the Soviet Union. This is the first time Russia has disclosed Albright's whereabouts, though the West
has known since May that he had defected. As in the case of
Pontecorvo, Burgess, Philby . . .*

Names, names.

A smudge of dawn was showing in the street. Laker stared
at it, thinking of Frenzel whose ghost would haunt him to
the end, Frenzel who had once defected too, earned a paragraph, if that, and whose life had then been balanced dia-
bolically against Patrick's.

He took up his cases and went stiffly into the morning's
pearly chill. "Provocation or necessity, Mr. Laker; they're
the two incentives. You're an instrument about to be put to
practical use."

Not anymore. Of his own will, of his own choice—as at
Gardelegen all that time ago, before Patrick ever existed.

He ate breakfast in a café where laborers and tram crews
apparently began their day. It was a quarter to seven when
he paid the bill and left; eight before he found a barber's
open and got a shave. A poster in a travel agent's window
enticed the world to visit the Leipzig Fair and Laker needed
no Danish to understand the significance of the boxed address. At half past eight he was in the Farimagsgade, waiting
for the Fair's office to start business. At nine sharp he was
admitted and by twenty minutes past he was out again, the
forms completed, his passport details logged, the fee paid,
the Fair Card in his wallet.

The SAS booking clerk was no less obliging. The Schöne-feld flight connected with one for Leipzig at 14:40; Leipzig arrival time was 15:10. Would that be satisfactory? A trav-eler's check? Certainly. . . . She bore no resemblance to the girl who yesterday had seemed to have loosed disaster upon him, but the SAS uniform and a certain similarity of speech dragged his mind back to the room and the window opposite and what he had prepared for then, what had bound him then. Watching her make out the flight ticket he pieced the broken jigsaw together once again, and with the clarity of hindsight he saw a pattern of inevitability in what had hap-pened, step by step: Slattery's use of him and Hartmann's use of him both doomed by time and mischance, sucking him down into the dark mouth of this funnel of vengeance in which he now found himself.

He rode in a taxi to the airport. He was there with more than an hour to spare. A dozen times on the journey he must have tested the locks on the black case, yet his trust in them diminished as his luggage was weighed and heaved out of sight. But it was early yet to worry on that score; the hazards were still three hundred miles away. He went into the de-parture lounge and drafted a bitter cable to Slattery, but even the most vicious phrasing was inadequate and, in the end, he sent nothing. Nothing to Gale & Watts either. Noth-ing to Roundwood. Nothing to anyone, lest in doing so he should somehow weaken and waver, remember friends, san-ity, remind himself that he might never get back.

When his flight was called he filed out with only a handful of others, fifteen at the most, and about half of them seemed to consist of a delegation of some kind; they all knew one another and solemnly filled a block of seats just aft of the wings. Except for a woman wearing a headscarf who sat im-mediately in front of him, Laker was quite alone. He had never seen a plane more empty. He felt exhausted, yet his thoughts were measured, held by the savage fatalistic mood.

He watched the runway blur beneath him, the airport sink below, the green earth bank and wheel and level off. Presently he took out the Fair Card and thumbed it through, drawing what encouragement he could from it, keeping his anxiety about the coming Customs' confrontation battened down. Over the Baltic he dozed fitfully, never quite under. A stewardess startled him when she served coffee and from then on he was wide awake, staring down at the broken German coastline dead ahead, then at the slow slide of the land itself.

The weather was clear as far as Berlin and for some of the time he looked westward in the direction of Gardelegen and the River Aller, recalling how his father often used to say that when a man turned his back on something it usually got him again before the end, seeing a resemblance between that wartime gamble and this, that prolonged bout of murderous rage and this, gazing out on the country once openly trampled and fought over which was now the hunting ground of backroom entrepreneurs who'd devised their stealthy games of blackmail and death, catch-as-catch-can, their own dirty laws, their own ethics. And hating them for it, each and every one; but Hartmann above all.

They whined into Schönefeld within minutes of the scheduled time. They had flown south, yet it was colder; on the walk to the airport buildings Laker felt a nip in the air. Along with the delegation and most of the others he was herded into the transit lounge, the same peeling place he'd waited in the other day with the same waxen-faced woman trundling a trolley around and the same take-away Fair leaflets scattered on the tables between the couches along the wall. *During eight centuries the servant of peaceful trade and understanding between the nations. . . . A many-sided event, much more than the normal Trade Fair, set in a city where the hospitality of its inhabitants has become a byword throughout the world. . . . Meet and relax in Leipzig. . . .*

Through the window he glimpsed his first Vopos—a pair of them patrolling the perimeter of a half-empty parking lot— and another kind of chill fingered him, releasing a sudden anthology of fears. He'd almost come full circle.

The delay was quite short. A juddering piston-engined aircraft punctually lifted them off, bucking on the up-currents after it had gained height and set course above the overcast. There was no passenger service now, no drinks, no cigarettes. Laker didn't unclip his belt. He sat alone, more closely hemmed about than before but insulated from the alien chatter by a steadily generating tension. He had the vaguest, the sketchiest of plans, but he couldn't grapple with what lay beyond the next thirty minutes or so. They would be down by then and everything would hang on some anonymous official's whim. That was part of the gamble, the one part over which he had absolutely no control. From the first he had known it, accepted it, and now it was coming. But without the rifle he would be harmless; impotent.

The minutes passed, elongated by stress. He listened to the change of tone which marked the start of the descent. Scarves of cloud streamed over the wings. "Fasten your seat belts, please . . ." With a pang he remembered the previous nosing in; Patrick's "Dead on time," as the wheels touched— and now it was beginning again, the plane's shadow racing across the tarmac to join them, the bump, the throttled roar, the ponderous run toward the hard, the final lurch and the silence.

The doors opened and the steps were angled into position. Laker took his turn, head buzzing with the sensation of continued movement. WELCOME TO LEIPZIG was emblazoned across the front of the Arrivals building. Inside, the metallic greeting of the public-address system vibrated in his altitude-clogged ears—"Passengers are requested to present their passports and Fair Cards at the Immigration Bureau . . ." Beneath Ulbricht's blown-up, stony stare he completed the formalities and changed his money. There were fewer passengers to be attended to than before and the queues were shorter, but nerves made everything seem more prolonged. The thin person in cadet gray who studied Laker's passport took his time, squinting carefully at the dates of the smudged visa stamps.

"You were here earlier in the week." It was a statement, but an answer was expected.

"Yes."

"On business?"

"Yes."

That was all, but there was a dragging sensation in Laker's stomach. He walked into the Customs bay, wondering which of the knot of waiting officials would pronounce sentence on him. To claim the black rexine case when the baggage arrived called for a feverish brand of courage. He picked it up and set it on the bench beside his suitcase; clumsily lit a cigarette. In a state of terrible fascination he watched the nearest official's technique with the person next to him. Further along someone's luggage was being rummaged. Then it was his turn: two hands descended on the cases.

"Both yours?"

"That's right."

Small brown eyes held Laker's as he struggled not to bluster; held them but told him nothing.

"You are here for the Fair?"

"Yes."

The man looked down, stroked the suitcase leather admiringly. Then he tapped the other one.

"And here you have—?"

"Samples." Laker could feel the sweat breaking like pins and needles in his neck hair. "Trade samples."

"Such as?"

"Precision instruments."

A gesture, a chalked hieroglyph, and he was dismissed. Relief cascaded through him. He nodded and backed away, moved into the crowded Arrivals lobby. He was trembling violently. There was no sense of triumph. He pushed out into the open and stood on the steps. For a full minute he paused there, trying to give the impression that he couldn't make up his mind whether or not to join the taxi queue; then, with a gesture meant to indicate to an observer that he'd that moment remembered something, he swung on his heels and returned inside. But no one seemed in the least interested; he knew the feeling now.

The delegate group was being officially greeted by a trio of smiling men with identification tags in their square-out lapels. Laker passed them all by, making for the battery of telephone booths in the far corner of the lobby. For hours he had known what he was about to do. He selected the center one of three vacant booths and pulled the door across; grimly fumbled for change.

Double three, four two, eight six.

"Like the emergency handle on a train, Sam. Long odds against your having to reach for the thing, but it's reassuring to know it's there . . ."

He thumbed in the coin. After the blinding decision back in Copenhagen this had been the first practical idea to come to him, and it had come effortlessly. And the awful irony was with him again as he dialed—that Slattery had his uses at last. "Salt it away, Sam . . ."

. . . eight . . . six.

He waited then, fingers drumming a tattoo, mind riveted by the repeated bleeps.

A woman answered with a marked Saxonian accent, almost adenoidal. For some reason he hadn't expected to hear a woman. He hesitated, then spoke the introductory phrase that had been buried in the retentive pit of his brain along with the number.

"Peter told me you have a room to let."

"Who?"

"Peter. I was told you had a room."

There was no change of tone. "That is correct, yes."

"Would it be convenient if I called to see it?"

"Of course. How soon will you be coming?"

"In about half an hour?" he suggested.

"Very well."

She enunciated the address carefully, like a schoolmistress dictating to a backward pupil. Laker hung up. As he slid the door open he found the exit blocked by someone in the black uniform of the S.S.D. and a spasm of fear gripped him. Self-control demanded a tremendous effort. But almost at once he realized that the man had stepped aside and was giving him the right of way. He brushed by, muttering thanks. Badly shaken, warned, he went outside and joined those waiting for transport.

At least he had somewhere to go, some kind of sanctuary. Next he needed information; more than that he couldn't expect. But he had to discover what had happened, exactly how, precisely where and when. What he did then was his concern, no one else's.

And Hartmann had armed him for it; the irony had no end.

Chapter
Fifteen

 HERE were a few isolated spots of rain, as heavy as bird droppings, before Laker reached the head of the queue. A converted Wartburg limousine picked him up. He didn't give the address, only the street, and he took his cases into the back with him, his eyes on sentry-go as they pulled away.

They went nowhere near the center of the city, turning right once they were past the outlying tenement blocks, dog-legging through the scruffy wilderness of the suburbs. But it wasn't a long run; fifteen minutes, if that.

Laker walked for a while after settling with the driver, then made his approach. It was a somber residential street and the house was as drab as its neighbors, of blemished brownstone and with tall windows draped with lace curtains; in the one to the left of the front door a ROOMS notice was propped against the inside of the glass and Laker guessed it had been placed there for his benefit. Some children squabbled on the pavement; a white cat fled from the steps. Chimes ding-donged softly when he pressed the bell and the door opened almost before he had glanced both ways.

The woman was in her middle fifties, dumpy, graying, red-cheeked, with an apron over a flowered dress. She was wearing slippers.

"Was it about the letting?"

He nodded. The smile was cautious, but it welcomed him in. She remarked on the weather. Wiping her hands on the apron she showed him into the front room, an overcrowded place in which the air seemed absolutely motionless, as in a museum. A horsehair settee, a weighty table as a center-piece with carved straight-back chairs, china cabinets, decorative plates around the walls. In the window, flanked by aspidistras on brass stands, was a caged macaw.

"Isn't he beautiful?" the woman remarked, removing the pasteboard notice.

She seemed a highly unlikely ally. The macaw clambered onto the side of the cage and tried its great beak on the woman's proffered knuckles.

"How long would you require the room?"

"I'm not certain."

"I let by the week." She quoted the rate, explaining that this was inclusive of meals. "Would you like to see it?"

"Thank you."

She wagged a finger at the macaw. "Naughty," she smiled, then took Laker upstairs. It was a back room, small, with an iron-framed single bed and an old-fashioned marble-topped washstand. They were there for only a minute or two. Downstairs again she asked if he thought it would be suitable, and there was something disturbingly ordinary about the whole business, as if Laker had made a fantastic mistake and arrived at the wrong house. There was no indication that he hadn't. As he counted out a week's money she told him that soap and towels would be put in his bedroom and explained various domestic details about hot water, times of meals, the lights on the upper landing. He wasn't really listening. Having to pay worried him. Did you pay for a bolthole? For that was what this was. Surely. "Just in case, Sam . . ."

"I imagine you'll be staying in for the time being?" the woman said.

"Yes."

"There'll be a key if you want one later."

"Thank you."

"You have only to ask." She took the money from the baize-covered table. The macaw eyed them beadily through the bars. "Don't you stick your little black tongue out at me," she reprimanded it. "And be nice to the gentleman. He's your guest—remember that."

She smiled at Laker, only then dispelling his anxiety. "Someone will come," she said.

"When?"

"Before too long." And with that she left him.

After a little while he heard her go upstairs and come down again. He went up himself then; towels and soap were on the washstand. He slid the catch on the door, then went to the window. The room wasn't overlooked. Walls jutted out to either side and there was a narrow view toward the rear of some other houses which were partially screened by trees. Beyond them was the silvered dome of a gas holder. He unlocked the rexine case and took out the dismembered rifle; fitted it together. It was only the second time he had looked at it and he remembered how the first had destroyed the last flimsy shreds of hope that he was somehow at the center of a vile, unfathomable hoax.

All the markings had been obliterated. He wiped it clean of the film of oil, slotted the telescopic attachment into position and removed the protective end-caps. It was a precision instrument, all right; self-loading, single-shot. He didn't fill the magazine, but he reckoned it would take six. The balance was perfect and the shaped cheekpiece fitted snugly against the side of his face. Standing well away from the window he sighted on the lopped end of one of the branches of the nearest tree and the magnification brought it in from about fifty yards to what seemed to be no more than arm's-length, so close that he could see the growth rings in the exposed wood. For perhaps twenty minutes he acquainted himself with the rifle's handling, selecting an occasional snap target—a bird, a man at work on a distant roof—and every alignment amazed him with its apparent shrinkage of distance, the hairline accuracy at his command. Frenzel wouldn't have had a chance.

He broke the weapon down and repacked it in the velvet recesses; put on the locks. The house was very quiet, though once he thought he heard the woman talking, perhaps on the telephone. It was a quarter to five. He lay on the bed, wondering who would come, thinking. Anguish could still prick his eyes with tears and the unrelenting fury smoldered like a coal. But he seemed to have absorbed fatigue and mostly his mind was sharp and clear, no longer fogged with stupefaction, not so frantic. Time was at a discount now. He'd got back; found shelter. The rest would follow—somehow, somewhere.

He smoked a cigarette and watched a drizzle begin to blur the panes.

The doorbell chimed soon after five. He got off the bed at once. He could distinguish voices, pitched low—the woman's and a man's. After a short while footsteps padded softly on the stairs and someone knocked.

"Come in," he said.

The man was shorter than Laker, and older, perhaps ten years older. He was wearing a dirty raincoat. His face was long and heavily lined, pallid, and his mousey hair was cut

short, like a soldier's or a prisoner's. The blue eyes seemed
to lack any capacity for surprise.

"Good afternoon." His grip was like a vise. "Is the room
satisfactory?"

"Thank you."

"There's no need to confine yourself to it. You can use the
living room if you wish. I'm sure my wife mentioned that."
There was a wine-colored birthmark on one side of his neck
just above the collar line.

"She did, yes."

"Shall we go down? It is more comfortable there."

"All right."

A bicycle had been wheeled into the hall and there was a
cloth bag slung on the crossbar. Perhaps he was a plumber.
Askew on the front of the cage the macaw clucked at them
drily as they entered the room.

"Do you want names?" Laker asked.

"The fewer the better."

"Mine?"

"No." The man shook his head. They continued to stand.
He said, "When did your friend Peter recommend us?"

"Earlier this week."

"Never before?"

"No."

"So this is your first time?" The glance implied that be-
ginners usually made their own trouble.

"Yes."

"And you arrived. . . ?"

"On Wednesday."

"When did anything go wrong?"

"That afternoon."

"Three days ago?"

"Yes."

"How wrong?"

"I was arrested."

"By?"

"The S.S.D."

"When were you released?"

Laker shook his head. "It wasn't like that."

"I'm sorry, but I don't understand. Where have you come from—today, I mean. Now."

"The airport. Copenhagen."

The man frowned. He motioned toward the settee and they sat down. "Tell me," he said. "Tell me from the beginning."

"And then?"

"We'll see what can be done."

"You don't know what I want."

"Tell me, and I shall."

It didn't take long. Laker phrased the story carefully, selectively. He mentioned only Patrick and Hartmann by name. Kromadecka and Karen he left out of it; Frenzel too. He didn't once refer to Slattery or to London. The man listened in silence, without interrupting, poker-faced; mostly he stared at his grimy fingernails. It was a mercy to be able to talk at last, like a letting of blood. Laker said nothing about the girl either. He kept to the essentials, beginning with the mock-execution in the pines and ending with the canceled reservation at the Metropol which had brought despair and hatred to a white heat. And as he underlined the pressure put upon him and the promised consequences of failure he felt that he was speaking to someone who understood the realities of living—the potential terrors, the springs of desolation, that only one in a million were aware existed. Whoever he was he looked a person who had suffered, for whom pain and violence weren't abstractions.

Laker finished and the man glanced up at him. For a long moment he was quiet, then nodded several times, lips pressed tight.

"You say you came on Wednesday?"

"To start with, yes."

A pause. "Kromadecka?"

"Yes."

"Ah." He had it now; Laker watched him; it was all of a piece. "Ah," he said and nodded again. Then he muttered, "Bad, this is bad," and his breath made a long sigh.

"Can you help?"

"With regard to your son?"

"I have to know what happened."

"Of course, of course." He got up, rubbing his birthmark, his attention seemingly held by something in the street. "How did you return? On a Card visa?"

"Yes."

"You'll never get out the same way—you realize that?"

Laker shrugged.

"Not even if you tried to go now, not in view of what you've told me. The machinery isn't slow to function. They'll have the shutters up already."

"I daresay."

"Something can be arranged, though. It can be done, but not before Monday." The man turned and studied him. As if it were a duty he said, "Don't pin your hopes for your son too high, my friend. I have to say this. Don't hope too much."

Laker made no reply. He didn't need telling, but to hear it said fell on his heart like a blow. He squeezed his hands together, looking down between his knees.

"Forgive me," the man said gently, "but I know Hartmann. I know the kind of person he is. He is warped; there is a flaw of honor in him. Himmler had the same kind of flaw. In his case he was incorruptible where money was concerned. Hartmann's flaw is that he keeps his word."

"For what?" Laker burst out. "He could force me to do what he wanted, but once I'd failed, once that reservation was canceled . . ."

He choked to an end, Hartmann's image looming in his mind. The macaw skittered amiably about the cage. The man went to a cupboard and filled a glass.

"Here," he said. "*Schnapps*. Take it." He sat beside Laker again, his lined face very grave. After a while he said, "I can help in two ways. I can find out about your son. I can also get you across the frontier." He waited, then went on: "What more is there? You can't stay here, not indefinitely."

Laker drained the glass. At last he had someone to rely on—at last, and too late. He rose from the settee.

"There's a third thing," he said quickly.

"Yes?"

"You can tell me where Hartmann lives."

"He has an apartment at S.S.D. headquarters."

"Nowhere else?"

"No."

"Where he goes, then. What his movements are."

The man regarded him quizzically.

"I want to know," Laker insisted.

"What can you do? What can you do with your bare hands? It would be suicide, my friend."

"He provided me with a sniper's rifle."

"In Copenhagen."

"I brought it back."

"Here?" At last there was surprise.

"Here, yes. It's upstairs."

"My God," the man said slowly. "Now I have heard everything." He stared, as if making a reappraisal of the forces at work in Laker. "You carried it with you? Openly?"

"Yes."

"My God," he said again, this time almost in anger, "the risk you ran. Do you realize the risk you ran?"

An obsession diminishes perception. With infinite weariness Laker lifted his shoulders, let them drop. "I've been out on a limb for three whole days and no one's lifted a bloody finger—not until now. You're the first." He hadn't meant to say this, but his voice had a steely edge. "London led me by the nose, then dropped me. Three days ago I was just another businessman. I was beginning a holiday with my fourteen-year-old son. There was also someone I knew— Karen Gisevius. . . . And now? Who am I now? What am I?" There was no self-pity; only the terrible emptiness, the unquenchable loathing. "I'm entitled to take all the risks I choose."

The man hadn't moved his eyes from him. "I can get you out," he repeated, the anger, the alarm, quickly gone. "Remember that."

"I want Hartmann first."

"But say your son is alive. Say, for once, Hartmann hasn't—"

"I don't believe he is."

"But you must have proof. At least you must wait for that."

"I know. I know." Laker's vision blurred. "I was told he was staying with someone called Rauter. I . . . I signed a letter, explaining my absence. He wouldn't have believed it, though. I don't write letters like that . . ." Again he didn't finish, sick with the numbness.

"I have a friend who will know where to inquire."

"How soon?"

"I can't tell. It depends. But I will go and see him."

"When?"

"Now. Immediately." The man started to button his raincoat; he hadn't taken it off. "Rauter, was it?" He tightened the frayed belt.

"That's right."

At the door he turned, and Laker saw a look of pity which was akin to another he'd glimpsed somewhere back in the nightmare—whose, he had forgotten. "My wife will be here," the man said. He made an attempt at a smile. "You'll find her an excellent cook if you want anything."

Laker heard him cross the hall; a muttered exchange—in the kitchen, he supposed. Then the front door opened and he saw the man wheel the bicycle out and pedal away, shabby yet nondescript, along the drenched, dusky street.

Almost at once the woman entered the room. She pulled the curtain carefully before switching on the lights, as if a blackout were in force. Normally they had supper at nine, but if he was hungry. . . ? Some coffee and biscuits, perhaps? Laker thanked her and went upstairs, threw himself on the bed. Hope was spent. There was nothing left to revive. He was sure about Patrick already, absolutely sure. All day he'd been sure; all night. Hartmann had conditioned him. Hope had shriveled and died in the Metropol's foyer in one chilling moment of certainty.

The room darkened; the last of the daylight vanished. He thought a thousand things, confusedly, without sequence, in the way the drowning are said to do—except that there was no rush, no panic-stricken compression. Strangely, it was the memory of Patrick's pen-friends which moved him most, as if only now he had discovered there must have been loneliness.

"Look after him for me, Sam . . ."

It had gone eight when he heard the chimes and the woman slop in her slippers into the hall. His pulse quickened sluggishly, but he didn't move. He listened to the steps approaching on the stairs, on the landing, and even before the knock sounded he knew exactly what he was going to learn. He was resigned to it, ready, and the man's reluctance to speak was proof in itself.

Yet he said, "Well?"

"It is as you feared, my friend."

Laker closed his eyes. There was silence.

Then the man said awkwardly, "Shall I put on the light?"
"No."
"There is a paragraph in *Neues Deutschland.*"
"What does it say?"
"Do you want me to read it?"
"Yes."
The man leaned into the wedge of light that came from the landing and peered shortsightedly at a clipping:

> "A foreign youth, identified from papers on his person as Patrick Laker, last night received fatal injuries believed to have been caused by a motor vehicle in the Walder Platz. He was dead on arrival at the University Clinic. Inquiries are proceeding."

Silence again, longer. "London will go along with our account of an accident, Mr. Laker. They'll accept our post-mortem certificate . . ."
"I'm sorry," the man was saying. "Very, very sorry."
He didn't seem to know what to do with his hands. He came to the side of the bed and, in the gloom, put the clipping on the table there. Then he went back to the door where he paused, his face strained.
"What can I say? . . . Such an act is senseless. Meaningless. . . . Is there nothing I can do?"
"No."
"When it suits you we will talk some more. Any time. . . . When you wish it."
No answer.
He closed the door behind him, shutting the darkness in.

An hour must have passed before Laker went downstairs. The man and woman were eating in the kitchen and he joined them, the worst of his agony shed. There was cold meat, bread and soup, and he ate a little. The other two didn't speak much; when they did their voices were subdued. Laker drank a good deal of wine, sullenly, without effect, and afterwards he and the man went into the front room.

The first thing he said was, "I won't involve you. It's my affair. You've got something to lose." He was quite calm. "All I want is information concerning Hartmann's whereabouts."

"That won't be so easy. He doesn't parade himself." The man slipped a dome of green baize over the macaw's cage. "And that's what you're asking for, isn't it—a sitting target?"

"I'll take what offers."

"Listen. I know something about abominations, my friend. Both of us do in this house, believe me. But we also know something about survival—and the way your mind is now you will never see London again. What's more, you *would* involve us—inevitably, and that would mean our involving others. A chain reaction would start. Few of us are ever as strong as we pray to be. A liter of castor oil, electrodes against the genitals, ice-cold immersion—the threat alone is often quite sufficient. I hardly need explain what fear can do to a man."

A car was splashing through the wet. He cocked his head, his eyes following the sound along the street.

"We operate an escape-route, my wife and I. People come here in order to survive, to get clear and lick their wounds in safety. That's our function." He drew in his breath slowly. "We tell ourselves it's a worthwhile occupation."

He opened a drawer in one of the china cabinets and extracted a map. "You've misunderstood me."

"I don't think so."

"I haven't said I won't help. But I *am* insisting on conditions." He glanced earnestly at Laker, and again there was that built-in pity. "I can't stop you from leaving this house whenever you choose. But they're on the lookout for you.

And they'll pick you up before you even get wind of Hartmann, let alone squeeze a trigger." He was spreading the map on the table, flattening the creases. "I can't stop you. But I can argue with you. I can make the point that you weren't given this telephone number in order to endanger others on account of a personal vendetta."

Laker gazed with suspicion at the gray, cadaverous face. "What conditions?"

"One, that you're patient. Two, that I decide what is possible, and relate it to the problem of getting you back where you belong." A bruised fingernail stubbed the map. "You're a hundred and fifty kilometers from the frontier. Even if you managed to get that far—alone—you'd never cross the death strip."

"How patient?"

The man shrugged. "Getting out may be secondary to you, but it isn't to me. I want you off our hands, my friend." He offered Laker a cigarette. "You aren't the first to have wished Hartmann dead. But yielding to instinct won't achieve it. If you're going to succeed you need more than a few scraps of information and advice. I'll give you all there is, and practical help as well, but you must accept that it will have to be tied in with getting you away."

He coughed. "Besides, I should imagine you have good reason for wanting to return to London. From what you tell me I'd say they also have something to answer for."

It was almost midnight before they finished. Laker was so weary by then that he could scarcely employ his mind, but he had a dread of being alone again. Toward the end he was using the man as a safety valve, unburdening himself, as confiding as a solitary drinker in a bar. The woman came in eventually and offered him a couple of sleeping pills. He took them and the session ended. At the foot of the stairs he said to the man, "Don't try to fob me off, that's all I ask. You'll be wasting your breath."

"I won't, my friend. I promise you"—and Laker gripped his bony arms in a spasm of emotion.

The clipping was beside the bed and the gun was in its case. But oblivion came fast and, mercifully, there were no dreams.

Chapter Sixteen

TWICE next morning Laker heard the telephone. The first time it woke him to the waiting desolation; the second took him to the bedroom door, listening. But he deciphered nothing: on both occasions the woman was speaking. He lay in the bed until ten o'clock, then slowly shaved and dressed. While he was in the bathroom he thought somebody used the front door, but he wasn't certain.

There was a place set for him at the kitchen table. The woman greeted him with the same ingenuousness as when he'd first arrived. "I thought you'd like to rest," she said, clattering at the stove. "Did the pills help?"

"Thank you."

"You can get overtired, can't you? They're useful then."

"Yes."

"It looks like rain again. And we had a lot in the night, too."

The perfection of the lie she was living never varied, somehow raising an echo of the blatant disbelief that had unsuccessfully tried to hold Laker in the moment of waking.

When he asked where her husband was she said, "He's just gone to the shops for cigarettes. He won't be long"—and he wondered how much she really knew, how much her red-cheeked smile masked a longing for peace and safety.

He finished her strong, *ersatz* coffee and went into the living room, restless already, watching the street. Last night, sprawled on the settee, he had talked with an abandonment that was rare for him, wretchedness loosening his tongue. It had come piecemeal, in no chronological order, yet it had made a kind of whole—mainly about Patrick, but about Helen too, about Weybridge, Gale & Watts, Roundwood, about the war and Karen Gisevius; all that. And now, remembering some of the things he had said, he also remembered how the man had listened and how his sympathy had once or twice mounted almost to visible distress so that his willingness to assist in dealing with Hartmann grew like a bond between them. In the hall, when they were about to go upstairs, there had been a glint in his eyes which had reminded Laker of that night in Green Park half a lifetime before when Slattery had suddenly raged: "You kill the bastards, Sam. Kill as many of them as you can."

Just one this time. Just one to clean something out of his mind, out of his heart, out of his insides. And then, with what was left over, to face Slattery.

No, he hadn't done with London; the man was right. If it were possible, Slattery wasn't going to get away with it either.

Half an hour elapsed before the familiar figure cycled shabbily into view along the street. The lack of haste wasn't encouraging. The macaw squawked and fluttered excitedly when the front door opened and again when the man entered the room: simultaneously the telephone rang. He hesitated, ready to go, ready to stay, waiting tensely as the woman took the call.

"Yes, he's here," she said, and the man returned to the hall.

"That's right," Laker heard. "Yes. . . . With pleasure. . . . Certainly. . . . But not for two or three days. On Wednesday, perhaps. May I call and discuss it with you? . . . Very well. . . . Yes, I'll do that. I will be in touch. Without fail."

He was smiling grimly when he rejoined Laker. "A lady wants her kitchen painted."

So that was his cover. He tossed his cap onto the table. He hadn't shaved and he looked tired. "It's early yet. Don't expect too much all at once. It's going to be like walking in long grass for a while. . . . Did you sleep well?"

Laker nodded.

"How good are you with a rifle?"

"According to Hartmann, exceptionally good."

The man savored that quietly. "You'll need to be. You won't find him hanging about, asking for it."

"Where is he now?"

"At headquarters. At least, his car's there."

"A green one? Dark green?"

"A Moskvitch, yes."

He took a folder from his breast pocket and shook it open —a street map of Leipzig. "Hopeless," he said. "Hopeless. You wouldn't stand a chance in the city. Yesterday, for instance, he was here . . . and here . . . and then here, in the Alte Markt." He used his hands dismissively. "Hopeless. Impossible. You're going to have to wait until he travels farther afield."

"When's that likely to be?"

"Perhaps days."

"For God's sake!"

"How should I know?" He seemed on edge. "I'm not a prophet. But I am a realist, and what might suit you tactically might not suit me. Be reasonable. . . . Yes, reasonable," he repeated tartly. "Don't expect me to produce Hartmann for you like something out of a hat. I shudder when I think what has been done. Words are inadequate. But what you are asking has to be planned, thought about, worked on. Without help you'd achieve nothing except the certainty of disaster for others. So save up what you feel, my friend. Be patient."

The morning passed. The man left the house around noon, on foot. Laker hadn't asked what his sources of information were, and he didn't want to know. But the restraint, the frustration, were almost unendurable. He went up to the bedroom for a while, assembled and practiced handling the rifle. Somehow he hadn't bargained on a lengthy delay. On a base, yes; but not on caution, not on being cooped-up, not on marking time. In the demented haze of his return he had imagined something reflexively swift, unaided, a snarling pent-up release that would find satisfaction in seeing Hartmann crumple and go down. Now he must wait for it; curb himself. He recognized the necessity. But grief was like a wound; the real pain was slow to come, and it was still spreading, raw now, giving existence to depths of him long since insensible.

And this was Slattery's territory; that worried him. Already Slattery would be wondering where the hell he'd got to. He would have begun to check and countercheck—and even a fool like Jackson would very soon find out. If Slattery put two and two together it was possible that he would attempt to warn the local network off. Almost certain, in fact. Karen had been lost to him already and he wouldn't want any more casualties. As a side issue he might approve of Hartmann's death, but not if it meant jeopardizing his listening posts, his contacts, his go-betweens—all those who earned him dividends, showed returns. Someone would replace Hartmann, anyhow. The game would go on, Hartmann or no Hartmann, and for people like Slattery the game was the thing. In that ivory tower of his what mattered was to keep his pins firmly on the map. . . .

Stay out of this, damn you, Laker thought. You've done enough—or haven't you heard yet?

He hung about the living room, anxiously watching the street.

The man was soon back, but only to shrug. Nothing yet. . . . Toward one o'clock the telephone rang and he grunted cryptically several times into the mouthpiece, but all he said to Laker afterwards was: "Still at headquarters."

The three of them ate together in the kitchen. It was strange, but when the woman was present it was as if Laker and the man shared a secret from which she was excluded: the masquerade took over. But this time, as they were finishing, she suddenly remarked, "You didn't mind about the money, did you?"

Laker frowned.

"The rent."

"No." He fingered his glass, puzzled, dragging his thoughts away from where they swarmed. "No."

The man leaned forward. "My wife always insists that the laborer is worthy of his hire, no matter what the circumstances. But we aren't mercenaries, my friend, and if she has given you that impression she does herself less than justice." Quietly he said to her: "Show our guest your arm. . . . Go on."

The woman slid back the right sleeve of her blouse. Three or four inches above the wrist a six-figure number was crudely tattooed on the pink skin. Laker had no need to ask what it signified or when it had been put there.

"Ravensbruck," the man said. "And memories are just as indelible. I told you, we know something about abominations." He gestured. "Perhaps our willingness to help you is more understandable now. London would hardly approve, but that is neither here nor there. They spin the webs, but they don't live in them."

It was as if he had been reading Laker's mind.

He went out again presently, on foot once more; where, why, he didn't say. He never said.

There was little movement in the street—an occasional cyclist, a scooter or two. A dog barked periodically from the broken railings on the other side and a handful of people walked by, women mostly, sometimes pausing to gossip. Laker's agitation reached a new peak; drove him upstairs. From the window there the dome of the distant gasholder had sunk from view: almost twenty-four hours had frittered away since he first saw it. He lay on the bed, but soon got up and returned to the living room. There was no sign of the man and the telephone remained silent. Past three . . . The macaw ground its beak furiously on the cage-wire; the clash of crockery sounded from the kitchen.

Half past three. He'd never stand another day of it. Another day chained like this and something would snap. For the second time that afternoon he returned to the bedroom and lay there smoking, staring at the ceiling, watching the sagging gray sky, his face recording ugly inner journeys.

It was twenty to four when the telephone rang. He listened, head cocked, but for all he could tell it was another false alarm. Then he heard the woman on the stairs and he didn't wait for her to knock.

"Yes?"

She might have been coming in to turn the bedcovers down, or change the towels. "My husband asked me to tell you to be ready in five minutes."

Laker's heart lifted urgently. He nodded. "Very well."

"With both your cases. And would you please wear these."

She dropped some old blue overalls onto the end of the bed.

"All right."

He didn't question why. She left him and he put them on, dry in the mouth, his pulse quickening. The overalls were tight under the arms, but otherwise the fit was good enough. After a momentary indecision he folded his topcoat and pressed it into the suitcase, then hurried downstairs.

"Would you like some coffee?" The woman amazed him to the end. "It's on the stove."

"No, thanks."

He followed her into the living room where she remarked to the macaw, "Our guest is going. Aren't you sorry to lose him?" The bird clawed clumsily around the cage. She stroked its gaudy head, but her eyes were on the gap in the draped lace curtains. Very soon she said, "This is him now," and Laker saw a small battered open truck rattling along the street.

"Stay here," she said, a soft command in her tone for the first and only time. "Let him come in first."

The truck shook to a standstill and Laker watched the man get out and saunter toward the steps. The woman waited for the bell before she went to open the door. "Is he ready?" Laker heard, and her quiet "Yes." He moved into the hall. The man looked at him and nodded meaningfully. The two cases were at the foot of the stairs. Laker picked them up, but the man took the suitcase from him. "I'll attend to this."

"Good-bye," the woman said. "Good-bye. I'm pleased to have met you."

She would baffle anyone, Laker felt, even under blinding lights and relentless questioning.

He shook her by the hand, moved suddenly. "Good-bye."

The man went first. He slung the suitcase into the back of

the truck and covered it over with a square of perished tarpaulin. Laker clambered into the driver's cab, shoving the black case between his knees. It was a rickety vehicle, the blue-gray paint chipped and scored and patched with rust; the off-side fender was badly concertinaed and Laker could see the ground through a hole in the flooring.

The man climbed in behind the wheel, fastening the door with a twist of string. He had left the engine running. With a crunch of gears they drew away. Laker didn't look back; never saw the woman again.

"Well?" This before they'd shuddered twenty yards.

"He's gone north, toward Dessau."

"How far's that?"

"Seventy, eighty kilometers. But he'll be turning around at the district border, which is only half as far, and coming south again. And he's had a fair start, so we're against the clock." They swung left, clipping the curb. "He'll be on the autobahn, understand?"

"Traveling?"

"Traveling, yes."

That meant anything up to a hundred miles an hour; perhaps more. Daunted, Laker screwed his eyes, doubts and protest rising together.

"Listen," the man said loudly above the clatter. "At one point the southbound slow lane is under repair. There are warning notices out. Traffic's down to about half speed over a longish stretch."

Sixty, say. Even so . . . It could be lunacy. Laker bit his lips, questioning his companion's judgment.

"You might wait a week and never have as good a chance. There's a party on its way from Berlin and Hartmann's taking over escort duty at the district border. It isn't often that he strays so far from home."

They were rattling between drab rows of suburban shops.

"How's the time?"

"Four," Laker said. Then, uneasily: "I hope to God you know what's possible and what isn't."

"You want everything guaranteed, don't you?" Suddenly the man was nettled. He wrestled the wheel, glowering. "You want the work done for you, the risks all—"

"No, but—"

"Wait and see, then." He jammed down the brake pedal to avoid a cyclist; swore. "I made conditions, remember. There are other necks at stake besides yours. I tell you Hartmann's as vulnerable now as ever he'll be, but more important as far as I'm concerned is what happens afterwards."

Laker was silent.

"I can get you away," the man said, calming again. "And that matters. Any fool can commit suicide. Tonight you'll be over the frontier. We aren't waiting for Monday."

They were nearing the city's center, the Fair's flags and streamers, the Sunday afternoon crowds. LEIPZIG—ANOTHER NAME FOR HOSPITALITY. . . . Laker felt exposed, the overalls no protection against the attention attracted by the truck's racketing progress. A siren wailed behind them and his heartbeat thudded; there was no rearview mirror. For an awful moment it seemed as if the man were pulling into the side, but he was merely getting out of the way. An ambulance slid past, and Laker's skin crawled with relief.

"There's a map under the seat," he was told.

Traffic lights delayed them as he groped. A black limousine drew alongside and its uniformed passenger stared broodingly at the truck from a distance of three feet.

"National People's Army," the man muttered from the side of his mouth. "General." Then, when the lights changed and they had jerked into the car's wake, "We're taking the Halle road . . . Halle, got it? Through Schkeuditz."

"Yes."

"We hit the autobahn after leaving Schkeuditz. It's marked E6. The slow section I mentioned is about four kilometers north of the junction. That's where I'll put you down."

"And then?"

"The details don't make sense until you've seen the ground. But west of E6, running parallel, there's a minor road."

Laker peered, trying to steady the map. "About a kilometer west?"

"That's the one. We'll rendezvous there."

The man's voice was taut, authoritative. He was allowing Laker no choice. His plans were made, but they had the vagueness of something hurriedly thrown together. Laker managed to hold his uneasiness in check, focusing his mind on an imagined stretch of autobahn, picturing a vehicle at speed, thinking about angles, height, time, distance. . . . It was going to be now or never.

"How will I know which car is his?"

"That's taken care of. I'll explain when we're on the spot."

A clock showed four-twelve. They passed the Ring-Messehaus and its frontal gardens, then the Astoria where the nightmare had begun with stuttered explanations from a stranger in a raincoat, then the square where Hartmann had driven to the shooting gallery.

Laker needed no reminders. He pressed his calves against the rexine case, keeping it steady. A few storm-drops struck the windshield and he willed the sky to hold off, clenching his hands as he squinted upward.

"Time?" the man asked hoarsely.

"Four-fifteen."

They were heading west now: a sign pointed to Schkeuditz and Halle. All the din in the world seemed to be concentrated inside the drafty cab as they passed through a succession of cobbled streets. Shops, houses, factories, a ruined church, more factories, wasteland, rubble—gradually the city fell away. A stream meandered in to flank them the left and there were meadows on either side, dotted with oaks and larches. The road was mostly straight but the truck swayed dangerously, buffeted by a gusty cross-breeze, and the man crouched at the wheel, working the loose steering. They covered the distance to Schkeuditz at a kilometer a minute, slowed there to the permitted maximum, sweated out a traffic jam, then picked up speed again, steam issuing from the radiator. The countryside widened, more thickly wooded, slightly undulating. Northward, slanting cords of rain darkened the horizon.

"How long have we got?" Laker shouted.

"You ought to be in position by five."

"That rain will be on us by then."

The man risked a sideways scowl and grunted. He looked drawn and the creases in his forehead glistened. The grunt was his only comment.

Five kilometers brought them to the autobahn's approach. The road climbed a shade, veering right, then topped a low crest, and all at once the autobahn was there, as wide as an airport's runway, split by a humped strip of grass. Tucked in behind an ancient Porsche they filtered into the first lane and the man opened the throttle again, steam flattening continuously over the shaking hood.

Hartmann would be coming south. South, on the other roadway.

The traffic there was light, unevenly spaced. Laker singled out two or three of the faster cars, watching them swell from the size of toys and flash past, blurring as they went. Short white markers were planted at intervals along the far verge, behind which was a post-and-rail fence and then a broken fringe of pines. He was going to need cover and it looked as if he'd get it twenty or thirty yards from the roadway; but the speeds had shaken him—even allowing for the fact that he was trying to assess them while the truck was flat-out in the other direction.

A slightly banked curve and the entire autobahn changed course, heading toward the blue-black clouds along the northern rim. As they roared beneath a bridge the man suddenly pointed half left. "There . . . there," and beyond the humped divide Laker saw the beginnings of a long line of red-and-white tar barrels which sealed off the opposite outer lane. They drew level; continued on by. The obstruction lasted a full two kilometers and the traffic was noticeably slower. The bulldozers and cement mixers were idle: Sunday. Beyond the heaps of sand and steel mesh and broken concrete and the gangers' huts a bank sloped up to the perimeter fence and the trees.

It would be there, then. Somewhere over there.

The man had the accelerator against the floor. Twenty to five. They continued north for another couple of minutes, then looped off, spiraled, crossed the autobahn, looped down and rejoined it, heading south. The warning signs began almost at once. ROAD WORKS . . . REDUCE SPEED . . . TWO LANES ONLY . . . NO PASSING . . . Then the first of the barrels were in sight. ROAD NARROWS . . . SLOW . . . SLOW . . . Brake lights blinked dutifully on the sedan ahead of them. Angled trestles squeezed them into what was normally the center lane and the man eased his foot from the throttle. They cruised for about a third of the obstruction's length before he chose a gap between barrels, nosed through and came to rest in the lee of a covered tarring-machine.

"Now," he said immediately. "Now what I tell you will make sense. Get out and pretend to look at the engine with me. For once she has boiled to order."

They climbed down. He lifted the hood. Steam rose in clouds from the spitting radiator cap. He nodded toward the crossing they had just used.

"That's where I'll be—on the northbound shoulder. I'll be pulled off with the hood up, the same as now. Hartmann's escorting two other cars, so they'll come together, the three of them in convoy. I've some binoculars here which I'll give you in a minute. Keep me in view from wherever you locate yourself. Watch me all the time. When Hartmann comes through the underpass you'll see me slam the hood down and prepare to drive away. Is that clear?"

Laker nodded.

"There will be three cars, remember. I'll give my signal immediately they emerge from the underpass. You can't possibly make a mistake. You'll see them all the way from there. And the green Moskvitch will almost certainly be in the lead."

Laker nodded again. A lorry whined by, wet, wipers still working. Speed and rain—it would be touch-and-go. A chill moved through him.

"Hartmann has a driver," the man said, "so he'll be riding in the back seat."

"What else should I know?"

"Afterwards go due west. Through the trees. Keep going until you reach the minor road you saw on the map. Then wait there. Wait until we pick you up."

" 'We'?"

"I'll have switched to a car, but I can't say what kind it will be. Possibly a Volga. Just wait, that's all. And get rid of your overalls."

"All right."

The man leaned under the steering wheel and brought out a pair of binoculars. Laker shoved them into a pocket and pulled the black case from the cab. Air beat over them from a passing car.

"Now it's up to you," the man said. "I've done the best I can. Select your position, then watch for me on the shoulder by the underpass. I'll be there in five minutes." He clamped the hood shut, heaved himself aboard and switched on. The engine raced. Pulling away he wound the window down and pumped his arm to indicate urgency. Above the road he shouted, "Good luck, Mr. Laker."

Laker didn't reply. He cut between the tarring-machine and a stack of steel pipes and loped up the grass slope toward the fence, bending low as if he were under fire. The grass was soggy, sucking softly at his shoes. He climbed the fence and made for the trees, a kind of nausea welling up. And as he ran he began asking himself how the man had got to know his name.

He went a short distance into the wood, then dropped onto one knee and snapped the case open. In the couple of minutes it took him to assemble the rifle the query persisted.

How? . . . Last night, when distress and fatigue had made him talk so much—had it slipped out then? He didn't believe so. And there was more. The man had known what name to look for in *Neues Deutschland*. Only now this other fact struck him, now when action was all that mattered.

He must have told him. *Must* have done. . . .

He broke open the carton of ammunition and loaded the magazine, thumbing the rounds in separately. He put in four against the pressure of the spring, hesitated with a fifth, decided against it and rammed the magazine home. Two was about all he'd be able to use and an over-full magazine could jam; from twenty years ago he remembered. He stood up, pivoting on his heels. He was deep enough into the trees for the autobahn to be almost invisible. The sound of the traffic was pierced by a bird singing somewhere overhead.

"Good luck, Mr. Laker . . ." It wasn't a time for question marks.

He left the case where it was and moved to the edge of the cover. He was ten yards from the fence and the fence was about fifteen from the white markers along the roadway's border and those, in turn, were ten from the line of tar barrels. There were better places: he was quick to decide. Off to his right the trees receded up the slope, then spread down again almost to the fence. He ran there, slithering on the carpet of pine needles, impelled by a devil of instinctive obedience that was unleashed at last—like the time he'd kicked the radio set to pieces and started his own war, skill and hatred fused, all the layers by which he recognized himself stripped away, peeling away now as he came to the fence and studied the line of fire the new position gave him, possessed by the same terrible hurt as then, the same elemental lust as then, except once it had been for Germans, any Germans, faceless, anonymous enemies, and now it was solely for Hartmann, Hartmann who had asked for this from the moment they first met and who, by keeping his word, had ensured that he got it.

Laker went prone behind the fence. Perhaps three-quarters of a mile separated him from the underpass; a quarter from where the southbound roadway narrowed. He was about eight feet above road level with an uninterrupted view between a steamroller and one of the deserted gangers' huts. SLOW . . . NO PASSING . . . . SLOW—over his right shoulder he could see the warnings repeated behind him along the whole length of the obstruction. He took out the binoculars and fixed them on the underpass: there was no sign of the truck, but the rain had spread nearer, blue and obliterating.

Five o'clock exactly. . . . The ground was uneven so he wriggled back a few feet, angling his body about fifteen degrees from the fence. Emerging from the underpass the cars seemed to crawl. Where the slow section began they rocked minutely in telltale fashion from a touch on the brake or a sudden easing of the throttle, yet when they were about two hundred yards away the head-on effect rapidly diminished and it appeared as if they were actually accelerating as their individual detail loomed and they bore obliquely past with a rubbery whine.

The truck crashed along the northbound track as he was slipping the end-caps off the telescopic sight. He watched it, the query renewing itself, niggling, the man's willingness to be an accessory suddenly suspect.

Disturbed, he sighted on an approaching Skoda, splaying his legs. It was sharp and clear when he picked it up at three hundred yards. For about four seconds the hairline cross centered on a heavy face in the dark V cleared by the windshield wipers; then the swift traversing movement began and Laker couldn't hold the aim without slewing. He took a line on the next two cars, concentrating on the rear seats through the spattered side windows, coldly, expertly, a culmination coming, the scent of the nearby pines a needless mnemonic of fear, manipulation and murder.

If the rain held off he had a sixty-forty chance. But would it? Christ, would it?

The truck had limped onto the shoulder just short of the underpass and the man had the hood up: the binoculars made him seem within shouting distance. Six minutes after five . . . Laker's mouth was as dry as a kiln and the truck moved in and out of focus with every hammerstroke of his heart.

Why such risks for a stranger? . . . What had been plausible an hour ago, a day ago, was increasingly in doubt. Who else could have disclosed his identity?

A solitary lorry crept through the underpass.

Slattery?

Sweat dribbled from Laker's eyebrows and he blinked it away.

Slattery?

A couple of cars, abreast. A light flurry of rain. And the growing confusion, the whirling suspicion that, even now, he was somehow being used.

The man was going through the motions of tinkering with the engine. The binoculars trembled in Laker's hands. With the distrust of the abused he tried to ask himself if it could possibly be that he was still a puppet, Slattery's now, led unknowingly as if he were in his sleep to settle some score that wasn't his. And as he groped for an answer that made even a freakish hint of sense he knew that such a thing was inconceivable. Patrick was dead; the score was his and his alone. "Between you and me, Mr. Laker . . ."

Nothing through the underpass.

Frenzel was alive and Patrick was dead. The equation was Hartmann's, *the weapon was Hartmann's.*

Another lorry, another gap, then an old gray sedan. In ten minutes the rain would have engulfed the underpass.

Five-twelve.

Laker eased his weight from one elbow to another, fiddling the binoculars into sharper focus. As he did so he saw the man suddenly drop the truck's raised hood and three cars came out of the underpass in line astern, the Moskvitch in the lead.

His scalp tightened. The overalls split at the armpits as he reached for the rifle. Three quarters of a mile . . . A deluge of noise was filling his ears. He pushed the safety catch forward, not hearing the click, deaf to everything except the crescendo of the bloodbeat inside himself. Vaguely he was aware of the truck moving off the shoulder and heading the other way but his stare was riveted to the convoy: the cars were still small to the naked eye, like models, one green and two black, seeming to inch clear of the underpass.

He shifted position slightly, tensing, raising the rifle. The gray sedan had swept by where he lay. At half a mile he saw the nose of the Moskvitch dip as it approached the warning signs and he knew it was cutting speed. Six hundred yards . . . Nothing but the noise in his head, no conscious thoughts, no last-second spurt of rage, everything instinctive.

Five hundred . . . He nestled against the cheekpiece and

took preliminary aim. The car was shedding a misty spray. Wipers going, peaked cap behind the wheel, Hartmann in the back, alone, blurred by the smeared side windows. A peepshow, crossed by the hairlines, enlarging. . . . First pressure already on the trigger, the squeeze beginning. Another second. The angle widening, the apparent acceleration. An infinitesimal moment more—

Now!

Laker felt the jolt, saw the glass splinter and the simultaneous clutching movement inside the car. In an intensity of awareness he fired again, the aim held, the window frosting a hand's-width from the first point of impact, the figure slumping, hat askew—all this he glimpsed in the identical jarring instant, all at telescoped distance.

Then the lightning traverse to the right began and his chance of a third shot had gone. And he was stumbling to his feet, discarding the rifle, running.

He ran with his head down. The trees hid him almost immediately. The roar in his ears cleared for a moment, like enormous bubbles bursting, and he heard the savage whimpering of tires. After a short distance he stopped and looked back through a gap in the pines. The three cars were at a standstill, askew on the track, men leaping from them. The driver of the Moskvitch had opened the off-side door and Laker could see the overcoated figure sprawled head and shoulders onto the roadway, motionless.

He didn't wait. One glance was enough. He turned again and ran on, a choking sensation rising in his throat. The sounds of the autobahn receded. After a little he slowed, but the possibility of pursuit kept him going. The pines gave way to fields and he felt rain on his face as he moved into the open. Six or seven minutes brought him to the road, the selfsame scenes flickering vividly across his vision. The road was sunken, unsurfaced, narrow. He stripped the overalls off and tossed them into a clump of bushes, then climbed some barbed wire and clambered down the bank. The rain was intensifying. He sheltered against the trunk of a huge beech, breathing hard, mind churning, an exultant shiver once racking him like an ague.

It seemed a long while before he heard something coming. Fifty yards away the road cornered gently and disappeared from view. He quit the protection of the tree and started to move in the direction from which the promised car was approaching. He'd taken about ten paces before he saw it, a mud-flecked Volga. He raised a hand in greeting and stopped. It came quite fast, in low gear, almost filling the width of the road. Several people seemed to be in it, but the rain hid their identities. As it braked to a standstill Laker started forward again, thumbs up. In the same moment doors opened on either side and the front-seat occupants got out. And with a blow of incredulous dismay he recognized the blond, black-jacketed driver and the man in the raincoat with the lopsided face who'd been his captors once before.

For a lifelong moment he was rooted where he stood. Then he turned and fled, mind and body temporarily dissociated—the one stunned, the other in a paroxysm of movement.

"Mr. Laker!"

He sprinted along the road. A stuttering voice repeatedly bawled at him to stop. Doors slammed and he heard the car start after him. With a despairing effort he flung himself up the bank, expecting a shot. He clawed his way up frantically, reached the top as the car drew level below, then went to vault the barbed wire. The post he grabbed for support broke off as he was in midair; one foot caught the topmost strand of wire. Falling, he felt the sickening impact as his head clubbed against an outcrop of stone and everything exploded into darkness.

They had him in the car and the car was moving. He heard someone moan, not realizing it was himself. In the dim beginnings of revival he struggled, fighting the hand that seemed to be holding him down. Through swelling pain he babbled defiantly: "I got him, anyway . . . I got him!,, —kicking, straining against whoever was there.

"What do you think?" someone asked a million miles away, but not of him, and someone else replied: "Perhaps you'd better."

He felt his jacket being dragged off, his left sleeve being pulled up, then the prick and deep slide of a needle in his flesh. Almost immediately the blackness started to lump and tumble into the featureless landscape of renewed unconsciousness.

"You should have told him about his son," another voice was protesting. "You should have told him that."

It was the last thing to register and he took it under with him, bewildered even then. For it was Karen who had spoken.

Chapter
Seventeen

HE floated in the darkness, sometimes totally unaware, sometimes with his mind beset with problems which had been with him since childhood, sometimes swept by eddies of weakness that seemed to suck him down to where it was darker still. In the delirium of this darkness people touched him, shifted him, talked to him and about him and several times a whisper echoed round the resonant cave of his skull—"Patrick's all right. Can you hear? . . . Patrick's all right."

How long he floated he pieced together afterwards. But a moment came when he felt himself once more being lifted, cradled, borne slowly upward toward actuality. In a daze of vagueness he opened his eyes, then clamped them shut, stabbed by a blaze of light that seemed to start his head hammering as if a switch had been thrown. For an incalculable period his thoughts streamed away in ribbons of jumbled pictures, the thudding in his temples like a pile driver. Then, fearfully, he began to blink, his hands to wander.

He was in a bed. A shaded light on a glossy wall beyond the hump made by his feet, a chintz-covered window, a silver-gray door, a silver-gray cupboard, a table . . . Gingerly he felt his head, discovering bandages: dully he noticed that he was wearing his own pajamas. The fevered condition of his mind prevented him from guessing where he might be, or even reflecting that it was different from what he ought to have expected. He called out, a hoarse croak, but no one came. His watch had been taken from his wrist, so he had no idea of the time. He felt sick and closed his eyes, yielding to the heavy drag on his senses, remembering the autobahn, the Moskvitch, Hartmann in his sights and Hartmann inert, sprawled like a rag doll on the tarmac; remembering the narrow road and the Volga and the shock of who was in it, remembering running, knowing that something had gone horribly wrong—all that part very clear. And then remembering the darkness in which, impossibly, Karen Gisevius had existed and another voice had gently whispered lies to him about Patrick.

He slept again before the chaotic wandering took hold.

Now the curtains had been pulled aside and daylight was furring the edges of the window. He stared at it for what seemed a long time without fully realizing he was awake. The pile driver had been replaced by a lazy throbbing and he sat up cautiously, surveying the room, mystified. A vase of bronze chrysanthemums stood on the bedside table and his watch was there beside it.

Eight-fifteen . . . Monday? An enormous effort was required: his mind was sore, as if it had been kicked. Impulsively he started toward the window, but he swayed when he got to his feet and sank back, dizzy.

From the bed he could see the tops of some trees. He pressed against the pillows, struggling to make sense of the neat room, the flowers, the comfort. A flask of water was also on the table and he started pouring some into a tumbler. As he was doing so the door opened and a dark-haired nurse looked in. The crisp headgear, the white crossbands over the lilac blouse, the starched cuffs and apron—none of it rang a bell with him.

"Where am I?"

He spoke in German. She hesitated fractionally, then entered, closing the door behind her.

"Where is this place?"

To his astonishment she answered in English. "I haven't passed my colloquial yet, but if you're asking what I think you're asking, the answer is the British Military Hospital in Hanover."

"*Where?*"

"Hanover, Germany. And I'm from London, England." She smiled pertly, looking down at him. "Have you been awake long?"

Hanover: it wouldn't sink in. "How in the hell did I get here?"

"I wouldn't know," the nurse said. "I only came on duty at eight."

"What's today?"

"Monday." She was feeling his pulse. "How's the head?"

"Spinning."

"You've got six stitches in it, so no wonder. Do you feel you can cope with a visitor?"

"Who?"

"I wouldn't know that either. I'm just responsible for your well-being. What do you think—yes or no?"

"Yes," he said.

"It's up to you." She studied him clinically. "Are you sure?"

He nodded.

"Very well. I'll get him."

She went away with a starchy rustle. A minute or two

elapsed before the door opened again, and in that time Laker's mind moved sufficiently fast through its labyrinth of bewilderment not to be entirely surprised to see who came in.

"Sam."

Slattery tiptoed across to the bed as if he were in church.

"How are you, Sam?" The brick-red complexion, the smooth-as-glass manner.

Laker spurned his offered handshake. "Where the blazes have you sprung from?"

"I've been waiting along the corridor. They gave me a cubbyhole in which to park myself. I wanted to be with you the moment you surfaced."

"Is that so?"

"There's something you must know, Sam—right away."

"Go on."

"I talked to you during the night, and you answered after a fashion. Do you remember?"

"No."

"About Patrick." Slattery couldn't seem to manage it first time. "He's come to no harm, Sam. He's safe and well, here in Hanover."

All his life Laker was to remember that tremendous leap in his heart. The delirious whispers echoed—"Patrick's all right . . . All right . . ." Yet, staring at Slattery, he heard himself say, "I don't believe you."

"It's true. As true as we're together."

"It can't be. *Neues Deutschland*—"

"It is, Sam."

"Prove it." Oh my God, he thought. Oh Jesus.

"I shall. But take it easy, take it easy."

"Where is he?"

"With friends, on the other side of town."

"Bring him over. Let me see him."

"Just as soon as I can. But give him a chance, Sam." A tentative smile. "He probably hasn't had his breakfast yet."

"Let me talk to him, then."

"Are you up to it?"

"My God," Laker said. "Where's the telephone?"

He started to scramble out of bed, beside himself with wonder and excitement, but Slattery checked him and went to the door, opened it and called the nurse.

"She's fetching one," he said, returning. "You're in no state to be walking about."

Laker closed his eyes. He was trembling. His voice had thickened. "There was a paragraph about him in *Neues Deutschland*. It said he'd been killed in a street accident."

"It was false, Sam. A lie. You'll see."

Laker sucked in air. He needed time; time. "How did you manage it?"

"Manage what?"

"Getting him out." Incredibly, they were talking about the living.

"I'll put you in the picture presently."

"Now."

"Presently."

"And me . . . What about me? I was picked up by a couple of—"

"Let it wait, Sam. First things first."

Slattery raised a finger to his lips as the nurse entered to plug in a telephone. Only when he'd thanked her and she'd gone did he speak again.

"There's just one thing before you have a word with Patrick. He's swallowed the business trip story, and so far as your being *hors de combat* is concerned, the line is that you had an argument with a door at the airport last night. There shouldn't be any awkward questions, but play it by ear."

Laker nodded. His mind was being asked to make too many somersaults all at once, but he was too relieved to be thinking clearly, too muddled, too grateful. A miracle had happened; at the moment he could forgive everything. He ran his hands over his face while Slattery gave the operator a number.

"There's quite a tale to tell, Sam." The smile was still a shade uncertain. "But this is what matters now."

Slattery hung on, twisting the telephone cord in his fingers, blinking away behind his spectacles.

Laker exclaimed, "Why did *Neues Deutschland* carry a false report, for God's sake? I shot Hartmann on the strength of it." He looked sharply at Slattery. The nightmare wasn't done with yet. "Hartmann's dead. I shot him with the rifle he supplied me with to kill Frenzel."

But Slattery had turned aside. "Yes?" he was saying. "Is Patrick there, please? . . . It's his father." And whatever reaction Laker had looked for in Slattery was forgotten as he grabbed the telephone.

"Patrick?"

"Hallo, Dad. I hear you've been in the wars again."

"It's nothing."

"I was expecting you last night. I wasn't told until first thing this morning that you'd been carted off to the hospital. . . . How are you?"

"Some stitches in the head, that's all."

"Did you have a good trip?"

"Fine, thanks . . . I'm sorry about Leipzig. It couldn't be helped."

"That's okay, Dad. Mr. Rauter explained."

"Rauter?"

"Your associate. He fixed it for me to come over to Hanover."

"Who've you been staying with?"

"Erich Meyer."

"Erich?"

"You know, Dad—Erich Meyer, one of my pen-friends."

"Yes, yes; of course. Stupid of me, but I'm still a bit woolly. . . . Have you had a good time?"

"Great. Mr. Rauter said you'd settle with him about the money and all that."

"Of course. . . . When are you coming over here?"

"Just as soon as I can."

"A colleague of mine will send transport for you."

"Oh, good."

"In about an hour, probably. . . . All right?"

How he controlled his voice he never knew. He was sweating when he hung up. Joy quivered through him, a kind of weariness in its wake. Slattery was at the window, gazing out, and Laker asked him for a cigarette.

As the smoke swirled, Laker said, "I don't understand. Rauter was the person . . ." Then: "Christ, I'm so confused. So bloody confused. When did you get him over? And how? He spoke as if—"

"We'll start unraveling it, Sam." Slattery pulled a chair across to the bed. "When you're ready we'll unwind the whole thing."

"The last I can remember is being in a car after I'd tried to jump some wire. Two of Hartmann's men were there, the same two who'd arrested me previously, the two who'd given me the firing-squad treatment. . . . When I went back to Leipzig I made use of that wise-virgin number of yours. It was the fellow at the house there who produced the *Neues Deutschland* clipping—and he believed it, too. . . ."

Haltingly Laker attempted to feel his way.

"Hartmann was traveling south on the Berlin-Leipzig autobahn. Afterwards I went west to a side road as arranged. Then something went wrong . . ." He frowned, trapped by another memory, another echo. "I was sure Patrick was dead, do you understand? I got a message from Hartmann in

Copenhagen which said as much, and then there was this
Neues Deutschland confirmation. . . ."

He shook his head. "That car," he said suspiciously.
"Karen was in that car."

Slattery's lips began to curl.

"Karen Gisevius," Laker insisted. "Wasn't she?"

"Yes."

"How the devil—?"

"She came over with you. You crossed near Duderstadt.
And it wasn't easy, the state you were in."

"But what about Hartmann's pair? Who squared them?"

"No one. They laid the crossing on."

Disbelief narrowed Laker's eyes.

Slattery leaned forward. "I told you the other day that
Karen was one of the best contacts we had. Well, she'd be
the first to admit that Hartmann knocks her into a cocked
hat."

"*Hartmann?*"

Slattery nodded.

"You're not serious?"

"Very much so."

Stunned, Laker ejaculated, "He's dead. I shot him."

"No, Sam."

"I got him twice. He was in a green Moskvitch—"

"Not Hartmann. Not Hartmann, Sam. . . . You got the one
we wanted you to get."

And with the sudden hindsight of one too long deceived,
Laker began to see the rough outline of the whole appalling fraud.

It didn't matter to him at the moment who the other person was. All he could grasp was that he had been terrorized,
debased, manipulated, led with a ring through his nose from
beginning to end, forced to grieve, made to hate, sited to
kill. . . . All to order.

His brain seemed to writhe. Shaking, he pressed back on the pillows. A full minute must have passed. And then, in a low voice he said, "Who was he?"

"A very elusive gentleman, Sam."

"Tell me," he flared.

"Matthew Albright."

"Who?"

"Matthew Albright."

He hadn't needed the reminder. *Sino-Soviet expert missing from the U. S. State Department . . . Known since May to have defected . . .* ALBRIGHT HERE, MOSCOW SAYS. . . . A key turned sharply in his mind, but there had been too many shocks for another to register. And that it was Albright wasn't the awful thing.

Woodenly he said, "He was in Hartmann's car."

"Hartmann switched him when he took over the escort role at the Leipzig district border. For safety's sake, do you see? Ostensibly there was a rumor of an attempt on Albright's life."

Slattery beamed without restraint.

"Albright was the Russians' prize piece, Sam. More precious to them than half a dozen nuclear physicists. He was *the* outstanding expert on Sino-Soviet relations and virtually the whole of the West's economic and military strategy in the Far East is based on his prognosis. Moscow was a long way from picking him clean, even after three months or so; he'd have been invaluable for plenty of time yet, particularly with the seesaw rocking as it is now. We had to get him, and the sooner the better. The Americans asked what we could do to help, and—thanks to you—our scheme paid off." Slattery lit himself a cigarette. "We knew where Albright was, but he couldn't be touched while he remained tucked up inside Russia. But directly we heard of this trip of his to satellite Party centers there was just a chance. I'm not a Kremlinologist, so why he was making the grand tour I couldn't say; perhaps Moscow has a *nouveau riche* compulsion to show off its assets. It's happened before—Burgess, Pontecorvo; they and others made the rounds. But in Albright's case the Russians were certain to be ultra careful—and so it proved. In Warsaw, for instance, they hardly let a chink of natural light fall on him. About the only time he was going to be at all vulnerable was when he was being shunted, and even then . . ."

Slattery went on, engrossed with the background, Slattery who at the Mitre had had the gall to say: "No hard feelings I hope, now or at any time." And when he next paused, Laker found his tongue.

"You bastard." He dragged it out. "You bloody bastard."

Slattery blinked as if to ward off Laker's glare. "There wasn't any other way, Sam."

"No one has the right to do what you've done."

"A duty, though."

"Balls. Oh balls to that."

"I could give you precedents, chapter and verse."

"To hell with precedents. I want an explanation."

"You're in the process of getting it, Sam."

"Am I?"

"I had you listed for this days before you got your name in the *Evening Standard;* that was a coincidence, pure and simple, though it couldn't have happened at a more convenient time as far as I was concerned." Slattery blew smoke and tried another tack. "Look at it my way. If I'd asked you to dispose of Albright, do you think you'd have agreed? Of course not. But I especially needed you. In the first place you were the finest marksman I've ever known. And whoever took on this job would have to be a whole lot better than good."

"I undertook to deliver a message—no more, no less."

"And you finished by killing a man."

"Thanks to you."

"Not entirely. Nobody made you."

"Oh no?"

"Nobody made you, Sam."

"I was put against a tree with a bag over my head. I was told Patrick was dead. . . . And you sit there and split hairs about who's responsible—"

"Listen. There's a second reason why I needed you. I haven't forgotten what you were like in Green Park that night during the war or the way you were when you got back from Gardelegen. No one who knew you in those days could ever forget. And we don't change, Sam—not underneath, not where it matters. Given the circumstances, the chances are we'll conform. So—" he spread his hands—"we set a sprat to catch a mackerel. And Hartmann couldn't be mealymouthed if he was to foster what I knew was in you."

Coldly, Laker said, "Is this the way you work?"

"If need be."

"Irrespective of consideration for those you exploit? Irrespective of what it costs them?"

"Albright had to be removed. It was vital."

"You didn't answer the question."

"The circumstances were exceptional. We put you through the hoop, I don't deny, but you qualified on that score, too. You're as tough as nails, Sam. You always were." Slattery beamed again, and his look implied: But not the smartest, not the most cerebral. "Fear and hatred are the best tools in the trade. It was a gamble, even so. You might easily have let us down."

"*You* down!" Laker rolled his head, seething. "I wish to God I had."

"At the moment, perhaps. But not at the time, not while you were waiting for Hartmann's car. You wanted him then as badly as we wanted Albright. And you made sure you got him, as I guessed you would."

There was silence. Laker took a deep, shuddering breath

and put his hands to his throbbing temples. He still hadn't grasped how completely he had been stage-managed.

Slattery said, "I expect you've tumbled to it—Frenzel never existed. A dozen things could have gone wrong, but not that." With a kind of relish, as if he were explaining a sequence of chess moves, he began to reconstruct the pattern of events. "It was all relatively straightforward as far as Copenhagen. We tried to keep the pressure on you there, though Ritchie Jackson tells me the tailing was a bit too erratic. You were hardly expected to land up with the police, of course, though that was a minor matter—and it helped in a way. After Ritchie telephoned the Hartmann message to the Metropol it was a question then of wait and see. That was *the* crucial period, and later it was also touch and go whether you'd bite on that Leipzig number. What made everyone gray, though, was your going back with the rifle. We hadn't reckoned on that. Your friend with the macaw would have equipped you, do you see?" He stubbed his cigarette. "He was in a quandary about telling you who would pick you up on the side road for the getaway. We certainly hadn't anticipated your knocking yourself out and having to be bundled across the frontier like a sack of coals. . . . However, by and large it all worked very well."

He was speaking about a certain operation which had been carried out in a certain way, for all the world as though Laker hadn't been involved and there had been no private agonies. Laker studied him, amazed and contemptuous. Even Hartmann had been unable to contain a fleeting show of feeling.

"That clipping from *Neues Deutschland*—"

"We had it specially set, Sam."

"Your idea?"

"After a fashion, yes."

"Then damn you."

"We have to do these things."

"Don't try to justify yourself. For Christ's sake don't start that—not to me."

"There's a war on, Sam. No one likes to admit it, but there is. For some of us it never ended. We fight it how and where we can." Slattery looked almost pained. "I thought you'd understand, I really did."

"Say I'd failed?"

"We'd have tried something else."

"Used someone else, you mean."

"If necessary. We'd have found a way."

"God forgive you."

Slattery got to his feet. "You're tired," he said. "But all's well that ends well. Ease off, Sam. A lousy trick—all right. A lousy, shabby, underhand trick, and I apologize for it." He was still smiling. "But only you went through the hoop. Patrick was never in the least danger and we had your own safety at heart all along the line. For instance, there was no message in that watch strap of yours."

Near the door he turned. "By the way, I gather you'll be fit enough to travel tomorrow. A word from you in the office downstairs and they'll see that you and Patrick are whisked off to Heidelberg or wherever you decide." He paused, as if to receive thanks. "There are just two other matters, then we can call it a day. Hartmann's stayed on. He's sticking it out, and he might get away with it. But Karen's been wanting to cry off for a longish while now, and finally she has. It's too hot for her there anyhow. Remember this, though, when you see her. She was almost as much in the dark about what was afoot as you were. All she was told was that someone would call at Kromadecka's. She had no idea who it would be and she had no idea why—though when she did she hated every part of it. In fact, you could say that we used her, too."

Slattery cleared his throat.

"And—lastly—there's the fact that you're in a privileged position. You know too much, but that's the price I had to pay. I can't gag you. You can blow your top if you like. We'd deny everything, naturally—though that wouldn't prevent a few heads rolling over there in Leipzig. I can also appeal to you, though in your present mood I doubt if doing so would cut much ice. So I can only stress one unpalatable truth. You're a killer, Sam. Given the circumstances you're a killer. That, *inter alia*, is what's on the files, but don't brand yourself publicly as such; people wouldn't understand, not in the midst of their peace and plenty. Let's keep it between you and me."

"Go away," Laker grated.

"I'm going, Sam. Good-bye—and thanks. Look after yourself."

Ten minutes before Patrick arrived the door opened again. It was Karen.

"Sammy?"

She moved swiftly across to the bed. Laker held out his hands, taking hers. Tears, bright and shining, filled her eyes, and as he drew her toward him he knew that she wasn't crying for him, or for herself, or even out of happiness, but for what men had always done to one another in the endless collision of their dreams and would go on doing by way of lies and violence and dedicated cruelty until the world burned itself to a cinder.